Look what *Romantic Times* magazine has to say about reader favorite Linda Turner!

"With a cast of characters and a story that draws you in from the first, [this] is a tale that will capture your heart."
—About *Always a McBride*

"Linda Turner takes readers into an exciting world most only dream of...."
—About *The Enemy's Daughter*

"Ms. Turner develops a luscious romance with great sensitivity...."
—About *The Best Man*

"Favorite author Linda Turner turns the heat up high...."
—About *A Ranching Man*

"Ms. Turner comes up with another winner...."
—About *The Loner*

Dear Reader,

The holidays are here, so why not give yourself the gift of time and books—especially this month's Intimate Moments? Top seller Linda Turner returns with the next of her TURNING POINTS miniseries. In *Beneath The Surface* she takes a boss/employee romance, adds a twist of suspense and comes up with another irresistible read.

Linda Winstead Jones introduces you to the first of her LAST CHANCE HEROES, in *Running Scared.* Trust me, you'll want to be kidnapped right alongside heroine Olivia Larkin when bodyguard Quinn Calhoun carries her off—for her own good, of course. Award-winning Maggie Price's LINE OF DUTY miniseries has quickly won a following, so jump on the bandwagon as danger forces an estranged couple to reunite and mend their *Shattered Vows.* Then start planning your trip Down Under, because in *Deadly Intent,* Valerie Parv introduces you to another couple who live—and love—according to the CODE OF THE OUTBACK. There are *Whispers in the Night* at heroine Kayla Thorne's house, whispers that have her seeking the arms of ex-cop—and ex-*con*—Paul Fitzgerald for safety. Finally, welcome multipublished author Barbara Colley to the Intimate Moments lineup. Pregnant heroine Leah Davis has some *Dangerous Memories,* and her only chance at safety—and romance—lies with her husband, a husband she'd been told was dead!

Enjoy every single one, and come back next month (next year!) for more of the best and most exciting romance reading around—only in Silhouette Intimate Moments.

Yours,

Leslie J. Wainger
Executive Editor

Beneath the Surface

LINDA TURNER

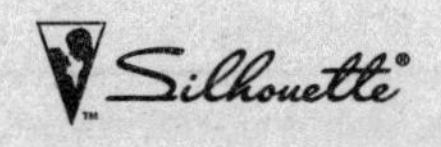

INTIMATE MOMENTS™
Published by Silhouette Books
America's Publisher of Contemporary Romance

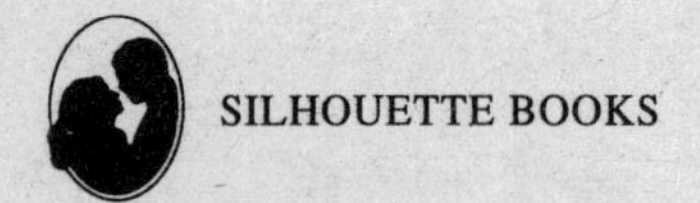

ISBN 0-373-27403-3

BENEATH THE SURFACE

This edition published by arrangement with Harlequin Books S.A.

Visit Silhouette Books at www.eHarlequin.com

Printed in U.S.A.

Books by Linda Turner

Silhouette Intimate Moments

The Echo of Thunder #238
Crosscurrents #263
An Unsuspecting Heart #298
Flirting with Danger #316
Moonlight and Lace #354
The Love of Dugan Magee #448
**Gable's Lady* #523
**Cooper* #553
**Flynn* #572
**Kat* #590
Who's the Boss? #649
The Loner #673
Maddy Lawrence's Big Adventure #709
The Lady in Red #763
†*I'm Having Your Baby?!* #799
†*A Marriage-Minded Man?* #829
†*The Proposal* #847
†*Christmas Lone-Star Style* #895
***The Lady's Man* #931
***A Ranching Man* #992
***The Best Man* #1010
***Never Been Kissed* #1051
The Enemy's Daughter #1064
The Man Who Would Be King #1124
***Always a McBride* #1231
††*Deadly Exposure* #1304
††*Beneath the Surface* #1333

*The Wild West
†The Lone Star Social Club
**Those Marrying McBrides!
††Turning Points

Silhouette Desire

A Glimpse of Heaven #220
Wild Texas Rose #653
Philly and the Playboy #701
The Seducer #802
Heaven Can't Wait #929

Silhouette Special Edition

Shadows in the Night #350

Silhouette Books

Fortune's Children
The Wolf and the Dove

Montana Mavericks: Wed in Whitehorn
Nighthawk's Child

The Coltons
The Virgin Mistress

Silhouette Christmas Kisses 1996
"A Wild West Christmas"

A Fortune's Children Christmas 1998
"The Christmas Child"

Crowned Hearts 2002
"Royally Pregnant"

A Colton Family Christmas 2002
"Take No Prisoners"

Under Western Skies 2002
"Marriage on the Menu"

LINDA TURNER

began reading romances in high school and began writing them one night when she had nothing else to read. She's been writing ever since. Single, and living in Texas, she travels every chance she gets, scouting locales for her books.

Prologue

Across the high-school cafeteria, the band launched into one of the biggest hits of the eighties, and the alumni from the Liberty Hill High School Class of '88 greeted the familiar song with a cheer of enthusiasm. Seated with her back to the dance floor, Abby Saunders didn't have to turn around to know that Dennis Coffman, her date for the evening, had decided she'd spent enough time reminiscing with her old high school friends. She, like everyone else within thirty yards of him, could hear every word he said as he strode toward her.

"Where's the beautiful woman I came with? I spent a fortune for the tickets to this shindig and I haven't got to dance with her once! Abby? Do you hear me, sugar? Enough gabbing. C'mon, let's dance. I want to hold that gorgeous body of yours."

Her cheeks stinging, Abby would have liked nothing more than to crawl in a hole somewhere and just disappear. She shouldn't have come…especially with Dennis. He was too loud, too obnoxious. He tried too hard to fit in, and in the process, couldn't have branded himself more of an outsider. She hadn't wanted to go alone, however, so she'd invited him to come with her. She should have known better. His compliments were too over the top to be sincere, and when he talked about money, which he did frequently, everyone within earshot seemed to cringe with embarrassment for him.

Seated with Lily, Natalie and Rachel at a table near the back of the cafeteria, Abby could imagine what her friends were thinking. What was she doing with *him?*

She'd asked herself the same question dozens of times over the last few months, and the answer was always the same. She didn't want to go through life alone. Unfortunately, she'd never had much confidence in herself as a woman. She was too thin, her breasts were too small and she'd never thought she was very interesting to a man…except Dennis. When they'd started dating, she'd tried to convince herself that everyone had faults, and at least Dennis didn't drink or play around on her or lose his temper and hit her. If he was a braggart and brash and liked to hear himself talk—well, she'd told herself she could live with that. Now she wasn't so sure.

She was embarrassed to be seen with him, and that made her feel horrible about herself. She'd known what he was like when she'd invited him to come with her. This was her fault. Suddenly needing to get out of there, she rose abruptly to her feet as Dennis reached their table. "I really don't feel like dancing," she told him quietly. "In fact, I don't feel well at all. Would you mind if we left?"

"Sugar, you don't know how glad I am to hear you say that," he retorted. "Not that I want you to be sick, but I've had about all the fun I can stand in this dump."

Abby winced. "Dennis—"

"Hey, the truth hurts. Hang on while I get the car. Then I'll take you somewhere where we can get some real food. That's probably why you're sick. I don't know who did the catering, but my dog wouldn't eat it."

With that loud announcement, he strolled out, not noticing the hostile looks that followed him. Abby saw them, however, and couldn't blame her former classmates for being irritated. He didn't have to be so rude.

"I'm sorry," she told her friends. "This was a mistake."

"Don't apologize," Lily told her. "You're not responsible for what someone else says."

"But I brought him here. I shouldn't have."

"You had a right to bring a date, Abby," Natalie said with a frown. "I just wish he appreciated you."

She grimaced. "He's not as bad as he sounds. Really," she insisted when her friends looked skeptical. "He's just got a lot of insecurities. I think that's why he boasts so much…to make himself feel better."

"You don't do that," Rachel pointed out quietly. "And you probably have just as many insecurities."

"True," she said ruefully. "I *am* one big walking insecurity, but at least I don't go around bragging about myself. I just make bad choices when it comes to men."

"I think we can all plead guilty to that," Lily said with a chuckle. "I've spent my entire life dealing with one controlling man after another. I just can't seem to get away from them."

"Hey, my story's better than that," Rachel retorted. "At least you didn't spend years trying to get pregnant by a man who'd had a vasectomy and didn't tell you. Do you know how dumb I felt when I found out?"

"If we're going for the stupid award," Natalie said, "then

I take the prize. I'm the only one who worked like a dog to put a husband through college and law school because he told me I'd get to go to school as soon as he could support us. Then what did he do? Used that same law degree to divorce me so he could marry his paralegal and run off to a tropical island. He doesn't even pay child support. Talk about dumb! And I never saw it coming."

"So we've all made mistakes," Lily said. "We don't have to keep beating ourselves up over it."

"We control our own destiny," Natalie added. "We just have to believe in ourselves and go after what we want."

Abby sighed in defeat. "I thought that's what I was doing when I started dating Dennis."

Rachel lifted a brow. "Whenever you think of meeting a great guy and falling in love, is Dennis the kind of man you dream of?"

Abby didn't even have to think about the answer to that one. "No, of course not."

"Then what are you doing with him when he is so obviously Mr. Wrong?" Natalie asked with a frown.

At that moment, Dennis pulled his car to a stop in front of the cafeteria doors and blared the horn. Abby swallowed a silent groan. If she'd needed a sign of how wrong Dennis was for her, he'd just given it to her. He wasn't the kind of man she could ever fall in love with—she was just wasting her time with him.

But breaking things off with him was the least of her problems. How was she supposed to believe in herself when she never had before? She didn't even know where to begin.

Chapter 1

"Don't be such a coward," Abby mumbled to herself. "People join dating services all the time. There's nothing to it. Pick up the phone and call!"

Taking her own advice sounded easy enough, but she cringed at the thought of throwing herself back into the dating scene. She hated dating. She just wasn't good at it. Men wanted a woman with curves and personality and sex appeal, and she lacked all three. Oh, she didn't think of herself as a complete loser—she was pleasant and easygoing and knew how to act in public. When it came to men, however, her confidence was nonexistent. And it was all her mother's fault.

"I think someone must have switched babies on me in the hospital. Look at you! You can't be my kid. You're skinny as a fence post, your face is covered with freckles and that red hair of yours glows in the dark. I never looked unattractive a day in my life. I was pretty."

Even now, twenty-three years later, Abby could see her mother fluffing her hair and preening before her like some kind of movie star. Concerned only with herself, she hadn't given a thought to what she was doing to her ten-year-old daughter's self-esteem. Not that that was anything new, Abby thought with a grimace. Her mother had never passed up a chance to point out that she didn't measure up, regardless of how hard she tried.

"Take my advice, sweetheart," her mother had told Abby countless times. "Learn all you can while you're in school, then get yourself a good job. You're going to need it. No man is his right mind is going to want you. You're just too plain."

Abby hadn't wanted to believe her, but time, unfortunately, had proved her mother to be right. Abby was thirty-three years old and could count the men who'd asked her out on the fingers of one hand. Which was why she'd agreed to date Dennis.

From the moment she'd met him, she'd known he wasn't the Prince Charming she'd been waiting for her entire life. Not even close. But she was so tired of being alone. And he wasn't a complete loser. At times he could be considerate. Though his constant bragging set her nerves on edge and he had even more insecurities than she did, she'd learned to close her ears to it. Things would work out, she'd told herself. They just needed some time.

Then she'd seen him through the eyes of her friends at her high-school reunion and was forced to face the truth. She could date Dennis for the rest of her life, but he just wasn't the type of man she was ever going to love. She was only dating him because she didn't want to be alone, and that wasn't fair to him or herself. The minute they'd arrived back in Austin after the reunion, she'd broken off with him.

That was two months ago, and she hadn't had a date since.

So what are you waiting for? that irritating little voice in her head demanded. *If you want a man in your life, he's not going to come knocking at your door. Step out of your comfort zone for once and go after what you want. Pick up the phone and call a dating service. It's the only way you're going to find someone!*

Reluctantly, she had to agree. She didn't have that many opportunities to meet people. She'd never liked the bar scene, and when she'd joined the singles club at church, the only man who'd shown her any attention was a fifty-year-old widower who was looking for someone to help him with his rebellious teenage daughter.

At least with a dating service, she would have an opportunity to meet someone who was close to her in age and possibly shared her interests, Abby admitted grudgingly. What would it hurt to try?

Her heart in her throat, she reached for the phone book in the bottom drawer of her desk and had just flipped it open to the yellow pages when Martin James, her boss, who was an Austin city councilman, stepped through the door between his office and hers. He'd been on the phone for the last twenty minutes with an unknown caller, and Abby only had to take one look at his set jaw to know that whatever business he'd discussed with the man had not gone well.

"Problems?" she asked.

"No more than usual," he growled. "I'll deal with it. I need you to make a bank deposit for me."

"Of course," she replied as he strode over to her desk and handed her a fat bank envelope. "Does it need to be in by two?"

"Just sometime today," he began, only to frown down at the yellow pages on her desk and the section she had circled. "What's this? Are you joining a dating service?"

With heat climbing her cheeks, she almost said no, but stopped herself just in time. What was wrong with her? She had no reason to be embarrassed. There was nothing wrong with using a dating service to find a date—people did it all the time.

Lifting her chin, she said, "Yes, I am. I was just about to call several and see how much it costs."

"I've heard it can be pricey. Are you sure you want to do this? I'd be happy to introduce you to some of my friends."

If anyone but Martin had made such an offer, she would have probably given it serious consideration. But she'd worked for him for three years, and that had given her plenty of time to get to know not only the man, but to meet some of his friends when they dropped by the office to visit him. Like Martin, they were charming, attractive, sophisticated…and far too smooth for Abby's peace of mind. From what she'd seen, they were nothing but good-looking womanizers who had no intention of settling down with one woman anytime soon. All things considered, she wanted nothing to do with them.

She could hardly tell her boss that, however. Instead, she laughed. "Are you kidding? Martin, your friends are gorgeous and they go out with women who are as pretty as they are. I'm not in the same category."

"That's not true—"

"It's okay," she assured him. "I know what I am. And short, redheaded women with glasses don't go out with hunks who like tall blond bombshells. So I'll just stick to the dating service and see if I can find an ordinary guy who's not looking for Miss America. I just want someone to go to the movies or out to dinner with, someone who's already sowed his wild oats and wants to settle down and have babies. I don't think your friends would qualify."

"You got that right," he laughed, not the least bit offended. Sobering, he added, "But do you want to go out with any Tom, Dick or Harry who joins a dating service? There are a lot of weirdos out there."

"I know," she said. "But I plan to be wonderful."

"So when were you going to sign up?"

She hesitated, grimacing. "I was going to check into it first…"

"So you can find a reason not to do it?"

He knew her too well. "I just don't want to make a mistake," she replied. "I've done enough of that already."

Not the least impressed with her practicality, he said, "Just remember, he who hesitates is lost. Sometimes you've just got to go for it. This could be one of those times."

"So you think I should just jump into this?"

He grinned. "With both feet. In fact, you can start right this minute." Walking around behind her desk, he rolled her chair back and urged her to her feet. "Go! Do it now! Make the bank deposit, then take the rest of the afternoon and go join your dating service. If Sonya and I ever break up, I may do it myself."

Abby doubted that, but before she could think of another reason to delay, he grabbed her purse and the bank envelope, shoved them into her arms, and hustled her toward the front door. Her heart pounding crazily, she had no choice but to go.

An hour later, after she'd made the deposit at the bank for Martin, Abby didn't know whether she wanted to thank her boss or shoot him. The second she walked through the front door of the Right One Dating Service, Judy Lake, an overly zealous staff worker, latched on to her like a duck on a june bug and hustled her into a small office. Before she'd even plopped her down in front of her desk, the woman was singing the praises of the dating service as if it was the greatest thing since sliced bread, and pushing her to join.

It was too much too fast, and almost immediately, Abby's insecurities kicked in. "I'm not sure I'm ready to do this," she said, abruptly rising to her feet. "I'll think about it and get back to you."

"Please don't rush off," Judy begged. "You're just nervous. Everyone is at first."

Torn, she hesitated. "I don't even know why I talked myself into this. I'm lousy at dating. I get all tongue-tied and sound like I don't have a brain in my head. And now I want to pay to put myself through that torture? It's crazy!"

Judy grinned. "Put that way, I have to agree with you. But this isn't about the money. You know that. It's about taking a chance, putting yourself out there and possibly being rejected. No one wants to go through that."

"My point exactly. So give me one good reason why I should do it?"

"I'll do better than that," she replied soberly. "I'll give you three." Holding up her hand, she counted them off on her fingers. "A husband. Children. Happily ever after. You'll never have any of those things if you're not willing to take a chance on love."

Just that easily, she brought the sting of tears to Abby's eyes. She *did* want all those things—she always had. She just didn't know how to get them.

Sinking back into her chair, she was horrified to feel the tears spill over her lashes. "I'm sorry to be such a baby. This is just so hard."

An understanding smile curled the corners of Judy's mouth. Reaching for the box of tissues on the corner of her desk, she held it out to her. "I've been where you are. I felt the same way, then I joined the Right One, and my life changed almost overnight."

Wiping her eyes, Abby arched a brow in surprise. "It was that easy?"

"No," she admitted honestly. "It took time and effort, but it was worth it. If you sign up with us, you'll get a printout on all the men we match you up with. I'll warn you up front that they all look good on paper. Unfortunately, even jerks and chauvinists and bores join dating services. But so do some really great men. It's your job to figure out which is which and find Mr. Right."

"Do you do any type of screening or background checks? I'd just as soon avoid the jerks and chauvinists, but it's the perverts and druggies and con men I'm worried about."

Judy didn't, thankfully, discount her concerns. "You have a right to be worried about that. Unlike some other dating services, we do a criminal background check on our prospective clients. Our dating counselors are very astute. If we have any doubts about a prospective client, even if we don't find anything on them, we don't sign them up. And everyone has to fill out a psychological profile. That tells us a lot about a person. If we're not comfortable with their answers, we suggest they go to another dating service.

"It's not a foolproof method," she acknowledged, "but we haven't had any complaints so far, and we've been in business ten years. So what do you say?" she challenged. "Are you game? I promise you you'll meet some wonderful men."

In the past, Abby would have thanked her for the information, then gone home and thought about it. In the end, though, she wouldn't have done anything...because she was afraid to take a chance. God, she hated being so timid! She'd been playing it safe all her life, and what had it gotten her? Guys like

Dennis! She was tired of hiding in the shadows and settling for obnoxious men because she thought she wasn't good enough to attract someone better. She was a good person and she was going to do this for herself. If it turned out to be a mistake, then she'd do like the rest of the world and live with the consequences of her actions. At least she'd be taking charge of her life and really living instead of just existing!

Straightening her shoulders, she said, "I'm game. What do we do first?"

"The psychological test," Judy replied with a pleased smile. "It takes about two hours— the first two hours of the rest of your life. Let's get started."

Already wondering if she'd lost her mind, Abby didn't even consider backing out. Reaching for the questionnaire the other woman held out to her, she quickly began to fill it out.

Logan St. John looked at his brother and sister as if they had lost their minds. "You did what?!"

"Now, don't get mad," his sister, Patty, said hurriedly. "We just wanted to help you."

His blue eyes dark with concern, his younger brother, Carter, agreed. "We're worried about you. Ever since Faith died, you've become a recluse. You go to work, then come home and just stare at her picture. I know you loved her, but dammit, Logan, it's been a year! You have to go on with your life."

"I'm not going to a dating service," he said flatly. "So you can just call whoever talked you into this and tell them you want your money back."

His sister and brother exchanged a look. "We can't," Patty finally admitted. "They don't give refunds."

"This didn't come cheap," Carter added.

When he named an outrageous sum, Logan swore roundly.

"You've lost your minds! Did either one of you ever stop to think that if I wanted to date, I would?"

"We were just trying to help," Patty replied. "Okay, so we should have asked you. But we knew you would say no."

"Because I don't want to date!"

"No one does when they're still mourning the death of a relationship," Carter retorted. "We know you loved Faith. You two were perfect for each other. But she's gone, Logan, and you're miserable."

"I'm coping."

"No, you're not," he argued. "Look at yourself. You haven't had a haircut in months, you need a shave, you don't laugh anymore."

"My wife died in a car wreck," he growled. "I fell in love with her when I was in ninth grade and never looked at another woman. She was all I ever wanted. Do you really think I care what I look like?"

"That's just it," Patty stated quietly. "You don't care about anything. You've cut yourself off from your friends and family, you bite people's heads off. I can't remember the last time I saw you smile, let alone laugh. And that makes me sad. You're not the brother I grew up with. You're not the man who loved Faith."

"Faith wouldn't be happy with you if she could see you," Carter added. "In fact, she'd probably tell you off."

Logan started to argue, only to shut his mouth with a snap. They were right. Faith had loved life, loved to laugh, loved to make him laugh. The last thing she would want was for him to hole up in the house, mourning her.

But he still loved her! He always would. How could he even think about going out with another woman when the only one he wanted to be with was Faith?

"You can't expect me to act as if she never existed," he said hoarsely. "I didn't stop loving her just because she died."

"Of course you didn't," Patty said, horrified that he thought they were asking such a thing of him. "You loved her since you were a freshman in high school. She will always own a piece of your heart. But you have to go on with your life, Logan. You have to get out, meet people. We thought this might be the best way."

He should say no. A *dating service?* What were they thinking? Did they even realize what they were asking of him? He was thirty-five years old, and he'd only kissed one woman in his life, only made love to one woman. Faith. The love of his life. How could he even consider taking out another woman? He'd feel as if he were committing adultery.

But Carter and Patty had paid a ridiculous amount of money to the dating service to pull him out of his grief. How could he throw that back in their faces?

"I should shoot you both," he growled. "You should have never spent so much money without discussing it with me first. Now I'm stuck with this."

"So you'll go?" Carter asked in surprise.

"What choice do I have?" he retorted. "I'm not going to let you guys waste that kind of money. But it's not going to do any good, you know," he added grimly. "I'll never love anyone but Faith."

Relieved, Patty stepped close to give him a fierce hug. "All we ask is that you give it a chance. Who knows? You might meet someone who'll make life worth living again."

Logan sincerely doubted that, but she was so pleased, he hated to burst her bubble. "What do I have to do?"

"Go to the dating service office and take a psychological test," Carter said, handing him the prepaid contract. "A counselor's already been assigned to you—she's just waiting for your call."

Rolling his eyes, Logan held the contract out in front of him as if it were going to bite him. "Just what I need—a psychological test. Maybe I'll flunk it."

Carter laughed. "Fat chance. You're saner than anyone I know."

Logan wasn't so sure of that. If he'd had an ounce of sanity, he would never agree to go to a dating service!

Still, he kept his word and headed for the place. When he arrived twenty minutes later, however, he couldn't bring himself to go in. This was crazy! Why hadn't he thought to offer Patty and Carter their money back? It would cost him a tidy sum, but it would be worth it if it meant he didn't have to pretend to be looking for a date.

"It's safe to go inside," a quiet feminine voice said. "They're really quite nice."

Looking up, Logan blinked at the sight of the woman holding the door for him. Slim and petite, with curly, dark auburn hair arranged in a thick braid down her back, she had a shy smile and understanding brown eyes that, for some reason, reminded him of Faith.

Taken aback by the thought, he frowned. What the devil was wrong with him? She looked nothing like his wife! His subconscious was just playing tricks on him and making him feel guilty for even thinking about dating another woman.

"Nothing personal," he said dryly, "but I can think of a thousand other places I'd rather be."

"Oh, I agree," she said with a twinkle in her eyes. "Like the dentist."

"Actually, I was thinking the opera, but the dentist will do." Wishing he could stand there and chat just to keep from having to go inside, he forced a smile that held little humor. "I guess there's no point in putting it off."

"It's better to get it over with," she agreed. "Good luck."

"My luck ran out a year ago," he said flatly, "but thanks, anyway."

With that cryptic comment, he turned and walked into the dating service. He'd hardly given his name to the receptionist when he was shown into the office of Nancy Hartfield, the counselor who'd been assigned to help him find Miss Right.

"So you're Logan," she said with a friendly smile, rising from her desk to shake hands with him. "It's a pleasure meeting you. Your sister was afraid you wouldn't come anywhere near the place when you found out what she and your brother had done."

"I almost didn't," he retorted. "I'm not looking for a date, let alone a wife."

"Well, that's blunt enough," she said wryly. "Obviously, Patty was right to be worried."

"There's a reason she and Carter didn't tell me what they were up to until it was too late," he said dryly. "They knew I'd never go for it."

"But you're here," she pointed out. "Obviously you intend to participate."

"Under protest. As much as I'd like to walk away, I can't. This cost my brother and sister too much money."

"I'm sure they appreciate that. And who knows? You may find a way to make the best of the situation. Just because you're not looking for a date doesn't mean you won't make friends with some of the women we set you up with."

Placing the psychological test in front of him, she explained how his answers would be fed into a computer, then matched with women whose test results were compatible with his. "So it's very important that you answer the questions as honestly as possible. Even though you're not looking for a date, we don't want this to be a complete waste of time for you. Shall we begin?"

Resigned, he had little choice but to agree. Over the course of the next two hours, he answered questions about his likes and dislikes, politics, religious beliefs, ethics, even his plans for retirement. By the time he finished, he felt as if the dating service knew him better than his own family did.

Nancy immediately entered the results into the company database, and the computer spat out names of five candidates who might become the woman of his dreams. As far as Logan was concerned, that position had already been filled and a replacement wasn't possible, but he obliging took the list, folded it and put it in his pocket.

Watching him, the counselor smiled. "At this point, I normally tell clients they can request another list of possible dates whenever they like, if they feel they're not compatible with any of the previous matches made by the computer. But you're different. I have an idea you're not going to even look at the list, let alone call any of the women on it."

"No, I'll make some calls," Logan assured her. "I gave Carter and Patty my word. I never said anything about being enthusiastic about the process. This wasn't my idea, remember?"

To her credit, Nancy didn't try to convince him to give the service more of a chance. Smiling slightly, she said, "Well, I guess that's it, then. Good Luck."

Surprised, he lifted a brow at her. "What? No pictures? Don't most dating services take a picture to show the prospective dates?"

"We're old-fashioned," she replied simply. "We prefer to

match people according to personality, not looks. That's why we're more successful than the others."

He didn't care how successful they were, they were going to strike out with him, Logan thought as he walked out of the building with a sigh of relief. Thank God that was over! He hadn't lied to Nancy Hartfield. He *would* call some of the women on the list...in his own good time. Maybe he'd get around to it next week, when he had nothing better to do.

But twenty minutes later, when he unlocked the front door to the home he and Faith had shared for fifteen years, silence hit him like a slap in the face, just as it had every day since his wife had died. He tried to tell himself that it wasn't so bad—he was getting used to it.

But the quiet made the house seem empty and cold, and loneliness tugged at his heart. Without thinking, he headed for the kitchen to grab a beer from the refrigerator. He'd just popped the lid on the can and started to lift it to his mouth when his gaze fell on the trash can next to the stove. It was nearly overflowing with empty beer cans.

Startled, he froze, scowling. Had he drunk that much beer over the last few days? He couldn't have. Sure, he had a couple when he came home at night because he was lonely and he missed Faith so much, but there was nothing wrong with that. It wasn't as if he was a drunk. He could control himself.

Oh, really? a voice in his head drawled. *Then why didn't you? What would Faith think if she could see you now?*

The answer to that was a no-brainer. She'd be thoroughly disgusted with him.

Logan couldn't say he'd have blamed her. He was pretty disgusted himself. This wasn't who he was. At least, he never had been in the past. He wasn't a teetotaler, but he'd never made it a practice to drink regularly, either. Or at least he hadn't until Faith died.

God, he missed her! He missed the smell of her, the taste of her, the sound of her voice. Given the chance, he would have done just about anything to feel her in his arms again. But he wouldn't become a drunk just because he didn't want to go through life without her. Stepping to the kitchen sink, he poured out the beer he'd just opened, then collected the rest of the cans from the refrigerator and tossed them in the trash. Not giving himself time to think about what he was about to do, he pulled out the list of women Nancy Hartfield had given him, then reached for the phone.

"Hello?"

Logan flinched at the eager female voice that shrilled in his ears seconds after he finished punching in the first number on the list. Was the woman sitting by the phone, waiting for it to ring? he wondered. "Hi," he said gruffly. "This is Logan St. John. Is this Missy Trainer?"

"Yes! Did you get my name from the Right One Dating Service? I didn't know if I should call or wait for someone to call me first. Have you called anyone else? This is just so exciting!"

In her too high voice, she rushed on to tell him how she'd never had a serious relationship, but this time she just knew she was going to meet Mr. Right. Logan hoped she did, though he knew it wasn't going to be him. Not that she gave him a chance to tell her that. Wound up like a battery-operated bunny, she just kept talking and talking and didn't give him a chance to get a word in edgewise.

"I'm sorry," he cut in abruptly. "But there's someone at the door. We'll have to talk another time."

"What? Oh...well, okay."

He hung up before she could say another word, then almost

threw the dating list in the trash. This was nuts! What was he doing? He loved Faith. He wasn't going to forget her by talking to someone like Missy Trainer!

So call someone else.

He almost didn't. But Patty and Carter knew he'd gone to the dating service today, and before the night was over, one of them would call to see if he'd set up any dates yet. Muttering a curse, Logan reached for the phone and punched in the second number on the list. He hoped they appreciated this, he thought. There weren't many people he would do this for.

Praying that the second woman on the list wouldn't be as bad as the first, he braced himself for God knows what as an answering machine clicked on and a mechanical voice said, "I can't come to the phone at the moment. Leave a number at the beep."

Disgusted, he sighed. Apparently, this wasn't his night. "Hello," he said, leaving a message. "This is Logan St.John. I'm looking for Abby Saunders. I got her number from the Right One Dating Service..."

Chapter 2

In the process of changing out of her work clothes into jeans and a T-shirt, Abby froze at the sound of the deep male voice rumbling from her answering machine. She'd left the dating service only two and a half hours ago and she was already getting a call? She wasn't ready!

Her heart pounding wildly, she stared at the phone as if it were a snake about to strike. She shouldn't have listened to Lily and Rachel and Natalie. They might think they could go after happiness and find the American dream, but Abby should have known she couldn't pull this off. There were some women who were just destined to go through life alone, and she was obviously one of them.

Her stomach in knots, her insecurities choking her, she almost let the answering machine finish taking the call. But she couldn't forget her high-school reunion, couldn't forget the expressions of her classmates on the dance floor. They'd been so happy, so in love with their partners. Watching them, she'd never felt lonelier…or more envious.

So talk to Logan St. John. This could be your chance…your only chance to have what you want! All you have to do is pick up the phone.

Still she hesitated. Men wanted someone who was pretty and flirtatious, who'd hang on their every word as if they'd just hung the moon. How could she do that? She *wasn't* pretty, and she was too insecure to flirt. Why hadn't she realized that sooner and spared herself this misery?

"If you want to talk, I'll be in the rest of the evening. Give me a call at…"

When he started to rattle off his home phone number, she panicked. He was going to hang up! Furious with herself for being such a coward, she reached for the phone and snatched it up. "Hello?"

Her tone was almost defiant. Taken aback, Logan wondered if he had the wrong number. "Is this Abby Saunders?"

"Yes, it is."

So the dating service had picked a defiant one for him, Logan thought with a groan. That was just great. First an airhead and now a woman full of anger. He was batting a thousand. Wait until he told Carter and Patty. Talk about a waste of money!

"I thought we might talk," he said stiffly. "But I obviously caught you at a bad time."

"No! Please don't hang up," she said quickly. "After the way I answered the phone, you must think I've got some kind of chip on my shoulder. I did sound pretty angry."

"Actually, the word *defiant* comes to mind."

"I'm sorry," she said sincerely. "It's nothing against you personally. It's just that when I heard your voice on the answering machine, all I could think of was that I must have been out of my mind when I signed up with the dating service. I'm not good at this kind of thing."

Logan had to admit that he liked her honesty. "I take it I'm the first *date* to call you?"

"And I've already blown it. I'm just so nervous."

"It's okay," he assured her. "I know how you feel. I wouldn't even be talking to you if my brother and sister hadn't signed me up for the dating service without telling me."

"You're kidding! They didn't even warn you?"

"Not until they'd signed on the dotted line and forked over a ridiculous amount of money. They were worried about me. I've...been keeping to myself a lot since my wife died last year."

"Oh, I'm sorry. Was she sick?"

"No, it was a car accident." Abruptly changing the subject, he said, "What about you? Have you been out of the dating scene for a while? Is that why you decided to join the Right One?"

"Actually, I don't know that I was ever a part of the dating scene," she admitted wryly. "Oh, I've dated, but none of the men I went out with were exactly winners. I never had much confidence in myself."

"Maybe that's about to change," he said easily. "What do you do for a living?"

"I'm a secretary. How about you? What do you do?"

"I'm a reporter."

Surprised, she gasped. "You're *that* Logan St. John? The one with the *Gazette*?"

He grinned. "Obviously, you've read my work."

"I love your unsolved crime stories. You're very good."

He wasn't one to boast about his writing or preen when praised. "Thank you," he said simply. "So tell me more about yourself. Are you originally from Austin?"

"Actually, I was born in Liberty Hill, Colorado. It's a small town—"

"Near Aspen," he finished for her. "I've driven through there on my way to Aspen. How'd you end up in Austin?"

"Work," she said wryly. "I was working for an insurance company in Denver and got transferred down here. I ended up quitting that job, but decided to stay in Texas. What about you? Are you from Austin originally?"

"Born and raised," he replied with a chuckle. "The entire family lives here—grandparents, parents, my three brothers and my sister."

"Oh, that's nice! I only have one sister, and my parents were both only children, so we didn't have any extended family when we were growing up except for grandparents…and they lived in Florida."

"Things were pretty chaotic when we were growing up," he admitted. "Christmas was always wild. It still is, in fact. Everyone has kids except me, and when we all get together, there's paper and ribbon everywhere and enough food to feed an army."

"It sounds wonderful."

"My family's helped get me through a lot," he said quietly. "Of course, I wanted to shoot Carter and Patty this afternoon when they told me about the dating service, but they were only trying to help." Forcing a lighter tone, he said, "Enough about me. What about you? What are you doing Friday night? Would you like to get together for a drink?"

Abby had relaxed as he'd talked about his family, but the second he asked her out, the nerves in her stomach knotted in alarm. "Oh, I don't know…."

"I don't bite," he assured her with a smile in his voice. "Or at least I don't if I'm fed regularly."

She smiled slightly, only to find herself suddenly fighting the need to cry. "It's not you," she said thickly. "It's me. I told you I'm not good at this. When I go on blind dates, I get all flustered and sick to my stomach and act like an idiot. It's awful!"

"Okay, so we won't go out on a blind date."

Defeated, she was glad he couldn't see her at that moment. She just wanted to drop down on her living room couch and cry her eyes out. Instead, she straightened her shoulders and forced a smile. "Thanks for calling...and for being so understanding. Good luck with your other dates."

With the opening she'd so generously given him, Logan should have thanked her for the conversation and hung up. In spite of the fact that he'd enjoyed talking to her, it was obvious the lady had a lot of insecurities, and he didn't need that.

But there was a loneliness in her voice that struck a chord deep inside him and reminded him too much of himself. *Don't go there,* he ordered himself sternly. *This woman's problems aren't yours. Remember, you only called her to get Carter and Patty off your back. You're not looking for a date.*

It didn't matter. Even as he asked himself what the hell he was doing, he heard himself say, "Whoa, not so fast! Let's talk about this. You paid a lot of money to meet people and go out. How are you going to do that if you're not comfortable going on a blind date?"

"I don't know."

"What would make you comfortable?"

"Not going out with a stranger," she said promptly.

He laughed, confused. "But you have to meet someone in order for them not to be a stranger. How are you going to do that if you won't go out with someone you don't know?"

"There's other ways to get to know people without meeting them face-to-face," she replied. "People do it all the time on the Internet. And there's always the phone. Why can't we have a phone date before we meet in person? Then if it goes well and we're both comfortable with the idea, we can meet somewhere for dinner or a drink."

"Are you serious? That would make you more comfortable?"

"I wouldn't feel like I was going out with a complete stranger," she said simply. "So what do you think?"

Logan almost laughed out loud. He couldn't have planned this better if he'd tried. In spite of the fact that he'd temporarily lost his mind and asked her out for a drink, it was only because he'd felt sorry for her. He didn't want to date anyone. He still loved Faith, dammit! But his siblings weren't going to quit harassing him until he convinced them that he was jumping back into life. What better way to do that than to call Abby occasionally for a *phone* date? Carter and Patty would think he was dating, so he'd get them off his back, and all he would be doing was talking to Abby on the phone. Just thinking about it made him grin. This could work.

"Friday night's good for me," he replied. "How about you? I could call you around eight, if that's okay."

Stunned, Abby couldn't believe he was agreeing so easily. If every man the dating service set her up with was as accommodating as Logan St. John, she was going to love dating! "You don't know how much this means to me, Logan. I was afraid you'd think I was weird or something."

"Not at all," he assured her. "I don't blame you for being nervous. Blind dates are the pits. There's nothing worse than having a drink or a meal with someone you don't know and sitting there in silence, trying to think of something to say."

"I know," she said. "It's awful! I just can't put myself through it."

"There's no reason you have to. We can talk on the phone as long as you like. If either of us decides that we don't have anything in common and don't ever want to meet, that's okay, too. No hard feelings, okay?"

"No hard feelings," she agreed. "Now that we've got that settled, I guess I'll talk to you Friday night."

"It's a date," he said with a chuckle, and hung up.

When the phone rang later that evening, Logan wasn't surprised to hear his younger brother's voice on the other end of the line. "Well, well," Logan drawled. "How did I know you would call?"

"I'm just concerned," Carter said defensively. "Patty and I got you into this. The least I can do is check and see how it went." When Logan only snorted, he said, "Oh, c'mon, don't be that way. How'd it go? I know you got a list of dates after you completed the psychological test, so what happened? Have you called anyone yet?"

Torn between amusement and irritation, Logan rolled his eyes. "It would serve you right if I didn't tell you a damn thing. You know that, don't you?"

"Hey, this was all Patty's idea—"

"And you were totally against it, right? That's why you put up half the money."

"Okay," he acknowledged, "so I let her talk me into it. I was just trying to help."

"You should have told me."

"We thought about it, but we knew you'd never agree."

"Exactly!"

"Look on the bright side," Carter said encouragingly. "There are a lot of nice women out there—you might actually meet a couple you like. And if you don't, you can always do a story on dating services. So? Talk to me! What happened?"

"I have a date Friday night," he retorted. "Are you happy now? Is that what you wanted to hear?"

"With who? What's her name? She must be nice if you asked her out already. Where are you going?"

"Geez, you sound worse than Mom!"

"Oh, God, I do!" his brother exclaimed, horrified. "Forget I said anything. Go out with your mystery date, have a good-time. I don't need the details."

When he told him good-night and hurriedly hung up, Logan laughed—truly laughed—for what felt like the first time since Faith had died. And it felt good...damn good. He'd have to thank Abby when he talked to her on Friday.

Logan had always been a morning person, but over the course of the last year he'd had little reason to get out of bed. He'd dragged himself to work and gone through the motions of doing the job he'd once loved, but he'd found no joy in investigative reporting, no joy in writing. He hadn't needed to go to a doctor to know that he was suffering from depression. His days were gray and dull and stretched one into another with no end in sight.

He expected the following morning to be the same, but as he rolled out of bed and headed for the shower, he found himself thinking about his conversations with Abby and his brother, and a slow grin of anticipation stretched across his face. Maybe this dating thing wasn't going to be so bad. He and Abby would talk on the phone, he'd put one over on his brother—who wasn't easy to fool—and his family would never know the difference. He almost rubbed his hands together in glee at the thought. This was going to be fun.

Imagining his brother's and sister's faces when they discovered that he'd pulled a fast one on them, he arrived at work an hour later with a spring in his step. The smile on his face didn't last long, however. He was just going over his notes for a story on fraud in the building industry when Nick Whitiker, his boss, buzzed him and announced, "We need to talk."

Logan knew that terse tone well. Nick was ticked off about something. Had Logan missed a deadline? He didn't think so, but he would be the first to admit that his work had suffered some during the last year. He and Nick had talked about it, and he'd done his best to be more focused. What had he missed? "I'll be right there," he promised.

Nick usually exchanged a few pleasantries with anyone he called to his office, but he didn't this time. Instead, he nodded toward the chair angled in front of his desk. "Sit down," he growled.

Logan preferred to stand and take whatever bad news Nick had for him, but he only had to glance at his boss's stern face to know this wasn't the time to push him. Without a word, he dropped into the chair. "If this is about the story on the poker games in the break room at the police department, I don't care what Chief Hawkins said, I've got proof."

Nick waved him off with a grimace. "If I thought you couldn't back up your stories, you wouldn't be on the crime beat. That's not the problem."

"Then what is?"

Leaning back in his chair, Nick looked at him over the top of his black-rimmed reading glasses. "I know the last year has been hard for you," he said gruffly. "And to be perfectly honest, I don't know if I'd have been able to hold myself together as well as you have if I'd lost Jackie the way you did Faith. Losing someone you love to cancer or some kind of health problem is one thing—you can understand it even though you can't accept it. But a drunk driver who's done this before? The jackass should have been shot!"

"I thought about it," Logan admitted honestly, "but killing him wasn't going to bring Faith back. Nothing will."

"So you have to move on," he said. "And that's the problem. Oh, you've been showing up for work, hitting your deadlines, keeping track of your assignments, but we both know you've only been going through the motions. Don't get me wrong," he added quickly. "I sympathize with you and everything you've been through, but that doesn't change the fact that I've got a paper to publish, and my number one reporter hasn't been writing up to par for nearly a year."

"You know I've been trying, Nick."

"Yes, I do, but unfortunately, trying isn't good enough. Sales are down, ad revenue has been dropping steadily for the last few months, and all departments have been ordered to tighten their belts and weed out the chafe."

"You're firing me?"

"No, of course not." He scowled. "Everyone knows you're the best damn writer I've got, but I'm getting pressure from upstairs. Porter isn't happy with the quality of the stories we've been putting out. He left me no choice but to hire his granddaughter's boyfriend to pick up the slack. He's right out of school—"

"Oh, c'mon, Nick! A college kid? You can't be serious!"

"I know," he said with a grimace. "I felt the same way when Porter told me about the kid. But then I read some of his stuff. He's good, Logan. Damn good. In fact, his writing reminds me of the way yours used to be. It's got an edge to it—"

"He's a kid, Nick! He's not me."

"No, he's not," he agreed. "But right now, you're MIA, and

he's the best I've got. I hope the two of you get along, but whether you do or don't doesn't change anything. Porter says he's here to stay."

Picking up the phone on his desk, he pressed a button and growled, "I need to see you in my office." When he hung up, he told Logan, "You came here right out of college yourself, so remember that. He's no threat to you. In fact, he may be just what you need to get out of the rut you're in. A little competition never hurt anyone."

Logan sincerely doubted that a kid who was still wet behind the ears could compete with an experienced reporter, but he himself didn't plan to compete with him or anyone else. He was handling his grief, and even though he'd lost interest in his writing after Faith died, he was still a damn good writer. And with time, he knew he would regain the sharpness he'd been famous for in the past.

A knock at the door distracted him from his thoughts, and he looked up to see a tall blond man walk in. He didn't look old enough to shave, let alone be out of college, and if Logan hadn't known better, he would have sworn he was a California beach bum who spent all his time surfing. Logan could almost smell the scent of the ocean as the younger man stepped into the office.

This was the crackerjack reporter with a sharp edge? Logan thought cynically. *Yeah, right!*

"You rang, boss?"

His tone was far from respectful, his stance slouched. Nick scowled. "I don't answer to *boss*. You can call me Nick or Mr. Whitiker."

The younger man only shrugged. "Sure. Whatever." Turning to Logan, he didn't bother to hold out his hand. "You must be Logan St. John. I'm Josh Garrison. I heard you were having some problems. Don't worry. I'll pick up the slack."

Logan liked to think he was fairly thick-skinned and didn't get insulted easily, but there was something about Josh Garrison's cocky tone and the look in his eye that irritated the hell out of him. "I don't need you or anyone else to pick up the slack where I'm concerned," he said coolly. "I'm quite capable of doing my job."

"Hey, man, don't get offended," Josh retorted. "I'm just repeating what Porter told me. The paper's in a slump and he brought me in to pull it out. If you've got a beef, take it up with the old man. I just do what I'm told."

He turned and strode out without another word. In the silence left behind, Nick swore softly. "Well, that went well. Dammit, Logan, you didn't have to get your back up!"

"The hell I didn't," he muttered. "You heard him. *I heard you were having some problems. I'll pick up the slack.* Smart-ass. I don't care what the 'old man' told him, I don't need him to do my job for me. I was winning awards for this paper when he was still playing tag on the playground in elementary school."

"Okay, so he wouldn't know tact if he tripped on it," Nick conceded. "He sets my teeth on edge, too. But like it or not, we're both going to have to live with him, Logan. He's the golden boy...and practically family to Porter. That gives him a get-out-of-jail-free card, so don't hold out hope that he'll wear out his welcome anytime soon. He's too good a writer, and you know how Porter is when he gets a bee in his bonnet that the paper's not pulling in enough money. He'd hire Attila the Hun if he thought it would bring in dollars."

"I don't care. The kid's arrogant."

Nick shrugged. "He's young. You were the same way at his age."

"I was never disrespectful," Logan said flatly. Staring at the door through which Josh had walked out, he scowled. "There's something about him I don't like."

"Just do your job and don't worry about him," Nick advised. "He'll show his true colors soon enough."

Logan had never been one to go out and look for trouble, but he also wasn't one to sit and wait for trouble to come to him without taking steps to ward it off. He intended to watch Josh Garrison very, very carefully.

Doing some much-needed filing at work, Abby should have rushed through the job, then started printing address labels for the fund-raising-campaign letter Martin wanted mailed by Wednesday. But as she completed the familiar task, she found her thoughts drifting to Logan. She still couldn't believe how understanding he'd been yesterday when he'd called her—or what a coward she'd been when he'd asked her to have a drink with him!

He probably thought she was scared of her own shadow, she thought with a silent groan. And she really wasn't. Granted, she had no confidence in herself when it came to men, but she wasn't afraid of them. The person she was afraid of was herself. And with good reason. She was a lousy judge of men. She'd proved it time and time again. She was thirty-three years old, for heaven's sake, and she'd never dated a man she wanted to introduce to her family and friends, let alone marry.

Just thinking about it made her cringe. Had she been desperate? she wondered. Was that why she'd gone out with anyone who'd asked her? She'd never felt desperate, just lonely. And horribly insecure. And Dennis and the others like him who'd asked her out had seemed so sure of themselves. She realized now, of course, that nothing could have been further from the truth—they bragged because they were as insecure as she was and didn't want the world to know it. But at the time, she hadn't been able to see through their facade.

Never again, she promised herself. She wanted a man who knew what he could do without having to boast about it. A man she could introduce to her friends without having to apologize for his behavior. After only a short phone conversation with Logan St. John, she refused to do as she had in the past and jump to any conclusions about what kind of person he was. He didn't seem to be insecure, but at this point, there was no way for her to know that for sure...which was why she intended to learn more about him *before* she decided if she really wanted to go out with him. If he turned out to be the type of person she thought he was, she would meet him for a drink and take it from there. If he wasn't, she wouldn't waste her time.

Satisfied that she was doing the right thing, she turned back to her desk to retrieve another stack of files that needed to be filed, only to spy a small piece of paper lying on the floor halfway between her desk and the filing cabinet. Scooping it up, she turned it over, thinking it was a piece of correspondence that must have fallen out of one of the files. She saw immediately, however, that it was a handwritten note to Martin.

"Martin, sorry I missed you. We need to talk about the deal. Meet me at the club at the usual time. J.N."

Who was J.N.? Abby wondered, surprised. Martin was a popular city councilman who had a lot of friends and contacts. She thought she knew most of them, but she couldn't think of any of his friends who went by the initials J.N.

Frowning, she stepped into his office after only a perfunctory knock. "Martin, do you know anything about this note? I found it on the floor. Was I supposed to file it?"

In the process of punching a number into his cell phone, he halted abruptly and put it away. "I don't know. Who's it from?"

Striding over to his desk, she handed the slip to him. "J.N., whoever that is."

Sitting back in his chair, he studied the note and abruptly laughed. "It's from John Nickels! We went to college together—he's just moved back to town. He got a job with Barnes, Tucker, and Smith. He called me this morning to tell me he was going to stop by. Since he never showed up, I thought he'd changed his mind, but I guess he came by during lunch and slipped it under the door. Damn!"

"You could call him," she suggested. "The afternoon's pretty booked, but you could fit him into your schedule around three. You have a meeting with Mr. Hawks at two-thirty, but he won't stay long—he never does. And you don't have another appointment until four. That'll give you plenty of time to visit."

"It would if I could reach him," her boss agreed. "But he hasn't started work yet, and doesn't have a cell phone." When she lifted a brow in surprise, he said dryly, "You heard me. He doesn't have one and doesn't want one. You'll have to meet John one of these days. He was born in the wrong century. He wouldn't have a cell phone if you gave it to him."

His tone was almost envious, and with good reason. His own cell phone rang all the time and was more of a curse than a convenience. "Maybe you can catch him at home."

Martin smiled slightly. "He forgot to give me the number, but that's okay. He'll call back. He wants to buy my car."

"The Corvette? You're selling your '58 'Vette? You can't be serious! You love that car!"

Grinning at her horrified tone, he shrugged. "Sonya says it's time I grew up. She wants to get married, and she's not going to be happy with anything less than a blowout." Wadding up the note, he tossed it in the trash. "Big weddings don't come cheap."

"But your 'Vette, Martin. Surely there's must be another way."

"It's just a car, Abby. I can get another one."

He could, but Abby knew it wouldn't mean nearly the same thing. The Corvette had literally been in pieces when he'd bought it right after he graduated from college and got his first job. He'd spent the last ten years restoring it, and just about everyone in town knew it was his pride and joy. He drove it in parades and car shows and had pictures of it all over his Web site. How could he sell something he loved so much for a wedding?

She almost asked him that, but she already knew the answer. He was a city councilman and always made an effort to keep up appearances. And his fiancée, Sonya, was just as bad as he was. She seemed to really enjoy being in the spotlight with him. Martin was right—she would want a fairy-tale wedding that would be splashed across the front pages of the paper and talked about for years.

Abby wrinkled her nose at the thought. A very public, impersonal wedding was the last thing she would want herself, but then again, she wasn't the one who was getting married. Changing the subject, she said, "You wanted me to remind you about the next city council meeting. The preliminary discussions about awarding the tax collection contract are scheduled to begin."

Straightening in his chair, he swore softly. "Damn. I forgot about that. Have we got anything in yet on the firms submitting bids?"

"I've been collecting it for the last three weeks," she said, and retrieved a thick file from one of the cabinets near the door. "Ben Coffman called again this morning while you were in a conference to see if you needed anything else. That's the third time this week."

"I never did like Ben," he said curtly. "He doesn't know when to back off and give a man some space. If he calls again, tell him he's going to lose any chance of getting my vote if he doesn't quit harassing the hell out of me and my secretary."

Abby would never be so rude to anyone, and Martin knew it. She would politely take a message, then pass it on to him. What he did about it was his business. "He's not the only one calling," she pointed out. "It's going to be a feeding frenzy until the August twenty-first deadline."

"I don't care. No one should get rude." His gray eyes hard with irritation, he growled, "The next time Ben calls, I'll take care of him."

Abby could handle Ben, but Martin was the boss. "No problem," she said easily, and turned back to her own office.

"Oh, and if John Nickels phones, put him through immediately," he called after her.

The words were hardly out of his mouth before the phone rang again. Abby stepped to her desk and had to smile when she recognized Ben Coffman's gruff voice. "Please hold, Mr. Coffman. I'll put you right through."

With the door between her office and Martin's open, she heard him mutter a curse at her words. Grinning, she stepped over and quietly shut it. She'd hardly returned to her filing when the phone rang again. Not surprisingly, the caller was from another firm that intended to make a bid to collect city taxes. She took a message, promised to relay it to Martin, then returned to her filing.

The pattern of her afternoon was set, and later, she couldn't have said how many times the phone rang. She finished filing, then printed out the address labels for the fund-raising-campaign letter, and began stuffing the envelopes. Considering how busy she was, she shouldn't have had time to do anything but concentrate on her job. Instead, she found herself once again thinking of Logan.

Troubled, she swore softly. "You have to stop doing this," she muttered out loud as she added stamps to the letters. What did she know about Logan? He had a nice voice and appeared to be understanding. That was no reason to daydream about the man, for heaven's sake! He was a reporter. For all she knew, he could be hard-nosed and pushy, and the type who didn't take no for an answer. Was that the kind of man she wanted to date?

"No!" she said grimly. She'd made mistakes in the past because she was lonely and wanted a man in her life. But she'd learned the hard way that there were worse things than being alone—such as getting mixed up with the wrong type of man. She was going to take it slow and easy this time and give *herself* a chance. She was a good person and she deserved the best. This time, she was going to get it.

So why are you only talking to Logan St. John? an irritating voice in her head demanded. *Why are you limiting yourself to just one man? The dating service gave you a list of five prospective dates. Call them. Then get another list and start the process all over again. That's why you joined a dating service—to meet men! What are you waiting for?*

Her heart pounded at the thought. She had never dated or

been involved with more than one man at a time. Not that she'd had the chance, she thought wryly. Few men had shown an interest in her. There had been months, even years, when she hadn't had a single date. While she'd sat at home, dreaming of Prince Charming and hating her solitude, every other woman she knew was having a full, active social life, getting to know any number of men before settling down with one. Wasn't it time she did the same thing?

Captivated by the idea, Abby felt sudden, foolish tears sting her eyes and had to laugh at herself. "Silly, there's no reason to cry. You can do this!" It wasn't rocket science. All she had to do was gather her courage and make some phone calls after she got home from work. Maybe then she'd be too busy to think about Logan.

Chapter 3

When Abby stepped through her front door three hours later, however, and her dog, Buster, greeted her with a joyous bark from the backyard, she found any number of reasons not to pick up the phone and call some of the other men on her dating list. She had to look at her mail and check her answering machine and spend some time with Buster. And then, of course, she had laundry to do and dinner to cook. She'd call later, after she did the dishes and settled down for the evening....

Then she realized what she was doing and stiffened. No! she told herself, swearing softly. She wouldn't do this. She would *not* act like a scared rabbit. Any bimbo could call a man. It didn't require any brain power. All she had to do was pick up the phone and punch in the number. The sooner she got it over with, the easier it would be.

"Yeah, right," she muttered as she pulled the list of prospective dates from the top drawer of her desk. "If it's so easy, why are my palms sweating?"

Because you're a coward.

She couldn't argue with that irritating little voice in her head, especially when it was right. Her heart slamming against her ribs, she frowned down at the first name. Frank Gurenski. What kind of man was he? she wondered. There was only one way to find out. Throwing caution to the wind, she quickly punched in his phone number.

"Hello?"

Up until that moment, Abby would have sworn she was working hard at not jumping to conclusions about a person without getting to know them first. But with a single word, Frank Gurenski revealed himself to be stiff and cool and hard to get to know. Disappointed, Abby almost told him she had the wrong number, but then reasoned that he could have had a bad day. Maybe he had call waiting and she'd caught him in the middle of another phone call. A lot of people didn't like to be interrupted.

So why would he have call waiting if he doesn't like to be interrupted? How dumb is that?

Sternly ordering the voice in her head to behave, she grabbed on to her courage with both hands and said with forced cheerfulness, "Hi. I'm Abby Saunders. Is this Frank Gurenski?"

"Yes."

"The Right One Dating Service gave me your name and number. I hope I'm not calling at a bad time."

"No. This is fine."

Whatever reaction Abby had been expecting, it wasn't such a total lack of interest. "Have you met anyone yet or are you still looking?"

"I'm still looking," he retorted. "It's not easy to find someone."

Especially if you don't talk, she thought, but she wisely kept that thought to herself. Instead, she waited for him to take up the conversational ball and ask something about her, but he didn't say a word. An awkward silence fell between them, and just that easily, all Abby's fears about dating came rushing back. Was *she* the problem? Did he find her uninteresting? Was that why he wasn't asking her anything?

Oh, please! At least you're trying. The man's a dud. Cut it short and put yourself out of your misery.

She didn't need to be told twice. "Well," she said brightly, "it was nice talking to you. I really just called to chat for a while to see if we had anything in common, but I really don't think we do. I wish you luck finding someone, though. Bye."

Yes! Now you're getting the hang of it! If you have to work that hard to carry on a conversation with someone, you don't *want to date him. Cut your losses and move on.*

Stunned, unable to believe that she'd hung up on the man, Abby stood in the sudden silence of her kitchen and didn't know if she wanted to laugh or cry. In the past, she would have continued a conversation that was going nowhere simply because she would have felt guilty if she hadn't. But not anymore, she thought, grinning. She didn't have to waste time on someone who couldn't string three or four words together just because she didn't want to be alone. She had choices!

Pleased, she punched in the second name on the list. Luke Templeton. What kind of man was he? Hopefully, he could at least talk.

Fifteen minutes later, Abby was finally able to hang up, but she had little positive to say about Luke Templeton. The man could talk, all right. And talk and talk! And although he hadn't boasted like Dennis had, he was definitely a man of strong opinions. He'd given her a laundry list on politics, religion, and money, and had given her little time to get a word in edgewise. He'd been so caught up in what he had to say that she doubted he'd even noticed when she hung up.

Amused, she wondered if Logan had run into the same type of problems with the women he'd called. Giving in to impulse, she quickly punched in his number and almost laughed aloud at her daring. Just days ago, she would never have dreamed of doing such a thing, but she truly felt as if she was getting the hang of using the dating service. She just had to keep her sense of humor and not take the situation too seriously.

"Hi. This is Logan. You missed me. Leave your name and number at the beep and I'll call you back."

Pulled from her thoughts at the sound of Logan's voice on his answering machine, Abby found herself smiling. He really did have a nice voice. It was deep and husky, really sexy. Did he look as good as he sounded? she wondered, her heart thumping at the thought. Maybe one day she'd find out.

"Hi, Logan," she said, suddenly feeling shy. "This is Abby Saunders. I just called a couple of the men on my list from the dating service and was wondering if you'd phoned anyone else. If you want to talk and share a laugh, give me a call."

Hanging up, she headed for her room to change into her running clothes. She was the new, improved Abby, she reminded herself. She wasn't going to wait by the phone for any man to call her back. Five minutes later, she locked the door to her apartment and went for a run with Buster.

The bar had been robbed less than fifteen minutes ago. Three police cruisers and an ambulance were parked out front, and customers were standing on the sidewalk in the weak glow of a nearby streetlight as detectives interviewed the witnesses. Finding a parking place across the street, Logan recognized Tim Bradly, one of the detectives, and headed straight for him.

Surprised to see him, Tim growled, "What are you doing here, St. John? You don't usually cover the penny-ante stuff. Must be a slow night."

"You would know that better than I, Bradly," he retorted with a grin. "You're the cop."

Tim swore good-naturedly. "Don't give me that bull. You've got the same scanner I do. Half the time, you beat me to a crime scene."

"Just doing my job," Logan chuckled, making no apology for the fact that he had a police scanner not only at work, but in his car. Tim understood that they both had a job to do and that they were both going to do it to the best of their abilities. "According to the report on the scanner, someone was shot during an attempted armed robbery. The robber was a woman?"

He nodded grimly. "It's not the first time we've had a woman running around town with a gun, demanding money, but it's not that common. From what we can tell, she was working alone."

Logan lifted a brow in surprise. "No kidding? She drove her own getaway car?"

"At this point, we're not even sure she had a car. She slipped out the back door and just seemed to disappear."

"And no one saw or heard a vehicle?"

"Most of the customers are half-lit, Logan," he said dryly. "The bartender was the only sober one in the joint, and when the robber started spraying the place with bullets, he ducked behind the bar. By the time it was safe to come out, there was no sign of the perp." A police helicopter approached from the west and began scanning the area. "If she had a car stashed down the block, she's probably long gone. If she's on foot, though, that's another matter."

"Let me know if she's spotted," Logan told him. "Mind if I interview the witnesses?"

"No, go ahead. We're still collecting evidence inside, but we've finished questioning everyone."

Thanking him, Logan began working his way through the customers who still lingered, obviously waiting for the police to finish their work so that they could go back in and resume drinking. As Tim had warned him, the customers had had a little too much to drink to know for sure what had happened, but they were all clear on one thing. The perp was a big woman with a gun.

A thought hit Logan, and he went in search of the bartender. "You must have got a good look at her when she pulled the gun out," he told him. "What did you think of her?"

"She was big-boned and ugly as homemade soap. And she had big hair."

Logan smiled. "You mean long hair?"

"Yeah, it was long, but it was also big. You know—like women used to wear back in the seventies."

"Could it have been a wig?"

Considering that, the bartender shrugged. "Sure, I guess so. Though I can't imagine why any woman would want to look like that. It wasn't attractive at all."

"Are you certain the perp was a woman? Could it have been a man in drag?"

"Sure," he said with a shrug. "Transvestites come in here occasionally. In fact, there's a brunette who shows up sometimes who's absolutely gorgeous. If I didn't know better, I'd swear *she* was the prettiest woman I'd ever seen in my life. I think he's really the superintendent for one of the school districts here in town. What do you want to bet he doesn't wear a dress to work?"

Busy jotting down notes, Logan was already formulating his next question when he suddenly realized what the bartender had said. He glanced up sharply. "Wait a minute. Back up. Did you say a school superintendent is a transvestite?"

"Well, I couldn't swear to it," he admitted. "After all, the guy looks a lot different without the makeup and wig and everything. But I'll bet last week's paycheck it's him."

"What makes you think so?"

"He's been in here a number of times, always dressed as a woman, and he always sits at the bar. I've gotten to know him pretty well. He goes by the name Elizabeth."

Taking notes, Logan could see the headlines already. "Has he ever told you anything about himself?"

"No, but I had to go to a program at my daughter's school one night, and the superintendent was there. The second I saw him, I knew he was Elizabeth. And he knew I knew! When he saw me, he turned his back on me."

"How long ago was this?"

"Three weeks ago."

"Has he been in for a drink since then?"

The bartender shook his head. "No, but he's not a regular. He only comes in a couple of times a month."

Logan pulled out his business card, which contained his office and cell phone numbers. "The next time he comes in, give me a call. Okay?"

"Sure," the man said, pocketing the card. "I don't want to cause the guy any trouble, but I don't want him hanging around my kid, either. I thought about calling the school board, but I didn't figure anyone would listen to me, being as I work in a bar."

"That doesn't mean you're not honest," Logan pointed out. "Or that you're not concerned about who's running your daughter's school. What's the superintendent's name?"

When he told him, Logan said, "I'll do some checking and see what I can find out. I doubt, though, that I'll find anything. The school district would have done a background check before they hired him."

"Then they didn't do a very good one," the bartender retorted. "It's not like this guy was raiding his wife's closet and parading around the house in her clothes. He's going out in public! And if he'll do this, what else is he doing? He works with kids, for heaven's sake!"

Logan could understand his worries, but just because the man liked wearing female clothes didn't mean he was a threat to the bartender's kids or anyone else. "I'll check it out and get back to you," he promised. "Thanks for the lead."

Excusing himself to question other witnesses about the robbery, Logan had to fight back a grin of anticipation. He couldn't wait to see Nick's face when he told him he'd gotten not one story tonight, but two. His boss would be shocked, and Logan couldn't blame him. He'd shown little interest in work over the last year.

That was about to change, he silently acknowledged as he headed back to the office. He didn't know what had happened to spark the change, but over the last couple of days, he'd found himself more interested in work, more interested in life. When his family heard about the change in him, they would say that he was finally getting over Faith's death and would thank God for it, but nothing could have been further from the truth. He missed his wife more every day and had never been lonelier. Maybe he was just coming to accept the fact that he would feel that way the rest of his life.

Thankful that he had work to distract him from that thought, he grabbed his notes on the bar robbery, booted up his computer and threw himself into the story. He wasn't one of those writers who had to sit and think and wait for the muse to strike. As a reporter, he just didn't have time for that. The second his fingers touched the keyboard, they were flying.

Lost in his story, he didn't realize he was no longer alone until Josh Garrison drawled, "Well, look who's busy burning the midnight oil. Not that it's midnight yet," he added, "but you don't strike me as a man who works overtime. I thought you left hours ago."

Logan barely bit back a curse. What the devil was *he* doing there? Tomorrow's deadline had come and gone, and the newspaper offices were practically deserted. Oh, Nick was still there—he always stayed after hours just in case a late story broke—but he was holed up in his office. Everyone else had either gone home or was out working on a piece for tomorrow's deadline…which was why Logan often came in after the paper had been put to bed. The phones were silent, and he had the place to himself. Or at least he usually did.

Wanting to tell Garrison to take a long walk off a short pier, he growled, "I could say the same thing about you, Garrison. What do you want?"

He made no effort to be nice to the guy. He hadn't liked him from day one, though he'd tried to be civil. Garrison, however, hadn't made it easy. He made snide remarks whenever he thought he could get away with it, then smiled like a politician and said all the right things whenever Nick was around. As far as Logan was concerned, the man was nothing but a two-faced brownnoser, and he wanted nothing to do with him.

Garrison, however, seemed to enjoy goading him. Far from being offended by his curtness, he only smiled smugly. "I'm here for the same reason you are—to work. Or didn't Nick tell you? He called me in to give me the Terry Saenz story. You do know who Saenz is, don't you?"

Logan didn't bother to answer. Of course he knew who Saenz was. The story had just broken an hour ago and was all over the airways. Saenz was an award-winning cop who'd taken a bullet for his partner last year when they'd been ambushed by a south-side gang. He'd nearly died from being shot in the chest. Once he recovered from his injury, he'd made it his mission in life to visit every school in town and warn the kids of the dangers of belonging to a gang.

The man was a bona fide hero—or at least he had been until he was arrested earlier in the evening for dealing drugs. According to the radio report, the shooting last year hadn't been just a random act of violence, as first thought. Saenz had been dealing drugs to the gang member who'd shot him.

"Congratulations," Logan told Josh sardonically. "It looks like you hit the jackpot."

"It's a hell of a story. You should have seen Nick—though I guess you know how gleeful he gets when a good story comes in. He's already called down to production and told them to save room for the piece on tomorrow's front page. And the story that broke today is only the tip of the iceberg. Once the police investigate Saenz further, there's no telling what they'll come up with. So you can expect to see my byline a hell of a lot over the next few months. Then there'll be the trial, of course. You can bet that's going to be heavily covered. I'm sure the news services will pick it up. Before this is over, I may be as well-known as you used to be."

He was deliberately trying to rile him, but Logan didn't

even flinch. What did old man Porter's granddaughter see in this jerk? Headlines and bylines weren't always a testament of how well someone did his job. Granted, before Faith died, *he* was the one who'd gotten the top assignments and whose stories regularly made the front page, but he'd never once taunted other reporters about it. That wasn't his way. Writing was personal for him—all he'd cared about was doing the best job he could. He didn't keep track of what his co-workers were doing. He didn't care because it had nothing to do with him.

In the world of print journalism, however, he knew he was the exception rather than the rule. Most reporters would do anything to get a front page story, and the competition was fierce. From what Logan had seen of Garrison so far, it was obvious the man would sell his own mother to get ahead. He thought he was hot stuff and it showed.

Idiot. Let him have the headlines and his fifteen minutes in the spotlight, Logan thought in disgust. He wasn't worried about Garrison or threatened by him. Logan was well-known in the city and had connections at the police department and informants who called him on a regular basis. He had plenty of stories to write, stories that Garrison wouldn't even know where to go to get.

So if the jackass expected him to be gnashing his teeth in jealousy over his big coup, he could think again.

"It sounds like you're going to be damn busy," he said dryly. "You'd better get started on tomorrow's story or you're going to have Nick breathing down your neck. If he gets it in his head that you can't meet your deadlines, he won't hesitate to assign someone else to the job."

"I guess you would know that better than anyone, wouldn't you?"

Disliking him more than ever, but refusing to be goaded,

Logan growled, "You're damn straight. I haven't been as dependable as I should have been over the last year—which is why you're here. If you don't want to meet your replacement, I suggest you don't miss your deadlines."

His point made, he turned back to his computer. A few long seconds later, Garrison stalked past him to his own desk. Logan never spared him a glance. His eyes trained on his computer screen, he cleared his head of all thoughts except the facts of the bar robbery, and focused on his opening sentence. Once he had that, it was easy. His fingers again flew over the keys, and just that quickly, he was caught up in his writing.

Later, he couldn't have said when Garrison finished his own story and left. Logan's eyes were glued on his computer monitor. Reading over what he'd written, he was, for the most part, more than satisfied. The last paragraph needed some work, but he wasn't worried about that. For the first time in a long time, the old edge that had been the trademark of his writing before Faith died was back. Nick would be pleased. Hell, Logan was pleased! He'd almost forgotten what it was like to write something he was proud of.

"Logan? I didn't know you were coming back tonight."

Glancing up from his writing, he found his sister-in-law, Samantha, walking toward him with a smile as big as Texas on her face. Amused, he had to admit that he'd always had a special place in his heart for Sam. It was through her that he'd met Faith at a high-school football game. Sam had arranged their first date without discussing it with either one of them, and when Faith died, the two of them grieved together over the woman they'd both loved. He'd helped Sam get a job in payroll at the paper several years ago, and every two weeks or so, they went out to dinner to catch up on each other's lives. She was family and always would be.

"Hey, Sam, what are you doing here? You're not usually around this late."

"There was a computer glitch," she said with a grimace. "And payroll had to go out tonight. We just finished." Glancing at his computer, she said, "What are you working on? I thought you were done for the day."

"I was…until I followed up on something I heard on the police scanner. I wanted to get it down on paper while the details were still fresh."

"Are you almost done? We could go to dinner…if you don't have any plans, of course."

She made the suggestion casually, but there was nothing casual about the emotions churning inside her. Logan was hers—he just didn't know it yet. She'd loved him since she was ten years old, but she was the younger sister and she'd never stood a chance once he met Faith. But Faith was dead and gone and in spite of his claims to the contrary, he wouldn't grieve for her sister forever. There would come a time when he would decide that he didn't want to go through the rest of his life alone.

And when he did, she intended to be there, waiting for him. Over the course of the last year, she'd played her cards carefully and she and Logan had become closer then ever. He trusted her. Once he finally got over Faith's death, she'd do whatever she had to to make him fall in love with her. It was just a matter of time.

His gaze drifting back to his computer screen, he said absently, "No, I don't have any plans. I was just going to go home and have a frozen pizza. Give me a minute here…" Frowning, he typed a few sentences, then quickly reread what he'd written. When he finally looked up, he smiled. "There! All done. So where do you want to go? What are you in the mood for?"

"It doesn't matter," she said with a shrug as he shut down his computer and rose to his feet. "I just didn't want to eat alone."

Frowning, he lifted a dark brow. "Don't tell me—you broke up with Wyatt, didn't you? Dammit, Sam, you two were so good together. What happened?"

She'd only been using Wyatt to try to make Logan see her as a woman. When it hadn't worked, she'd dumped him. "He was too controlling. The longer we dated, the more he wanted to take over my life. I couldn't take it anymore."

"No kidding? I would never have thought he was the controlling type. That's too bad."

Heading downstairs with her, he escorted her across the street to the Front Page Diner. Not surprisingly, the place was virtually deserted after the newspaper was put to bed. They took a corner booth and gave their orders to the waitress without having to look at the menu.

"It seems like ages since we've had dinner together," Samantha said after the waitress set glasses of iced tea in front of them. "So…what have you been doing? You look great. In fact, you look better than you have in a long time. What's going on?"

Sitting back, he grinned. "Patty and Carter signed me up for a dating service."

"What?"

He chuckled. "Yeah, that's what I said. They were worried about me. They felt like I needed to get out in the world more."

"Out in the world!" she said sharply. "What are they talking about? When you're working, you go all over the city, talking to all kinds of people. If that's not getting out, I don't know what is."

"They meant dating, Sam. They don't want me to spend the rest of my life alone."

"But you're not going to date anyone from a dating service!" When he didn't reply, she frowned. "You're not, are you? You didn't already go out with someone, did you?"

"No, of course not. Though I did call someone," he admitted. "Patty and Carter spent a lot of money to sign me up for this and I couldn't just let them throw that away."

The waitress arrived with their food then, but Samantha didn't even look at hers. Logan didn't notice. "So?" she asked when he dug into his chicken as if he hadn't eaten in a week. "How did it go?"

"Fine," he replied. "She was nice. Believe it or not, I even asked her out."

"I thought you said you didn't go out with anyone."

Even to her own ears, she sounded like a jealous girlfriend, and she wasn't surprised when Logan's eyes narrowed. But all he said was, "I didn't. She turned me down."

Startled, Samantha nearly choked on a sip of tea. "Are you serious? Why?"

He shrugged. "It wasn't anything personal. She doesn't have a lot of confidence in herself. She just wants to talk on the phone. I'm calling her Friday."

Samantha almost laughed. Let him talk to her. She didn't need to fear a woman who was afraid to even go out with a guy. Talk about a loser! Logan would never be interested in a woman like that. And he was going to be hers, she silently vowed. She already knew that he cared for her. Now all she had to do was wait until he was open to loving someone again, and she would have the inside track on winning his heart. As for the loser who paid for a dating service, then was too much of a chicken to actually go out with someone, she could call someone else. Logan St. John was Sam's. It was just a matter of time.

Smiling confidently, she relaxed and dug into her meal as heartily as he was.

From there, the conversation drifted to politics and news stories and what various family members were doing. Samantha could have sat there and talked to him all night, but not long after they both finished their meal, he called the waitress over for their bill. "I hate to break this up," he told Samantha as he pulled out his wallet, "but it's getting late, and I want to work on my screenplay some before I go to bed."

"Of course," she said, and reached for her purse.

They'd always gone dutch whenever they went out, and this time was no different. Leaving their payment on the table for the waitress to collect later, they naturally fell in step as they crossed the street to the *Gazette*'s employee parking lot. Twilight was falling, but it wasn't completely dark yet. Still, Logan escorted Samantha to her car.

"You know, you don't have to do this," she told him with twinkling eyes as she unlocked her door. "The parking lot's well lit and your car's only three aisles over from mine. I'm perfectly safe."

"If you don't like it, take it up with my mother," he said with a grin. "She raised all of us boys to walk a lady to her car. Anyway, you can't be too safe, so indulge me. It's a man's job to protect his family."

Her smile never wavered, but deep inside, she winced. She wasn't family dammit! Rising up on tiptoe, she pressed a kiss to his cheek. Ever since Faith had died, she'd started kissing him on the cheek whenever they parted. And his response this time, as always, was the same. He ruffled her hair as if she were a four-year-old and growled, "Call me if you need anything."

What she needed was for him to hold her and kiss her like

she was the love of his life. Unfortunately, her dead sister still held that position.

Fighting the need to throw herself into his arms, Samantha told herself he had to feel the chemistry between them. He just wasn't ready to acknowledge it. He would, though, she promised herself grimly. She just had to give him more time.

"Let's go to the movies next week instead of going out to dinner," she said. "I'll call you."

Giving him a quick hug, she slipped into her car and drove away. Watching her disappear down the street Logan frowned. He hadn't missed the anger in her eyes or her sharp comments. Obviously, she was more upset about breaking up with Wyatt than she'd let on. And that was a damm shame. She was a good kid, he thought affectionately. She always had been. But losing Faith had been as hard on her as it had on him. She and Faith had been best friends, and her death had left a huge hole in Sam's life. Over the last year, she'd lost a lot of weight. And there was a sadness in her eyes that broke Logan's heart.

He'd thought she was getting better—ever since she'd started dating Wyatt Christian, she'd seemed so happy. Logan had thought they were perfect for each other, but obviously, he'd been wrong. And that was too damn bad. She deserved someone special. Maybe he'd ask some of his friends if they knew someone she might be interested in. She'd be horrified when she found out about it, but she'd just have to live with it. That was what family was for.

Chapter 4

"Hi, Logan. This is Abby Saunders..."

Grabbing a cold soda from his refrigerator as his answering machine rattled off his messages, Logan found himself smiling as Abby's voice, wry with amusement, filled his kitchen. So she'd called some of the other men on her list of possible dates, had she? he thought with a grin. Considering her shyness, he was surprised she'd worked up the nerve. From the sound of it, her calls hadn't gone any better than his.

At least she could laugh about it, he thought, as he listened to the rest of her message. He wondered if she realized how special that made her. Probably not. From what he'd been able to tell, she didn't appear to think that she was the least bit remarkable, which was a crying shame. She was upbeat and positive...and flat-out nice! The only negative thing he'd heard her say had been about herself. She didn't seem to have a clue how rare that was. Why was she so insecure? Who had made her doubt herself? Her parents? Her first boyfriend? Whoever it was, Logan hoped he got the chance to one day tell them off. It was no less than they deserved.

Her message ended and the next one started. Not even listening to the reminder that he a dental checkup scheduled for the following day, he quickly looked through some papers on the kitchen table and found Abby's phone number. It wasn't until he'd placed the call that he realized that it was nearly ten o'clock at night. She was probably getting ready for bed—

"Hello?"

He recognized the lilting softness of her voice immediately and felt something shift inside him that he couldn't put a name to. Frowning, he didn't give himself time to analyze it. Instead, he told himself it was just his imagination, then proceeded to ignore it. "Hi, Abby. I hope I'm not calling too late."

"Logan! Oh, no, not at all," she said in a pleased tone. "I was just—Buster, no!"

When she gasped, then giggled, Logan grinned. "Why do I have a feeling I caught you in the middle of something? Buster's not one of the men on your date list, is he?"

She chuckled. "Not hardly. He's my dog. I'm giving him a bath and he decided this was a good time to shake."

Even though he didn't have a clue what she looked like, Logan could picture her on her knees next to the bathtub as a big shaggy dog shook water all over her and her bathroom. Most of the women he knew wouldn't dream of bathing their dogs themselves, and they certainly wouldn't laugh when they got soaked, but Abby couldn't stop giggling even as she warned Buster to behave.

"It sounds like you've got your hands full. I can call back later, if you prefer."

"Oh, no!" she protested quickly. "Now that this mangy

mutt of mine has soaked me and the bathroom, he's curled up on the bath mat, cleaning his paws. Let me throw a towel over him and we can talk."

A few seconds later, she sighed in relief. "There! What a workout! I hadn't planned to bathe him tonight, but he loves water, and I forgot to shut the door when I was filling the tub for a bath."

Moving into the living room, Logan sank down into his favorite chair, a recliner Faith had bought for him on his thirtieth birthday, and popped his feet up in one smooth motion. "When I was a kid, we had a German shepherd that used to do that. He drove my mother nuts. So what kind of dog is Buster?"

"A boxer mix. He can be a spaz sometimes, but he's a great watchdog. And he's always willing to listen anytime I need someone to talk to."

She was far less reserved than she had been the last time they spoke, and when she didn't remember to be nervous, Logan found himself liking her all the more. What did she look like? he wondered again, and realized it didn't matter. She was a good listener at the other end of the phone line.

"Tell me about your German shepherd. How old were you when you got him?"

Lost in his thoughts, he blinked. "What?"

"The dog you had when you were a kid," she prompted with a smile in her voice. "You said you had him when you were a kid. How old were you when you got him?"

"Six," he answered. "His name was Hank." Just thinking about the dog that had always been by his side when he was growing up made him smile. "He was a great dog. We couldn't keep him in after he learned to climb the fence, so everywhere I went, he was right behind me. At night, he slept at the foot of my bed. I guess that's why I was never afraid of the dark like some kids. Hank was always with me."

"How old was he when he died?"

"Sixteen. I was away at college."

"I didn't think to ask you last time if you liked dogs. Do you have one now?"

"Faith was allergic to both cats and dogs," he replied simply, "so we never even fenced in the backyard. We had a goldfish. It didn't fetch very well."

Abby laughed. "No, I don't imagine it did. Though I did have a fish that jumped through hoops when I was a kid. Or at least it did until the cat caught it in midjump and ate it."

"You're making that up!"

"I beg your pardon."

"You can beg all you like," he retorted with a chuckle. "You're making that up."

She didn't deny it. Instead, she teased, "This is the story of a lifetime and you're questioning its authenticity? Don't you know the truth when you hear it?"

"My point exactly," he said dryly.

When she just sniffed, Logan grinned. All right! This was a woman he could like. In fact, there was nothing he enjoyed more than a woman who liked to tease. Given the chance, he would have told her that, but for the first time, she had let down her guard enough for him to catch a glimpse of the real Abby Saunders, and he didn't want her to withdraw back into her shell.

"I can see right now that I'm going to have to watch you," he stated easily. "So tell me about the men you called from the dating service. I bet one of them's Brad Pitt, isn't he? If we're talking tall tales, let's make it good."

"Brad Pitt's married," she retorted, chuckling.

"Damn! Don't you hate it when that happens?"

"Will you stop it! I'm trying to be serious."

"Anyone who tells a story about a goldfish that jumps through hoops doesn't have a serious bone in their body."

Grinning, she had to admit that he was right. "Okay, so I made it up. I just wanted to make you laugh. But this is serious, Logan. You should have heard these men I called. They were awful!"

"In what way?"

"One of them barely said two words, and I had to pull those out of him! And the other one was the exact opposite. He was so busy talking about himself that he didn't even notice when I hung up. He was still talking!"

"Maybe he was trying to impress you."

"Well, he picked a lousy way to do it. I don't even think he heard me when I told him my name."

"What an idiot," Logan declared. "He doesn't have a clue what he missed out on."

Just that easily, he touched her heart. A soft smile curling her lips, she said, "Thank you. I thought so, too, but I couldn't very well say it."

Absorbing the sound of her voice as he was, it was several long moments before Logan actually heard what she'd said. Bursting out laughing, he said, "I love your honesty, Abby. Don't ever lose that."

"Not everyone appreciates it—which is why I generally keep it to myself," she confided. "Tell me about the women on your list. Did you call any more of them? They've got to be better than the men I talked to."

"I don't know about that," he replied dryly. "Besides you, I only called one, and she had this shrill voice that hurt my ears. She was probably a nice woman, but she didn't sound like she had a brain in her head."

"I thought men loved empty-headed women."

"Not this man! I like an intelligent woman who can give me a run for my money when we discuss politics and religion and anything else that comes to mind. Not that I'm looking for any kind of woman, smart or otherwise," he quickly amended. "Not for a romantic relationship, anyway. I told you that."

"Yes, you did," she said easily. "I haven't forgotten. Relax, Logan. You're safe with me. I've got my own problems. I can't even work up the nerve to go out with anyone."

He smiled. "There are worse things in life. Think about it. There are all kinds of phobias out there. You could be afraid of dust or hot dogs. Can you imagine going through life with that kind of phobia? And I'm not just talking about being afraid of drinking water. That's nothing! What if you were so afraid of water that you were terrified of rain and wouldn't even take a bath or a shower? People would call you Stinky…"

He paused dramatically. "You're not afraid of water, are you? Tell me that's not the reason you don't want to go out!"

Abby laughed gaily. "No, of course not! I was bathing my dog when you called, remember?"

"Oh, yeah. So what's the problem? I can handle the truth. You're afraid of neon lights, aren't you?" he teased. "That's why you don't want to meet for a drink. Or is it small talk? You're bored with us menials trying to get your attention. That's it, isn't it? You don't want to be bothered with someone who's not as smart as you are."

"Stop!" she laughed. "I love neon, and as for small talk, you seem to be pretty good at it. I haven't hung up screaming, have I? You're not a menial. In fact, I'm sure you could run circles around me when it comes to brain power. It's not that at all. I just need to get to know you better."

"So how am I doing?"

"That's debatable," she said with a chuckle. "I know you love to write, and you're obviously a tease. But there are a few thousand other details you failed to mention. Like whether you like mustard or mayonnaise on your hamburger, if you like sugar in your coffee, that kind of thing. And then there's the Grand Canyon."

She'd caught him off guard again. Grinning, he crossed his ankles and leaned farther back in his chair. "I'm sure I'm going to regret asking this, but what's the Grand Canyon got to do with anything?"

He expected her to give him some kind of flippant remark. Instead she said quite seriously, "I've stood at the rim and watched the sunrise and felt like I could do anything. I was just wondering if you'd experienced the same thing."

Logan felt as if she'd just punched him in the heart. He'd never told anyone, not even Faith, how he'd felt when he'd seen the Grand Canyon for the first time. The experience had been intensely private, and even as he started to tell Abby that he knew exactly what she was talking about, he knew he couldn't. Not without somehow betraying Faith.

Guilt tugging at him, he said with forced lightness, "I felt something like that when I put on in-line skates for the first time. Then I fell and cracked my head. Some things you can only do when you're young."

"C'mon," she replied, "you're not that old. You couldn't be. When I filled out the survey at the dating service, I was very particular about not wanting to date anyone over sixty-five."

"Sixty-five!" he sputtered, shocked. "You'd date someone thirty years your senior?"

Delighted, she laughed. "Gotcha!"

"Damn! I guess I just got left in your dust, didn't I?"

"Um-hmm."

"That wasn't a compliment," he growled.

Listening to the sound of her laughter, Logan grinned. She might be too insecure to meet him in person, but with the telephone between them, she was a trip.

They talked for another hour, and when Logan finally hung up, he was still smiling. The next time he had an awful day, he had to remember to call Abby. Thanks to her, he'd completely forgotten about Josh Garrison and his taunting behavior earlier at the paper. For no other reason than that, Logan could have kissed her.

Not that he would even if he could have gotten his hands on her, he assured himself as he stepped into the bathroom and turned on the shower. She was just someone he was starting to consider a friend. What did she look like? he wondered yet again, grinning at the memory of how she'd shrieked and laughed when her dog had splashed her. She obviously wasn't one of those women who freaked out if her hair was mussed or she got a little dirt on her. Did she know how appealing he found that? If he ever got the chance to meet her face-to-face, he'd have to tell her.

Later, after he showered, he worked on his screenplay, just as he did whenever the silence of the night got to him. That helped the evening go by quicker, and distracted him from the loneliness of his existence. It was the hours after turning out the lights that he'd grown to hate. He would lie in bed for ages, thinking of Faith and missing her, until he finally fell asleep from sheer exhaustion around two or three in the morning.

Every night was like the last, or at least they had been up until now. Lying in the darkness, his conversation with Abby replaying in his head, Logan didn't think of Faith, let alone miss her. For the first time since she had died, he was asleep the second he closed his eyes.

Late the following afternoon, Logan paid little attention to the hustle and bustle of his fellow reporters as they raced to get their stories in before the afternoon deadline. He had his in and was already working on setting up several interviews for tomorrow. On the phone, he didn't notice that Samantha was waiting for him to hang up until she slipped into the chair angled in front of his desk and dropped an envelope in front of him.

"What's this?" he asked as he finished his call and picked up the envelope.

"Tickets to Faith Hill," she replied with a smug grin. "I know how much you like her music, so I thought I'd surprise you with an early birthday present."

"My birthday's in April, Sam," he said dryly. "This is August. You're either very late or really, really early."

"I just thought it would be fun," she said. "If you're finished here, we need to be going or we'll get caught in traffic."

"What? What do you mean? Are you saying the concert's *tonight?*"

"Of course it's tonight!" she said, laughing as she tugged him to his feet. "That's why we've got to go. We don't want to be late."

Normally, Logan wouldn't have hesitated. Ever since Faith had died so unexpectedly, he and Sam had done a lot of things on the spur of the moment. She'd been a godsend, distracting him often from his grief and loneliness, and he didn't know what he would have done if she'd hadn't been there for him, especially in the first few weeks and months after the accident. He didn't want to hurt her feelings, but he had planned to call Abby again tonight, and if he went to the concert, he wouldn't get home until nearly midnight. That would be much too late to phone her.

"Logan? Is something wrong? I thought you'd be thrilled."

"I am. Well, I would be if I could go," he added. "I'm sorry, sweetie, but I've got to work."

"Oh, c'mon, Logan, you can work anytime. We're talking Faith Hill," she said, smiling as she waved the tickets in front of his face temptingly. "You can't miss this."

Sitting back in his chair, he surveyed her steadily. "Did you get the tickets from Ivan?"

Ivan Dividian worked for one of the ticket outlet companies in town and was absolutely nuts about Sam. If she'd given him the least encouragement, he would have married her in a heartbeat. But she just wanted to be friends. She didn't, however, say no whenever he gave her tickets to the hottest concerts in town. That bothered Logan. She was using Ivan, but she didn't see it that way.

"He wanted me to have them," she said with a sassy smile. "And it wasn't as if he could take me himself. He has to work tonight."

"So do I," Logan said quietly. "I'm sorry, Sam."

"But if you're just doing research, I could help you...tomorrow night. You shouldn't work all the time, anyway. You need to play more, to get out and have some fun. This'll be so much fun!"

"I know. And I wish I could go, but I really can't. I've just got too much work to do. I'm sorry."

She was angry—she couldn't hide the temper that flashed in her eyes, but Logan had to give her credit—she didn't blast him with the sharp side of her tongue. Lifting her chin, she drew herself up to her full height and said,

"Then I guess I'd better let you get to it. I'm sorry I bothered you."

She turned and stormed out, leaving Logan feeling like a heel. He almost called her back. What had gotten into him? He'd made her mad and that was the last thing he wanted to do. She was as much a part of his family as Carter and Patty and the rest of his siblings, and he didn't know what he would have done if she hadn't been there for him after Faith died. He would do anything for her, but he didn't want to go to a concert or anything else tonight. He just wanted to go home and call Abby.

Guilt tugged at him. He'd apologize tomorrow, he promised himself. He'd stop by her favorite pastry shop on the way to work and buy a couple of chocolate covered doughnuts for her. Then he'd explain to her how stressful work had become since Josh Garrison had been brought on board, which was why it was so important for Logan to give all his attention to his writing right now. Hopefully, she would understand.

She'd understand even more if you told her the real reason you don't want to go tonight, the irritating voice in his head drawled. *Why don't you just tell her the truth? You don't want to go to the concert because you prefer to go home and call Abby.*

He couldn't deny it. She was just so damn easy to talk to. There was nothing romantic about his conversations with her, but Sam would never understand his need to just talk to someone. She would think he and Abby were dating, and he didn't need to discuss that with her to know that she would see his involvement with any woman as a betrayal of her sister. It was better to keep his private life to himself.

Returning his attention to his work, he made two more appointments for tomorrow, read over what he'd written earlier, then shut down his computer for the night. Thirty minutes later, he stepped into his house just as the phone rang. Hoping it was Abby, he snatched it up, only to scowl when a telemarketer tried to sell him credit card protection.

"I've already got it," he growled, and hung up. He hadn't realized that he'd memorized Abby's number until he picked up the phone and punched it in.

He told himself that he just had a good memory, but there was no denying that he was disappointed when her answering machine picked up after four rings. At the beep, he said, "Hi, Abby. This is Logan. I just got in and thought I'd give you a call. Guess I missed you. If you want to talk, call me whenever you get in. I'm going to be up late writing."

Hanging up, he glanced at his watch. It wasn't too late to change his mind and go to the concert with Sam—she'd be thrilled. The thought, however, didn't tempt him in the least. He just wasn't interested. So he strode to the kitchen to figure out what he was going to do about dinner.

Abby hated fund-raising dinners—she always had. The food was usually tasteless, the speakers boring, and by the end of the evening, her mouth hurt from smiling so much. Unfortunately, there was no way of avoiding them in an election year, and she'd learned to live with them.

Something odd was going on this year, though, she thought with a frown as she headed home after Martin thanked the last guest for coming. Over the years, she'd helped her boss organize more of these dinners than she could count, and the same wealthy constituents always seemed to attend. Or at least, they had until tonight. She'd found herself talking and socializing with people she'd never seen before—sleazy lawyers and smooth-talking business people who made her more than a little nervous.

What was going on? she wondered as she reached her house and unlocked her front door. She knew about Martin's finances, and although he made a decent salary, he was far from wealthy. So where had hc comc up with the funds for such an elaborate dinner? When he'd told her he was having the fund-raiser at one of the city's most famous seafood restaurants, she'd thought he was just going to rent the party room for an hour and serve hors d'oeuvres and wine while he glad-handed his wealthy constituents. Instead, he'd rented the entire restaurant, then served dinner, complete with champagne! She didn't need to see the bill to know that it had to cost the earth.

Thankfully, it had paid off. He'd raised twice as much money in a single night than he had with his three previous campaign dinners combined. But he'd taken a huge risk. Why? She didn't understand his mind-set right now. Just that morning, he'd told her he was thinking about buying a Lexus and possibly going to Europe for Christmas! How? she wondered, confused. Yes, he'd raised a lot of money tonight, but that could only be used for his reelection campaign. So where was the money coming from? When she'd asked him if he'd won the lottery, he'd just laughed.

What was going on? she wondered as Buster greeted her with a happy bark and circled her excitedly while she fed him. She didn't normally consider herself a suspicious person, but she couldn't help being curious when the numbers didn't add up. Obviously, Martin had funds he hadn't told her about, which was, of course, his prerogative. But he wasn't usually secretive. Was he hiding something from her? Why?

Not liking the doubts that nagged at her, she frowned as she stepped over to the phone to listen to the messages on her answering machine. "Hi, Abby..."

At the first sound of Logan's voice, she smiled. After such a tense evening, he was just the person she wanted to talk to. She couldn't discuss Martin with him, of course—Logan was a reporter and she couldn't take the chance—but that was all right. There was just something about him that lifted her spirits. She didn't care what they talked about. She just enjoyed her unexpected "dates" with him.

It wasn't that late, barely nine-thirty, and he had told her to call whenever she got in. Her heart pounding, she punched in his number. Four rings later, the answering machine picked up. Surprised—he must have stepped out unexpectedly—she was waiting for the beep to leave a message when he suddenly picked up the phone. "H'llo?"

His voice was rough and groggy and somehow made Abby's heart ache. The few men she'd been involved with over the years hadn't been the type to lie in bed with her and just snuggle and talk in the dark, but at the sound of Logan's voice, she could imagine herself wrapped close in his arms, lying in his bed, talking about her day.

Her cheeks heated at the thought. What was she doing? "I'm sorry," she said stiffly. "I didn't mean to wake you up. Go back to bed. We can talk another time."

"Abby?" Abruptly coming awake, he said, "Wait! Don't hang up. I wasn't asleep…well, I was, but I was just catnapping on the couch while I waited for the news to come on. I meant to work on my screenplay, but I couldn't really get into it. So what's up?"

Amused, she laughed. "You called me, remember?"

"Oh, yeah." Expelling his breath in a heavy sigh, he said, "I just wanted to talk. It's been one of those days." He sighed again and, after a brief pause, continued. "I told you about Josh Garrison, didn't I? The new reporter? The only reason

Porter hired him is because he's his granddaughter's boyfriend. It can't be because of his people skills—he doesn't have any. He's an arrogant jackass. I don't trust him as far as I can throw him."

"Why?"

"I don't know," Logan replied honestly. "You know how it is when you meet someone for the first time, and you take an instant dislike to them without even knowing them? That's how I feel about Garrison. Of course, he's cocky, which is hardly surprising—he's dating the owner's granddaughter. He could be a complete moron and he'd still never have to worry about losing his job."

"Can he write?" Abby asked. "Surely Mr. Porter wouldn't have made him a reporter if he can't write."

"Oh, yeah," he said. "He's good, thank God. If Porter had to saddle us with nepotism, at least he had the good sense to make sure the man knew how to report the news before he hired him. No, Garrison's talent as a writer isn't the problem. It's his attitude. He's got it in his head that there's some kind of competition between us, and he takes every opportunity to let me know he's winning. Like I care! As long as I can write my stories, he can have the front page. That's not my standard of excellence. It's his, though. From what I've seen, he's as ambitious as hell, and that makes me nervous. Anyone who wants to be number one at all cost will do anything to not only get to the top, but to stay there."

Abby had to agree. Ambition could be a dangerous thing. She found herself thinking of Martin, and frowned. Something was going on with him—he'd changed over the last few weeks—and she was afraid to guess what he was up to.

Worried, she started to tell Logan about it, only to bite back the words just in time. No. Martin was an elected official and

Logan would see it as his duty as a reporter to investigate any suspicious behavior. And for all she knew, there *was* no suspicious behavior. She could just be imagining it.

Wishing she could ask Logan, she said instead, "I can see how someone like that could make you hate going to work. You're lucky you're able to get away from the office so much. That's got to help."

"I'm out on the streets as much as possible, investigating stories and avoiding the man whenever I can. Unfortunately, I can't do that indefinitely. Every time I go back to the office, Garrison seems to be either coming or going, and he can't wait to let me know about the next big story he's been assigned."

Suddenly realizing how he sounded, he chuckled. "Feel free to jump right in at any time and tell me I sound like a whiny baby."

Abby smiled. "I wasn't thinking that at all. You don't like the man. There's nothing that says you have to."

"True," he agreed. "It's just that today he was particularly irritating, and the day went downhill from there. I made my sister-in-law angry—"

"Is this your brother's wife?"

"No, Faith's sister, Samantha," he explained. "She works at the *Gazette*, too. She had tickets to a Faith Hill concert and surprised me with them this afternoon. She knows she's one of my favorite singers, but I just didn't feel like going."

Whatever Abby had been expecting him to say, it wasn't that. "I didn't know you were dating anyone," she blurted out. "I thought that was why your brother and sister signed you up for the dating service."

"What?" Surprised, he laughed. "Whoa! Back up a minute. You've got the wrong idea. Sam and I go out to dinner occasionally, but she's like a little sister to me—she always has been. We're not dating. In fact, I thought she and her boyfriend were pretty serious about each other, but they broke up last week. She says it's over, but I'm not so sure. They were pretty crazy about one another."

"Was Faith her only sister?"

"Her only sibling, period," he replied. "Their father died years ago, and after Faith died, their mother moved to Florida, where Sam's grandparents live."

"So you're her only family in Austin? That must have been very difficult for her when her mother moved away."

"It's been rough on her, but Sam's pretty tough." Changing the subject, he said, "So how was your day? I hope it was better than mine."

"Well…"

"Uh-oh, that doesn't sound good. Is your boss giving you a hard time about something?"

She hesitated, fighting the need to confide in him. "No, it's nothing like that. I had to go to a business dinner with some…new clients. I didn't enjoy myself at all."

"You know, I could make that up to you," he said lightly. "We could go out Friday night instead of having a phone date."

Abby felt her heart stop in her chest at the very suggestion of meeting him. "Oh, Logan, I don't know—"

"C'mon, don't be that way," he coaxed. "You said you wanted to get to know me some before we met so you wouldn't be going out with a stranger. We've done that. I'm no longer a stranger, am I?"

Her pulse pounding, she said, "No, but—"

"It's just a drink, Abby. If I turn out to be some kind of a cyclops, we'll say good night with no hard feelings and go our separate ways. Okay? What do you say?"

More nervous than she'd ever been in her life, she hesitated. Could she do this? she wondered wildly. He was right—even though she could pass him on the street without knowing him, he was no longer a stranger. She *did* want to meet him, but the old insecurities kicked in at the very thought of coming face-to-face with him. What if he thought she was too thin? Or her wiry red hair turned him off? She liked him—and she desperately wanted him to like her. Maybe they should wait. It was too soon.

"It's not too soon, Abby," he said quietly, reading her mind. "Let's meet. What's it going to hurt? I promise there'll be no pressure. Even if you don't ever want to go out again, we can still be friends and talk on the phone, just as we have been. C'mon. Let's go to Charlie's, down on the river. Have you been there?"

"No."

"We can sit on the patio, have a margarita and just talk. We can even set a time limit if it will make you feel more comfortable. Fifteen minutes, not a second more."

Amused, in spite of her doubts, Abby had to laugh. "Okay, okay! But I don't need a time limit, Logan. We'll just see how it goes."

"That sounds good to me," he said, pleased. "Do you know where Charlie's is?"

"Fourteenth Street at the river," she replied promptly. "What time shall I meet you?"

"How about seven o'clock Friday night? I'll be at the bar wearing a green polo shirt and khakis. How about you? How am I going to know you?"

"I've got curly red hair," she said dryly. "I don't think you're going to be able to miss me, but just in case you do, I'll be wearing a white shirt and pink skirt."

"Then I guess I'll see you Friday," he said easily. "And if

either one of us decides we're not suited for each other, no one gets offended. This isn't personal."

She agreed, and Logan hung up. Standing in his kitchen, he found himself grinning like an idiot. He couldn't believe she'd agreed to meet him in person. They'd been talking less than a week, but it seemed longer. If it worked out—and he didn't see why it wouldn't since he already knew he liked her—maybe he could talk her into going to dinner. After all, she didn't have to worry about him putting a move on her. He'd made no secret of the fact that he was still in love with Faith and had no intention of ever getting romantically involved with anyone again. That's what made Abby so perfect. She wasn't interested in jumping into the dating scene, either. Like him, she just wanted a friend. This could work.

More excited than he had been in a long time, Logan went to bed with a smile on his face. And in the darkness of his bedroom, he thought of her, and the night seemed a little less lonely.

Abby tossed and turned all night. What had she done? she wondered, panicking as the darkness of the night seemed to press in on her. She never should have let Logan talk her into this. She wasn't ready. She might be able to talk to him on the phone, but she knew herself too well—she would freeze up when they sat down to talk in person. She'd get all tongue-tied and flushed, and he'd think she was boring and shy and didn't have a single social skill.

It was going to be awful, she worried, swallowing a sob. She should call him and tell him she wasn't going to be able to make it because she'd forgotten about a previous engagement she couldn't get out of. It was a lie, of course, but so what? After all, it was only a matter of time before he quit calling her altogether. He'd been patient with her insecurities so far, but how long could that last? He was a man who fairly oozed self-confidence. Sooner or later, he would grow tired of her hang-ups, and their friendship would be over.

Tears welled in her eyes at the thought, and with a sob, she rolled over and buried her face in her pillow. On the floor beside her bed, Buster whined in sympathy, and that only made it worse. She had to stop this! she told herself firmly. She hated being so insecure, hated constantly doubting herself and any man who showed the least bit of interest in her. She didn't have to be alone. She just had to give herself a chance.

Exhausted, she finally fell asleep, but the morning brought different doubts as she replayed in her head last night's conversation with Logan. He'd assured her he wasn't dating anyone, but what was his relationship with his sister-in-law? They went out to dinner frequently and Samantha even invited him to go to concerts with her. To Abby, that sounded as if they were dating—or at least Samantha was.

Abby believed Logan, however, when he claimed he wasn't interested in dating anyone. Every time he talked about Faith, she could hear the pain in his voice. He still loved his wife and probably always would.

So why was she even thinking about meeting him? Abby wondered. What was she setting herself up for? She believed in love at first sight. What if she took one look at him and lost her heart? He was in love with another woman. What difference did it make if she was dead? Love was love—you couldn't turn it on and off like a light switch.

Maybe she should just cancel, Abby thought as she headed to work. It would be the wise thing to do. She'd waited all her life for the right man to come along—she'd dreamed of him, fantasized about him. After all these years, she'd thought she'd imagined everything there was to know about him. Not once had she dreamed that he might be in love with his dead wife.

Chapter 5

When she arrived at the office a little before eight o'clock on Friday morning, Abby wasn't surprised to find the place deserted. Martin hadn't put in an appearance before eleven all week, and even then, he was long gone by two in the afternoon. What was going on? she wondered as she unlocked the front door to the office and let herself in. The city council was meeting later that afternoon to discuss the tax collection bids, and Martin didn't even seem interested. That just wasn't like him. He loved his job, loved serving on the city council and helping people. She'd never known him to be so neglectful of his duties. Something was obviously very wrong, and as soon as she got the chance, she intended to ask him what it was.

But eleven came and went, and he still hadn't reported in for work. Usually, he phoned if he wasn't going to be able to make it, but she hadn't heard a word from him. Concerned, she was seriously considering calling his house to make sure he was all right when the phone rang. "Thank God!" she sighed, and quickly snatched up the receiver. "Martin James's office."

"This is Trent Holloway. I need to talk to Martin."

His tone was curt and cool, and Abby wrinkled her nose in distaste. Trent wasn't one of her favorite people. A junior partner in one of the law firms bidding on the tax collection contract with the city, Trent seldom bothered to greet her with even a "hello," let alone a "please" when he demanded to speak to Martin. He wouldn't know common courtesy if he tripped over it.

Wishing she could tell him to take a hike, she was as cool as he when she said, "I'm sorry, Mr. Holloway, but he's not here. Would you like to leave a message?"

"I need to talk to him as soon as possible."

"I'll give him the message as soon as he comes in," she said smoothly.

"You don't understand," he snapped. "This can't wait! I've got to talk to him before the city council meeting this afternoon!"

"I'm sure he'll call you—"

"He has to understand what getting the bid means to my firm. Without it, we could go under."

"The second he comes in, I'll tell him to call you," she assured him. Her other line rang then, and she silently sighed in relief. "I'm sorry—you'll have to excuse me. I have another call."

"If you hear from Martin—"

"I'll give him your message," she said, and quickly hung up.

Over the course of the next twenty minutes, she took ten calls for Martin. They were all from lawyers like Trent Holloway, and they all had the same message for Martin: their firms would do just about anything to get the city tax collection contract.

Adding the last message to the stack she'd placed on her boss's desk, Abby frowned. What had Trent Holloway meant when he'd said that Martin had to understand what getting the bid meant to his firm? What did that have to do with anything? The bids were sealed and the city council would choose the company that submitted the lowest one. End of story. There was nothing else to discuss. So why did he think talking to Martin would make a difference?

Confused, she didn't like the direction her thoughts were going, but they'd taken on a life of their own. Lightning quick, one suspicion jumped to another, then another, and in the time it took to draw in a sharp breath, the word *bribe* was circulating in her head like a tornado.

No! she thought, horrified. Martin would never take a bribe. She'd been working for him for four years, and she knew him better than most. He had a hard edge and he could be demanding, but she'd never known him to be anything but an ethical man. She might not know where he was getting the money he seemed to have right now, but she couldn't believe that he was taking bribes to somehow influence the city council into giving the tax contract to a particular firm. The bids were sealed, for heaven's sake! Even if he wanted to, there was no way he could pull off such a thing.

Even as she tried to reason away her suspicions, however, she couldn't forget how little Martin had been in the office lately. He'd had lunch at some of the most expensive restaurants in town, then spent the afternoon playing golf…with members of firms bidding for the tax contract. He knew he wasn't supposed to be fraternizing with anyone wanting city contracts, so why was he? Did he realize how guilty he looked?

Troubled, she was tempted to discuss the matter with him

when he came in...just in case she'd misjudged him. She loved to read mysteries and she'd be the first to admit that at times her imagination got carried away. For all she knew, this could just be a huge misunderstanding. Maybe she was missing the obvious. She'd talk to Martin and ask him what was going on.

But even as she considered how she could delicately bring the subject up, a voice in her head warned her to not even think about going there. The tax contract was worth millions of dollars and Martin was a public servant. If he really was taking bribes from any firms bidding on the contract, then he was committing God knew how many felonies. He had to know that. He wouldn't take kindly to being questioned, let alone exposed.

She paled at the thought. Would he hurt her? If someone had asked her that last week, she would have said, "No, of course not!" without even thinking about it. But he wasn't the man she'd thought he was. Obviously, she didn't know him at all, and that worried her. A man who betrayed the public trust and took bribes could be capable of anything.

Should she call the police? Her stomach twisting in knots, she immediately rejected the idea. If she notified the authorities, the media would immediately find out about the story, and Martin's reputation would be destroyed before he could say a word in his own defense.

She couldn't do that to him, she decided. She didn't have any proof that he was doing anything illegal, just suspicions that could be all wrong. He'd been a good boss and had always treated her fairly. She owed him the loyalty of discovering the truth before she said anything to him or anyone else. It was the fair thing to do.

Still, her heart was pounding like crazy when Martin

opened the door to the office thirty minutes later and walked in. Abby took one look at him and was suddenly terrified that he could see her suspicions in her eyes. She quickly glanced at her computer screen. "Good morning," she said quietly. "Your messages are on your desk. I also called your nine and ten o'clock appointments and told them something came up and you'd have to reschedule. I hope that's not a problem."

"Are you kidding? I completely forgot I had appointments! Thanks, Abby. You're a godsend."

"I wasn't sure what you wanted me to do. I couldn't get in touch with you."

"I forgot my cell phone and left it at home," he said in disgust. "John Nickels showed up on my doorstep right before I was about to leave for work and wanted to take the 'Vette for a drive. Before I knew it, he'd tied up most of my morning." Flashing a grin, he held up a check. "It was worth it, though. He bought it."

"You sold it!"

"He wanted it so badly, he paid me an extra two thousand to convince me to sell it."

"You're kidding!"

"I know," he said with a laugh. "Can you believe it? Only a fool would have turned that down, and my momma didn't raise any fools. I was going to sell it eventually anyway, so why wait? I took the money and ran."

"But you always loved that car. I don't see how you can be so happy about getting rid of it."

"I love Sonya more," he retorted. "And as I said, she wants a big wedding. Anyway, it's too late to back out now. We went to the DMV and did the paperwork. John already has possession of the car. It's a done deal."

Abby wasn't normally a suspicious person, and just a few

weeks ago she would have believed his story without even thinking about it. But nothing he did made sense anymore, and she was no longer so trusting. People didn't generally pay thousands of dollars more for a car than the seller was asking, especially when there were no other prospective buyers. How stupid did Martin think she was?

"It just seems like you rushed into this," she said with a frown. "I hope you won't regret it."

"I only regret the things I don't do, not the things I do." A smug smile curling the corners of his mouth, he handed her the check. "Take this by the bank later and deposit it for me when you're out running errands, okay? I've already endorsed it. Just put it in my private savings account."

"Of course. Don't forget the city council meeting. Trent Holloway has phoned several times. He's very anxious to talk to you before the meeting."

Martin grimaced. "He's becoming a pain in the butt. I'll get back to him if I have a chance. Right now, I've got other calls to make."

He strode into his office and shut the door, surprising Abby. He rarely shut the door between their offices. In fact, in the four years that she'd worked for him, she could think of only a half-dozen times when he'd made calls in private. She was his secretary, for heaven's sake. They were the only two people in the office, so she knew just about everything that was going on, anyway.

Obviously, not everything, her conscience pointed out. *Otherwise you'd know where he's getting all the extra money he seems to have.*

There was no denying that. Disturbed, she frowned down at the check from John Nickels. She didn't believe for a second that he'd paid two thousand dollars more than the asking price for the 'Vette. It just didn't ring true. So what was the check really for? Was this a bribe? Was Martin going to somehow help John get the city contract? After all, Barnes, Tucker, and Smith had submitted a bid. She should make a copy of the check.

Glancing at the phone on her desk, she saw that he was on line one. Who was he speaking to? she wondered. And how much longer would he talk? She just needed a few seconds.

Her heart in her throat, she studied the closed door for what seemed like an eternity, afraid to move. What would she say if he caught her making a copy of the check? Her mind a blank, she told herself she'd think of something. Then, before she could change her mind, she quickly stepped over to the copy machine and slapped the check onto the glass. A heartbeat later, she grabbed the copy and the check and turned back to her desk.

With no warning, Martin jerked open the door between their offices. "Abby, I need the file on— What's wrong?"

Trapped in the no-man's land between her desk and the copier, she froze. "Nothing!" she said too quickly. "Why?"

"You look a little pale," he replied, studying her with sharp eyes. "Are you feeling all right?"

Grabbing at the excuse like a swimmer caught in a rampaging river, she swallowed thickly and pressed a hand to her temple. "I've got this killer headache," she said faintly. "I took some aspirin this morning, but it hasn't even phased it. I think it's allergies. Ragweed is back in season, and it always gives me trouble."

"Have you got any allergy medication with you? Maybe you should go home…."

"Oh, no! I'll be fine," she assured him as she returned to her desk and smoothly inserted the check and the copy between some other paperwork. "I've learned to live with it over the years. Anyway, I've got work to do." Gathering up the stack of papers in which the copy of the check was hidden, she added, "I think I'll go ahead and run to the bank and the post office before I get started on something else. Is there anything else you need me to do while I'm out?"

"Not that I can think of," he replied. "I've got some more calls to make, then I'll head over to city hall for the council meeting. It'll probably run long, so I doubt that I'll be back to the office today."

When he once again retreated and closed the door between their offices, she released her breath in a shaky sigh of relief. A split second later, she grabbed her purse and hurried out the door with the stack of papers she'd hidden the check in pressed tight to her breast.

Her pulse thundering, she half expected Martin to yell, "Stop!" at any moment, but he was still holed up in his office and probably never heard her leave. Shaky with relief, she couldn't get away fast enough.

That was far too close for comfort, she thought as she raced to the post office. If he'd opened his office door three seconds faster, he would have seen her pull the check out of the copier. She could have told him that she made copies of all checks just in case there was any question or problem, but he would have only had to check the files to know that wasn't true.

She'd keep the copy at home, she decided as she reached the post office and mailed her already stamped letters in the drop box outside. She might not ever need it—she hoped she didn't!—but she wasn't taking any chances. If there was ever any question about Martin's activities, she would have proof she could give to the authorities.

Shocked by her own thought processes, she drove to the

bank and deposited the check. Then she headed for city hall, wondering how she'd come to distrust him so quickly. She wasn't by nature a distrusting person, and in the past, Martin had given her no reason to question his ethics. Everything had changed, however, during the last few weeks. How could she trust him when he tossed aside his ethics to play golf with members of the firms bidding on the tax contract? Then, on top of that, he was spending money as if he'd just won the lottery! Of course she was suspicious! How could she not be?

Sick to her stomach at the thought of how this could all end, she parked in the garage across the street from city hall, then quickly made her way to the council chamber. Stepping inside, Abby wasn't surprised to discover that the place was packed. A multimillion-dollar contract was up for grabs, and every law firm in the city wanted it.

The council meeting had already started. Abby didn't normally attend, and she was afraid Martin might be suspicious if he saw her there. So she slipped into a seat at the back of the room, right behind a woman with big hair. Abby couldn't see Martin, but she didn't need to. She could hear him, and that was all that mattered.

"As you know, Mr. Mayor, I've spent the last few weeks doing background checks on the firms wishing to make bids on the tax collection contract. Unfortunately, some of them need to be eliminated from the bidding process due to a lack of financial stability. If you'll check your report, you'll see that I've put an asterisk by each of the firms that didn't make the grade."

Flipping through the report in front of him, the mayor quickly read through the list, then looked at the other council members. "The floor is now open to discussion. You've all read the report. If there's no objection—"

"I object!" Trent Holloway said loudly, hotly, from the audience. "My firm's on that list, and I resent the implication that we're financially unstable! We're more fiscally sound than half the firms bidding on the contract, and Councilman Jones is well aware of that."

"The facts are there for everyone to see, Mr. Holloway," Martin said coldly. "I'm sure Ms. Johnson will agree with me. She's an accountant. I seriously doubt that she'd recommend giving a multimillion-dollar contract to anyone with such shaky books. Ask her."

Put on the spot, Alice Johnson didn't, to her credit, squirm. "I haven't had a chance to take a good look at the books, but from what I've seen so far, there are some concerns."

"Holloway's books are a mess," Martin said flatly. "If he can't handle his own money, how can we expect him to take care of the city's tax revenues? We need someone like Linsey and Young…or John Nickels. Maybe Holloway needs to look at *their* books to see how it's done."

Shifting slightly so that she could see past the big hair that blocked her view, Abby wasn't surprised to discover that Martin's mouth was curled slightly in that smug smile she'd never liked. He was gazing right at Trent, silently daring him to object further. For a moment, Abby was sure the other man was going to race to the front of the council chamber and rip him to shreds. He was furious, and she couldn't say she blamed him. For the last two weeks, Martin had been playing golf with him, meeting for drinks after work, taking his calls and treating him as if they were best buds. They'd even gone fishing together! Then, just yesterday, everything had changed.

Why? she wondered. What had happened? Martin was exaggerating the problem with Trent's finances and seemed to be deliberately blackballing him. And for the life of her, she didn't understand why. Trent's books were no worse than some of the others'. After all, she knew. She was the one who'd typed up the report!

Then it hit her. John Nickels was Martin's old friend! He'd sold him the 'Vette, even though he'd always sworn he would never sell that car. And yesterday afternoon, they'd played racquetball together. Had they made some deal and used the sale of the 'Vette as a kind of cover-up? she wondered, stunned by the thought. Was that what was going on? No wonder Trent Holloway was livid! He'd obviously thought they had some kind of arrangement, and Martin was reneging on it. And there wasn't a damn thing Trent could do about it. After all, it wasn't as if he could go to the police. *He* would be charged with trying to bribe an elected official. And despite any charges he might make, Abby doubted that anyone would believe him. Martin was one of those politicians who seemed to be coated with Teflon—he could charm his way out of just about anything. And he wasn't a stupid man. If he was accepting bribes, he'd already found a way to cover it up.

Shaken, hating the suspicions that churned in her gut, but unable to dismiss them, she realized she couldn't sit there any longer and listen to Martin taunt Trent. It sickened her. *He* sickened her. She had to get out of there, to think about what she was going to do. Because one thing was clear—if Martin was in this up to his neck, as he appeared to be, she couldn't bury her head in the sand and pretend it wasn't happening. That would make her as guilty as he was.

Taking advantage of a comment from someone in the audience who drew everyone's attention to the far side of the room, Abby quietly slipped outside. Walking to her car, she was tempted to go to the police right then and there and tell them her suspicions. But what good would that do without proof? Martin was one of the most popular members of the city council—there was even talk of him running for mayor in the next couple of years. Considering that, the police and D.A. weren't going to put their careers on the line to investigate her suspicions without some kind of proof.

But how could she possibly prove he was taking money on the side to influence council decisions? she wondered as she headed home. She didn't have access to his private bank accounts. And the check she'd made a copy of could be easily explained. He'd sold his car. Of course John Nickels would pay by check. There was nothing suspicious about that.

If Martin had actually sold the 'Vette.

If she hadn't had a line of traffic behind her, she would have stopped dead in her tracks at the thought. Would Martin lie about such a thing? If he was taking bribes, that was a no-brainer. Of course he would! After all, what were the odds that she would ever discover the truth? They didn't socialize. In all the years she'd worked for him, she'd never even been to his house. He could tell her he'd sold the car to the president himself, and there was no way to know if he had or not.

Unless she went to his house and checked his story out for herself.

Her heart thundered at the thought. Did she dare? Just because he'd never invited her to his house didn't mean she didn't know where it was. Right after she started working for him, she'd driven by it just to see what it looked like. Whatever she'd been expecting, it wasn't a redbrick Tudor in one of Austin's most expensive historical districts. Martin just didn't seem the type. In spite of the charming face he showed the public, he was hard and cynical and didn't have a sentimental bone in his body…except when it came to his 'Vette.

He hadn't sold it, she thought grimly. She was sure of it.

Now all she had to do was prove it. Without hesitating another second, she turned down Congress and headed for his house.

Ten minutes later, she reached his street with her heart in her throat. For what seemed like the hundredth time, she looked in her rearview mirror to make sure she wasn't being followed. She knew she needn't worry—the city council meeting would continue for at least another hour—but she couldn't help but be paranoid. If for some strange reason he left the meeting early and caught her driving down his street, the fat would be in the fire. He'd know she was up to something, and there wouldn't be a damn thing she could say to defend herself. She *was* up to something!

His house came into view then, and she almost cruised by without stopping. But she hated being a coward. It seemed as if she'd played it safe her entire life, and she was so tired of it! So what if he caught her trespassing? she thought. If he showed up unexpectedly, she'd use the excuse that her parents had some friends that had just moved into the neighborhood and she was looking for their house. He wasn't going to show up anyway. The council meeting was still in session.

Satisfied that she was safe, she pulled over to the curb in front of his house and sighed in relief when she saw that there were no cars in the driveway. She knew he had a maid who came once a week, but from what she remembered, the woman normally worked on Thursday, not Friday, so the coast was clear. Her heart in her throat, Abby quickly stepped out of her car and only then realized that Martin might have security cameras. She swore softly, but it was too late to worry about that now. If he had cameras, he'd already caught her on tape.

Throwing caution to the wind, she hurried down the driveway to the old-fashioned carriage house that served as a detached garage. The doors were closed, of course, and she didn't dare try to open them in case there was an alarm. Instead, she stood on tiptoe and looked through the paned windows that faced the street. And there, sitting in a place of honor in the middle of the garage, was the 'Vette.

"That lying dog!" she gasped. He *had* taken a bribe! And she'd deposited the check in his bank account for him!

Outraged, she felt like a fool. Even though she'd suspected he hadn't sold the car, there'd been a part of her that refused to believe he would sink so low as to accept a bribe from anyone. And on top of that, he'd outright lied to her. What else had he lied about? How many other bribes had she deposited for him without even knowing it?

Hurrying back to her car, she drove away without having a clue where she was going. What was she going to do now? she wondered wildly. Turn him in? Did she have enough evidence? The check she'd deposited for him said it was for the purchase of the Corvette, but she could just imagine what he'd say if the police questioned him about it. *I did sell the car—we're just waiting until the check clears before we do the paperwork.*

"Yeah, right," she muttered. He'd told her they'd already done the paperwork, but he would, of course, deny that. And then what? It would be her word against his, and with no other evidence, the police wouldn't be able to do anything.

Frustrated, she desperately wished she could talk to Logan. He would know what to do. She was meeting him later for their "date," but she didn't want to wait that long to speak to him. She didn't have his work number, but he'd given her his cell phone number and told her to call him whenever she liked. He would tell her if she was being paranoid, she thought, or if her suspicions were well grounded. He investigated crime stories every day. He would know what to do.

Pulling over to the curb, she parked, grabbed her own cell phone and punched in his number. His phone rang and rang and her heart sank. Where was he? She really needed to talk to him—

"Hello?"

"Logan?" She was so relieved, she would have hugged him if he'd been within touching distance. "Thank God! This is Abby. Are you busy?"

"Hey, Abby," he said in a pleased tone. "I was just on my way back to the office. Why? You sound a little frazzled. Is everything okay?"

She opened her mouth to tell him about Martin, then hesitated. What was she thinking? she wondered, suddenly wanting to cry. She couldn't talk to him. He was a reporter. A crime reporter! Once she told him about her boss, how could she ask him not to write what he knew? That would hardly be fair to him, especially when the new reporter at the *Gazette* seemed to be getting all the best stories and loved rubbing it in.

Defeated, she couldn't remember the last time she'd felt so lonely. She just wanted to talk to him, to confide in him, to lean on him when she needed advice. Was that so much to ask? Why did she have to always be alone?

"It's nothing," she said huskily. "Really."

Logan frowned. Something in her tone set alarm bells clanging in his head. Immediately pulling over to the curb so he could concentrate on her instead of his driving, he quickly put his car in Park, then cut the engine. "Talk to me, Abby," he said quietly. "Something's wrong—I can hear it in your voice. What is it? You know you can talk to me—"

"That's just it," she interrupted. "I want to, but I can't forget that you're a reporter."

"Is that what this is about? I don't report what my friends tell me, Abby. I thought you knew that."

"I want to," she confessed. "It's just that…"

"What?"

For a moment, he didn't think she would be able to explain the doubts that pulled at her. She didn't say a word, and in the silence, he could almost hear her inner struggle. "I give you my word that whatever you say will go no further than my ears," he stated quietly. "Tell me what's wrong."

There was no doubting his sincerity, but Abby couldn't tell him everything, not yet, not when she still didn't trust her own judgment where men were concerned. "This is just so hard for me," she choked out. "My insecurities kick in and…" Hesitating again, she finally blurted, "I have to tell someone or I'm going to go crazy! I don't know if I'm being paranoid or what, but I'm afraid my boss is taking bribes."

"From whom?"

She hesitated, then said cautiously, "From some businesses bidding on contracts with the company I work for."

She knew he was too sharp not to realize she was leaving out some important details, but he didn't call her on it. Instead, he said, "What makes you think he's taking bribes?"

"He's spending a lot of time with representatives from some of the companies making bids, and he's spending money I know he doesn't have. I don't know what to do."

"What do you want to do?"

She didn't have to think twice about that. "If he's really taking bribes, I can't just turn my back and pretend it's not happening. I have to report it to the authorities."

"Of course you do," he said promptly. "I would expect no less of you. So what's the problem?"

"I don't have any real proof that he's doing anything illegal," she replied, "just suspicions. He's well-known here in town, Logan. I can't trash his reputation without knowing for sure that he really is taking bribes. He'd be ruined for life."

If Logan had had any lingering doubts about the type of woman Abby was, she'd just reassured him that there was no reason to question her character. Damn, he liked her! She was a good person. Why was she so shy? Surely she had to know how special she was.

One of these days, he'd tell her that, but for now, he said, "If I were you, I'd just keep my eyes and ears open. If your boss is on the take, you'll come across evidence of it soon enough. You just have to be patient."

Logan couldn't have said anything that could have reassured Abby more. He didn't ask any questions about her boss or where she worked or even what had happened to make her so suspicious. And she could have kissed him for that. He'd given his word, and deep in her heart, she knew he meant it. He wasn't just telling her what she wanted to hear. He was an ethical man, which was why he had such a difficult time accepting the new reporter at the *Gazette.*

She could talk to him, she thought, relieved. One day soon, she knew she would tell him everything, but for now, it was enough just knowing that she could talk to him without having to worry whether whatever she said ended up on the front page.

The tension that had knotted her stomach all day eased immediately, and she suddenly couldn't seem to stop smiling. "Thank you. You don't know how much I needed to hear that."

"You're welcome," he chuckled. "I'm glad I could help."

"Me, too. I've never been involved in something like this before, and I guess I was panicking. I didn't know if I was imagining things."

"I haven't known you that long, but you seem like you've

got a level head on your shoulders. If you think your boss is on the take, he probably is."

"I just want to shake him," she confided. "I don't understand why he's doing this. He has a wonderful career. He's risking everything and he doesn't even seem to know it."

"Oh, he knows it," Logan replied. "If he's got any sense at all, he's got to know. But he can't resist the lure of the money. I see it all the time. People think they'll never get caught. And sometimes they aren't. Just don't let this tear you up. Whatever's going to happen is going to happen. Okay?"

"Okay," she said with a sigh. "Thanks, Logan. I guess I just needed to unload on someone."

"Hey, don't worry about it. I told you you could call me at any time. So what about tonight? Are you ready?"

It was only then that she remembered that not only did they have a date later, but she had a hair appointment for four o'clock. "Oh, my God, I forgot! I'm getting my hair cut in half an hour! I've got to go!"

Laughing, he said, "Then I guess I'll see you later. Hey, you're not getting your hair dyed, are you?"

"No, of course not!"

"Just checking," he said with a smile. "Did I happen to mention that I've never gone out with a redhead before? I'm looking forward to it."

He hung up before she could say another word, and Abby found herself sitting parked at the curb with a goofy smile on her face. "Idiot," she said softly. "If you don't get to the hairdresser, Logan's going to be horrified at the sight of your mop of red hair. Move it!"

She didn't have to tell herself twice. Putting her car in gear, she checked the mirrors to make sure no one was coming, and pulled away from the curb. Twenty minutes later, she arrived at Jonathan's Hair Salon. She'd never been there before, but she'd heard rave reviews about Jonathan Clark, the owner and head stylist. That didn't, however, stop her heart from pounding as she walked in the door. She'd never been to a hairdresser yet who could do anything with her hair.

The man who greeted her was tall and slender, with the hands of an artist. He took one look at her and smiled kindly. "You must be Abby."

Self-consciously, she lifted a hand to her flaming wild curls. When she'd called to make the appointment and told him about her hair, he'd assured her he could help her. "You must be Jonathan." Pulling a tight curl away from her head, she grimaced ruefully. "This is it. What do you think? Can you do something with it?"

"I've seen curlier hair," he assured her. "And whether I can help you or not is up to you. If you're willing to put yourself in my hands, I promise you you won't be disappointed. If you want to keep it long, and just have it trimmed, well, I'm not sure either one of us is going to be dazzled with the results, but I'll do what I can for you. It's your call."

For as long as she could remember, she'd hated her hair. It was thick and impossible to comb or brush, and any time there was the least bit of humidity in the air, it frizzed. For years, she'd scraped it back tightly into a ponytail and braided it because that was the only way she could contain it. Just the thought of cutting it short and letting it frizz all over her head terrified her.

Hesitating, she studied him with fearful eyes. "If you cut it short, are you sure I'll be able to control it? I won't be able to braid it when it frizzes."

"You won't need to braid it," he promised her with an understanding smile. "Trust me. You'll love it."

Every hairdresser Abby had ever gone to had said the same thing, but as she studied the quiet confidence in Jonathan's dark blue eyes, she believed him. "I have a date tonight with someone very special who's never met me before," she said huskily. "I don't want him to see me looking like this. Do what you have to."

Grinning, he said, "You're going to knock his socks off. Come with me."

Abby was in the mood to be daring. Her heart in her throat, she followed him into the shop and never looked back.

Chapter 6

The woman who looked back at Abby in the mirror was a stranger. A pretty stranger with beautiful, short red hair that fell in soft curls to just below her chin. Amazed, she lifted fingers that were far from steady to a curl that was smooth and sleek and oh so soft.

"I can't believe it," she told Jonathan, meeting his gaze in the mirror as he stood behind her with a wide smile on his face. "Are you some kind if magician? How did you manage this?"

"It all starts with the right cut," he replied with a smile. "I take it you like it?"

"Like it? Are you kidding? I love it!" Giving in to impulse, she jumped up to give him a fierce hug. "Thank you so much! I don't recognize myself. I look almost pretty."

"What do you mean, you look *almost* pretty? Do you need glasses? Of course you're pretty! If you don't believe me, wait until your date sees you. He's going to be blown away."

"Oh, my God! My date!" Horrified that she'd taken one look at her new hairdo and completely forgotten about Logan, she whirled to grab her purse. "I've got to get out of here! What do I owe you? Whatever it is, it's not enough. Did I say thank you?"

Laughing, he took the credit card she handed him. "More than once. So what are you wearing? You'd look fantastic in black."

Her face fell. "Oh. I was going to wear a white blouse and a pink skirt."

Before the words were out of her mouth, he was shaking his head. "Not for a first date. You want to knock him over. I'm telling you black is the color for you. A short, sassy dress in black. Not too fancy, but not too casual, either. He needs to know that you were interested enough to put some effort into dressing up a little."

Abby smiled wryly. "Who knew dating was so complicated? No wonder I haven't been very successful at it."

Grinning, Jonathan handed her her credit card and receipt. "Trust me, you will be now. Just get a black mini, heels and smile prettily. You can't lose."

Abby didn't think it was going to be as easy as that, but she couldn't remember the last time she'd felt so good about herself. Could she really wear a mini? She was thirty-three years old, for heaven's sake! She hadn't worn short skirts even when she was younger. Maybe she should just stick with her knee-length pink skirt and white top. That was how Logan was expecting her to be dressed.

So shake him up a little bit, the little voice in her head whispered. *You've played it safe all your life and where has that gotten you? Alone! Indulge yourself for once. Don't you want to see yourself in a mini?*

A smile playing with the corners of her mouth, she had to admit that she did. She'd always had nice legs. And if she wore something to show them off, she was almost positive Logan wouldn't complain. The dress shop around the corner from her house always had something cute and sassy in the window. She'd never shopped there—in the past, she'd never needed something short and sassy—but if she hurried, she could stop and check it out. If she didn't find anything, she could always wear what she'd originally planned.

Her pulse pounding with excitement, she hurriedly drove there and parked. Once she was inside, it took her five minutes to find exactly what she was looking for.

It was perfect. It was black, as Jonathan had suggested, with spaghetti straps and a short black-and-white ruffled skirt set at an angle. The second she pulled it on and zipped it, Abby felt not only pretty, but utterly feminine. She loved it. It cost the earth, but she didn't blink as she paid for it. Some things were worth the price.

Later, she didn't even remember driving home. All she could think about was tonight. Would Logan be surprised? Attracted? He'd made it clear he wasn't looking for anything but a friend, and that was okay. As much as she wanted to knock his socks off, she'd really brought the dress for herself. Because of the way she felt in it—pretty and fun and young. If Logan liked it, then all the better.

Twenty minutes later, she strapped on her favorite black high-heeled sandals and stood in front of the mirror. Tomorrow she would have to send flowers to Jonathan, she thought with a grin. How had he taken one look at her and known how to make her look beautiful? She'd lived in this body all her life, and she hadn't had a clue! The hair, the dress, her makeup were all perfect. She didn't even look like herself! And Logan would never know it. He'd never laid eyes on her before.

It would be her little secret, she told herself as she headed downtown to Charlie's a few minutes later. That should have given her all the confidence she needed to wait for him in the bar and greet him with an easy, natural smile. But her heart was in her throat and she'd never been more nervous in her life. As she drew closer and closer to Charlie's Patio and Grill, old insecurities stirred, raising their ugly heads. Sick to her stomach, she wanted to drive right past the restaurant and go back home. She'd call Logan and tell him she wasn't feeling well.

Her cell phone rang at that moment, startling her. Taking her eyes off the road for a split second, she looked down at her cell phone and had to smile. Logan. She should have known. Pulling into the restaurant lot, she quickly parked and reached for her phone. "Hello, Logan."

"Hi, Abby. Are you okay?"

Surprised, she said, "Why do you ask?"

"I don't know. I just had a feeling you might be panicking about now. You are, aren't you?" he pressed when she didn't deny it. "You're thinking about canceling."

"Maybe we're rushing this," she said worriedly. "We don't have to meet in person. We could just have a phone date."

"We could. But tonight isn't a date, remember? You're just having a drink—and possibly dinner—with a friend. We are friends, aren't we?"

"Of course. But—"

"And you do meet friends for dinner, don't you?"

"Yes, but—"

"And we agreed there'd be no kissing. Right? As much as you want to throw yourself at me, I have to insist that you control yourself. Okay?"

Her lips twitched. "I'll do my best."

"I appreciate that," he said wryly. "Now that we have that settled, I don't see any reason why we can't meet as we'd planned. Do you?"

What else could she say but *no?* He'd neatly stripped her of every argument, and they both knew it. Amused, she said, "You're very tricky, Mr. St. John. Has anyone ever told you that?"

"More often than you would imagine." He chuckled. "Where are you?"

"Outside in the parking lot."

He laughed out loud. "I should have known. Shall I meet you at the door?"

She smiled. "If you don't mind."

"I don't mind at all. I'm on my way now."

Her heart thumping like crazy, she locked her car and started toward the entrance to the restaurant on shaky legs. She told herself it still wasn't too late to cut and run. Logan might not ever speak to her again, but she didn't have to put herself through this.

Then she saw him. There was no question that the man who stepped through the restaurant entrance was Logan. He wore a green polo shirt and khakis, just as he'd promised, but she hardly gave his clothes a second glance. It was the man himself who drew her gaze.

His eyes met hers from across the parking lot, and her steps slowed, then stopped altogether. This was Logan? she thought, the thunder of her racing heart loud in her ears. During all their phone conversations, she'd come to know his voice as well as she knew her own. She'd dreamed about him, fantasized about him, and created an image of him in her head that went with his wonderfully sexy voice. But the man who stood thirty feet away from her, his eyes roaming over her as hers were roaming over him, looked nothing like what she'd expected.

He was six-one if he was an inch, and lean and rangy as a cowboy, with dark brown hair touched with gray at the temples. It was his face, however, that stole her heart right out of her lungs. She'd never expected him to be attractive. He'd told her that his wife, Faith, was the only woman he'd ever dated, and Abby had assumed that his brother and sister had signed him up for the dating service because they didn't think he'd be able to find anyone else. She couldn't have been more wrong.

She didn't know if a man would appreciate being called gorgeous, but she could think of no other way to describe him. He wasn't pretty-boy handsome, but then again, that wouldn't have appealed to her. Instead, he had a rugged face and square jaw that looked hard as granite. Dimples framed his sensuous mouth, and though he had yet to smile at her, her heart kicked just at the thought.

She knew he was still grieving for his dead wife, but what in the world was this man doing walking around single? she wondered. She would have thought some lucky woman would have snatched him up months ago.

Even standing thirty feet away from him, she could see that his blue eyes were twinkling as they met hers. Then his gaze dropped to her flirty black dress, and in the time it took to draw her next breath, she found herself fighting the need to cut and run and end this before it even began. She'd been a fool to think that she was going to attract a man like Logan with nothing but a new haircut and a cute dress. She couldn't possibly be the type of woman he'd be interested in. He would want someone as good-looking as he was, someone who was outgoing and confident and would be comfortable in just about any situation. Abby was afraid to even date!

From across the parking lot, Logan watched one emotion after another chase across her expressive face and saw the exact moment her insecurities crept in. To distract her, he called out teasingly, "You can't be Abby Saunders. I was told to look for a redhead in a white shirt and pink skirt."

She tried to smile. "I decided I needed something different to boost my confidence, but it's not working very well."

"Why?"

"Because you're gorgeous!" she blurted out. "And I'm just…me."

His heart aching for her, Logan took a step toward her and unconsciously gave her a smile he reserved for the people he really cared about. "Have you looked in the mirror lately?"

"Are you kidding? I spent half the afternoon looking in the mirror. I got my hair cut, then I bought this dress."

"And did you like what you saw?"

"Logan…"

At her protest, he took another step toward her and teased, "You did, didn't you? That's why you bought the dress."

"Yes, but—"

"You should. It looks fantastic on you."

When she still hesitated, her brown eyes dark with doubt, he couldn't believe it. Could she really not see how pretty she was? No, she wasn't Miss America, but she had the kind of natural, old-fashioned prettiness that was seldom appreciated nowadays. She had a splash of freckles across her pert nose, her chin was slightly rounded and her soft mouth was a little too big for her oval face. She'd still look young when she was eighty.

It was her large brown eyes, however, that stopped him in

his tracks. They mirrored her every emotion, but there was nothing wrong with that. A man would always know where he stood with a woman like Abby. He liked that. Faith had always worn her heart on her sleeve, too, and he'd loved that about her.

Not that Abby looked anything like Faith, he quickly assured himself. She was slender as a wand, with small breasts and a waist that he could easily span with his hands. There had been nothing petite about Faith, but when he'd held her, she'd filled his arms in a way no woman ever would again.

Tonight, however, was about Abby, not Faith, and he wanted her to know how great she looked. Taking a few more steps toward her, he said quietly, "I like your hair."

Short and curly and a deep red that glistened with gold highlights, it gave her a sassy look that was incredibly appealing. His fingers itching to touch, he grinned and continued toward her. "What did it look like before?"

For the first time since they'd spotted each other, an easy smile curled her mouth. "A Brillo pad comes to mind."

"Oh, c'mon! It couldn't have been that bad!"

"Trust me, it was. I had to wear it braided all the time or I looked like a wild woman."

"I like you like this," he said sincerely, and came to a stop less than three feet away from her. Several more cars pulled into the nearly full parking lot, and from the restaurant patio, laughter carried easily on the evening air, but Logan never took his eyes off of Abby. "When we set this up, we agreed that there would be no pressure. We were just two friends getting together for a drink. That hasn't changed just because we now have a face to put together with the voice on the other end of the phone. So will you let me buy you a drink? Charlie makes a great margarita. We can sit on the patio and have a couple of drinks and swap war stories."

"I don't have any war stories."

"Neither do I," he said with a wicked grin. "So we'll make some up. It'll be fun."

She shouldn't have. He was far too good-looking for her peace of mind, not to mention charming, and when he smiled at her like she were the only woman on the planet, she felt beautiful for the first time in her life. Why couldn't she have a drink with him and enjoy the feeling for a little longer? After all, it wasn't as if anything could come of it. He wasn't ready to let go of Faith, and Abby wasn't going to make the mistake she had with Dennis, and jump into a relationship with anyone. Not yet. Not until she had more confidence in herself.

Cocking her head, she smiled and lifted a delicately arched brow. "Did I ever tell you about the time I was in Tunisia during World War II?"

Delighted, he grinned and took her arm as they headed for the restaurant patio. "No, as a matter of fact, you didn't. And since you weren't even born yet, this should be quite interesting."

"Just wait," she assured him with a sassy wink. "You ain't heard nothin' yet."

Later, Abby couldn't remember when she'd enjoyed herself so much. With Logan's encouragement, she came up with the most outrageous stories, and he followed suit, making her laugh until she cried. Anyone eavesdropping on their conversation would have thought they'd both lost their minds.

Chuckling over a tale she'd made up about being a spy for England during the Revolutionary War, of all things, Logan grinned. "You're older than you look. And you're too damn good at this. You should be writing fiction. You are going to have dinner with me, aren't you?"

He slid the invitation in so smoothly that it was several seconds before his words registered. In the time it took to draw in a quick breath, her smile faltered. "Oh, Logan, I don't know."

"Don't get all tense on me," he said quickly, shooting her a reassuring smile. "This has just been so much fun I hate for it to end."

"I know," she said huskily. "I've had a great time, too. But—"

"You have to go home and wash your hair."

"No!" When she saw his lips twitch, she laughed. "Stop that! I'm trying to be serious here."

"You don't have to explain, Abby. I understand. We agreed to meet for a drink, so let's stick to the original plan."

"It's not that I don't want to," she explained earnestly. "I just have a history of jumping into relationships too quickly. I swore I wasn't going to do that when I joined the dating service. I promised myself that regardless of how much I liked someone, I was going to take things slow. And I do like you. You've been wonderful."

"So have you. So let's have dinner. Your heart is safe with me. I won't hurt you. I promise."

He wasn't just saying easy words to reassure her. He meant it—she could see it in his eyes. And he had no idea how incongruous his words were. When was the last time he looked in the mirror? Didn't he realize how sexy he was? How attractive? How could he think her heart was safe with him? Just looking at him made her bones melt!

"What?" he asked when she just grinned at him. "Why are you smiling?"

Because she desperately wanted to have dinner with him

and every instinct she had told her she'd be crazy to pass up an opportunity to spend more time with such an incredible man. After all, he wasn't asking her to marry him, just have dinner. "I can't think of anyone I'd rather share a meal with," she said honestly. "Is it too late to change my mind?"

"Are you kidding? Waitress, we need a table!"

The dinner that followed was the best that Logan had had in a long, long time, and he couldn't even remember what they ate. He had eyes only for Abby—her smile, the laughter in her eyes, the beautiful flush in her cheeks. He hadn't realized how lonely he'd been until he found himself sitting across the table from an incredibly attractive redhead who made him laugh. Over the course of their meal, she made him completely forget his grief, and that stunned him. Warning bells clanged in his head. If he wasn't careful, he could find himself doing exactly what Abby had feared and rushing into something just because he missed his wife. That wouldn't be fair to Abby or himself.

Still, he was disappointed when the meal—and their evening—came to an end. "Come on," he told her huskily after he paid the bill. "I'll walk you to your car."

He almost took her hand, then thought better of it. They were just friends! That should have been easy to remember, but as he escorted her outside, her delicate scent seemed to wrap around him, teasing his senses. He found himself watching her, imagining what it would feel like to kiss the freckles that dusted her nose, to trace the soft, enticing curve of her mouth with—

"Logan? Did you hear me?"

Jerking back from his heated thoughts, he frowned. "I'm sorry. What did you say? My mind drifted for a second."

"I just wanted to make sure there's no misunderstanding

between us," she said, gazing up at him earnestly. "I had a wonderful time. The only reason I turned down your invitation to dinner is…"

"Because you got burned the last time you were so impulsive," he finished for her. "It's okay, Abby. I understand. Anyway it's a woman's prerogative to change her mind. And," he added with twinkling blue eyes, "you know a good thing when you see it."

"Of course I do," she said seriously, only to blush when she realized what she'd said. "Logan! Stop that!"

Grinning, he stared down into her laughing eyes and found himself enchanted. How could she not see how pretty she was? She had the most incredible skin—creamy and dusted with freckles. Just looking at her made him smile.

"Logan, you're not listening again."

"Yes, I am," he growled. It wasn't her words he heard, however. It was the vibrations that seemed to hum between the two of them with no effort. He hadn't felt this good since Faith had died, and it was all thanks to Abby. She was like a breath of fresh air and she didn't even seem to know it.

"We passed the first test," he said. "Tonight proved we could have a drink and dinner and talk just like we do on the phone. We're both presentable—in fact, you're a hell of a lot more than that, though you don't believe it—so there's no reason why we can't do this again. That's why I'm going to call you next week and invite you to dinner again and you're going to say yes. Right?"

The worry lines wrinkling her brow vanished. "Well," she said with a short laugh, "you seem to have covered everything."

"Not quite," he replied, and surprised them both when he leaned down and pressed a kiss to her lips.

The laughter and music from the patio floated on the early

evening air, but in that instant, the entire world seemed to turn silent, and all Logan could hear was the roar of his blood in his ears. He'd kissed her, he thought, stunned. Had he lost his mind? When they'd agreed to meet tonight for a drink, he'd assured her that she didn't have to be nervous—he wasn't going to try to kiss her or anything. And then he'd done exactly that! Idiot! Now she was never going to trust him, and he couldn't say he'd blame her. He'd gone back on his word.

Because he couldn't stop himself.

Shaken, he stepped back. When their gazes met in the glow of the lights that illuminated the restaurant parking lot, there was no question that he'd surprised her. Her eyes were wide with an emotion he couldn't read.

Swearing softly, he said, "Abby, I'm sorry! I told you there'd be no pressure, that you didn't have to worry about me kissing you—"

"It's okay, Logan. It was just a kiss."

"I know, but I gave my word—"

"I'm not offended," she assured him. "I'm certain you have a lot of women friends you kiss."

"Yes, but—"

Her brown eyes glinted with amusement. "Then why are you getting all bent out of shape? I'm not. We're friends, aren't we? You're not pressuring me at all. And just in case I gave the impression that I'm a prude, I'm not. I just don't want to rush into anything."

"Point taken," he said ruefully. "Did I mention that I had a really good time?"

She grinned. "As a matter of fact, you did. So did I."

"Then I guess it's time to say good night." Taking her keys from her, he unlocked her car, then opened the door. "I'll call you tomorrow," he said huskily, handing her her keys. "Okay?"

"Okay," she said softly. "Good night."

"Drive carefully."

This time, she kissed him—on the cheek. Then before he could say anything, she slipped quickly into her car and drove away. Standing in the parking lot, Logan watched her taillights disappear in the distance and wondered if this was what it felt like being struck by lightning. His heart was racing, his pulse pounding and he couldn't seem to think straight. And he didn't like the feeling at all!

What the hell was wrong with him? he wondered with a scowl. Faith was the woman he'd given his heart and loyalty to, the woman he'd promised to always love. Even though she was dead, there was a bond between them that not even death could destroy. He was never going to share something that special with another woman. How could he? He still loved Faith.

So why did he feel as if he'd been living in a cave for the last twelve months and he'd just stepped out into the sunshine? he wondered with a frown. That was a question he didn't have an answer for, and he didn't want one. He just knew he was angry and he didn't know why.

When Abby walked through her front door twenty minutes after she'd left Logan and the restaurant, she couldn't have said how she got home. Her mind was in a daze and she couldn't seem to stop smiling.

You're going overboard. It was just a kiss, nothing more. He said himself that he kisses his women friends in exactly the same way, so don't read anything into it. The operative word here is friends! *That's what you want, too, isn't it? Isn't it?*

Irritated with the annoying voice of her conscience, she dismissed it with an airy wave of her hand. This had been one of the most incredible days of her life and she wasn't going to let her conscience ruin it for her. She had a new dress, a new hairstyle, a new lease on life and she felt fantastic! And it was all because of Logan.

When the alarm bells once again went off in her head, she laughed and assured herself that there was nothing to be worried about. She knew Logan just wanted to be friends, and she wanted the same thing. For now, anyway, she amended as she twirled like a schoolgirl in her living room. She hadn't lost her head—or her heart, for that matter—she was just having fun. What was wrong with that?

It seemed as if she'd waited her entire life to meet a man like Logan, and she planned to enjoy getting to know him better. And why shouldn't she? He was fantastic looking, charming, funny, a perfect gentleman. And best of all, he wasn't try to rush her into bed before she was ready for that kind of relationship.

She could have kissed him for that.

She had! she thought with a giggle. She would next time, too, she promised herself as she floated dreamily into her bedroom to change out of her new dress. Somehow he brought out the best in her, and she couldn't wait to see him again.

When Logan didn't call the next day, she told herself that he was probably busy. The following day was Sunday, and when there was no word from him, she wasn't surprised. A lot of people spent the day with their families. For all she knew, he might even have had to work. He was busy.

By Monday, she was completely confused. She'd have sworn that he'd enjoyed their time together as much as she had. But maybe she'd misunderstood. Maybe he wasn't the person she'd thought he was. Maybe he'd just said what he thought she wanted to hear. Maybe with his silence, he was trying to tell her that he didn't want anything to do with her now that he'd met her.

Don't! her heart cried. *Don't do this to yourself. He did like you. You couldn't have misjudged him so completely. You're a better judge of character than that.*

She liked to think she was, but with every day that passed and he didn't call, the confidence she'd gained with her new hairstyle and her to-die-for dress was quickly fading. A dozen times she picked up the phone to call him, to ask him if anything was wrong, only to hang up. She readily admitted that his silence intimidated her. She couldn't call him. She'd made it clear that she really liked him. The ball was now in his court. He would phone her if he was interested in seeing her again.

But even though she considered herself a patient person, waiting for him to call was the hardest thing she'd ever done. She found herself thinking about him at all hours of the day and night, dreaming about him, reliving every smile, every laugh, every word he'd ever said to her in the short time they'd known each other. And when she couldn't find a reason in those memories for his continued silence, she once again found herself examining her own actions. It was a never-ending cycle, and she'd never been so frustrated in her life.

On Monday, she thanked God for work. It was one of those wild days when nothing seemed to go right, and she had little time to turn around, let alone think of Logan. Late in the day Friday, after the city council had discussed the merits of the firms bidding for the tax contract, the council members had narrowed the field from thirty to five. After further study of the firms competing for the contract, the council would award the contract—in two weeks. Abby didn't fool herself into thinking that the next two weeks would be anything but a nightmare.

And it was all Martin's fault.

He was practically gleeful over the fact that two of the

firms he'd spoke highly of had made the cut. He made no apology for the fact that Trent Holloway had not. In fact, he continued to ignore the messages Trent left for him, then made it clear to Abby that she was not to put through any more of the lawyer's calls. He hadn't got the bid—there was nothing more to say.

Abby couldn't believe Martin's coldness. He and Trent were supposed to be friends! How could he forget that so easily? He knew how badly the lawyer had needed the contract to stay afloat, but he showed no sympathy for his plight. In fact, he couldn't have cared less. And that really bothered Abby. After all the years she'd worked for him, she would have sworn that she knew exactly what kind of man he was. Nothing, however, could have been further from the truth. He wasn't someone she considered a friend, but she'd always respected him as a councilman. Now she couldn't even do that.

Even though she still had no evidence that he was taking bribes except for the copy of the check for the sale of his Corvette, she could no longer give Martin the benefit of the doubt. Her gut told her that whatever he was doing was at the very least unethical, and, in all likelihood, illegal. And looking him in the eye was getting more difficult by the hour…especially when he was now being wined and dined by two of the five firms in the running for the contract. The phone had been ringing off the hook all morning, and his social calendar was nearly booked solid for the next two weeks. Just thinking about it tied Abby's stomach in knots.

Was it common knowledge that he was on the take? she wondered. Was that why he was getting so many calls? And if it was, why hadn't someone like Trent Holloway come forward and complained to the authorities? He might be incriminating himself, but he was about to lose everything. Was he really going to stand silently by and let Martin pocket God only knew what kind of bribes while he himself went under?

The phone rang sharply, and with a grimace, she answered it, half expecting it to be Walker Sutton, the only bidder who had yet to call Martin to arrange a meeting. But the caller was Liz Green, the secretary for Paul Ortega, one of the other city council members. "Hi, Abby."

"Liz!" Pleasantly surprised, Abby sat back in her desk chair with a smile. "I've been wanting to call you, but it's been crazy around here. I guess it's been the same for you."

"Hasn't it been awful?" she said with a groan. "Every time I turn around, the phone's ringing. Paul's in and out, people I've never heard of are demanding appointments. It's nuts."

Her story sounded all too familiar. Shocked, Abby felt the knot in her stomach tighten again and could do nothing to stop it. "Martin's been playing golf a lot lately," she said carefully. "How about Paul?"

The other woman hesitated, and in the silence, Abby heard words Liz never said. When she did finally speak, she was as cautious as Abby. "He's spent quite a bit of time at the country club over the last few weeks. I was surprised. He doesn't really like golf."

"Martin's not really interested in it, either," she admitted. "But he does like rubbing shoulders with club members. He likes the finer things in life."

"So does Paul," Liz said quietly. "His ambition is sometimes...misplaced."

Abby would have said that Martin's ambition was misplaced more than *sometimes*—lately, it seemed to be most of the time. "Are you as concerned as I am, Liz?"

"I think I'm getting an ulcer," she replied simply. "I've never been so stressed in my life."

Her heart pounding, Abby wanted to ask her flat out if she thought Paul was taking bribes, but Liz was as careful with her words as Abby was. "Are you planning to do anything about that…stress?" she asked.

Liz hesitated, then finally admitted, "I'd like to, but I have…no insurance. I can't afford it."

Abby didn't pretend to misunderstand her. Liz wasn't going to say anything incriminating about her boss, regardless of what she knew, and Abby couldn't blame her. Liz was a single mom with three kids and a deadbeat ex-husband who had chosen to go to jail rather than pay child support. She couldn't afford to say anything that might cost her her job.

"I understand," Abby said. "You have to do what's right for you."

"If circumstances were different—"

"It's okay," she assured her. "Don't worry about it. How are the kids? Your oldest is in high school, isn't she?"

"She graduates next year," Liz said with pride. "She wants to go to UT, then she can live at home."

The University of Texas was a state school, and when compared to other universities, it was a great buy for the money. But college—any college—was expensive. And that was just one more reason why Liz couldn't afford to turn her boss in. She couldn't take the chance. If he somehow proved to be innocent, he would, no doubt, fire her for all the trouble she'd caused him. And if he was guilty, well, she'd still lose her job when he went to prison. Either way, she was screwed.

They talked for ten more minutes and never once mentioned their bosses. Abby laughed about a party they'd both attended last month, and when she finally hung up, she was smiling. But her good humor faded almost immediately. When Liz had told her what Paul was doing, Abby had hoped she would come forward with her to expose what was going on. That obviously wasn't going to happen. Like it or not, she was on her own.

Chapter 7

"You're awfully quiet. Anything wrong?"

In the process of printing out thank-you letters for everyone who had made contributions at the last fund-raiser for Martin's reelection campaign, Abby didn't realize he was watching her until she looked up to find him standing in the doorway between his office and hers. Her gaze met his, and for reasons she couldn't begin to explain, fear suddenly clutched at her heart.

Had he somehow guessed she was suspicious of him? she wondered in horror. Fighting panic, she forced a smile and prayed he couldn't see how he'd startled her. "I'm just tired," she lied. "I made the mistake of starting Stephen King's newest book last night and was afraid to go to sleep. I kept hearing noises all night long."

For a moment, she was sure her boss didn't believe a word she said. His eyes narrowed with an emotion she couldn't put a name to, but then, just when she thought he was going to call her a liar to her face, he said, "That's what you get for reading that stuff. When you finish printing the mail out, take it by the post office, then go home early and catch up on your sleep. I want you sharp tomorrow."

"I will be. I promise." Feeling as if she'd just dodged a bullet, she added huskily, "Thank you, Martin. I really appreciate this."

"Everybody has a bad night once in a while," he replied with a shrug. "Don't worry about it."

When he turned and strode back into his office, Abby sank into her chair before her trembling legs gave out on her. What had just happened? she wondered, fighting tears. She wanted to believe that he didn't have a clue how suspicious she was of him, but she couldn't forget that expression in his eye when he'd asked her what was wrong. He'd never looked at her in quite that way before. With nothing more than a glance, he'd turned her blood to ice.

She couldn't take this much longer, she thought shakily. She wasn't that good an actress. She'd never been successful at hiding her emotions, especially when she was nervous, and Martin made her a nervous wreck. It was those piercing eyes of his…and the fact that the charming facade he presented to his constituents was nothing more than a clever disguise. Although he appeared to be caring and generous, the real Martin James was self-centered and ambitious. At times, he could be downright cold. He wasn't above using people to get what he wanted in life, and he wanted a hell of a lot.

If she had any sense, she'd walk out and never look back. Unfortunately, finding another job in the current economy might turn out to be next to impossible. She couldn't risk quitting without having something else lined up. And even if she could find another position, her conscience wouldn't let her just walk away as if nothing was wrong. If Martin really was taking bribes—and she was convinced now more than ever that he was—he was betraying the public trust and costing the taxpayers thousands of dollars by manipulating the bidding system. She couldn't pretend it wasn't happening or she would be as guilty as he was.

He would slip up, she told herself as she began to fold the thank-you letters and stuff them into envelopes. He was cunning, but eventually, he'd drop his guard and leave some kind of evidence lying around for her to find. And when he did, she'd go to the police. She just hoped it was sooner rather than later. Martin wasn't the only one who might slip up.

The second Logan stepped through his front door, he found himself heading for the small bedroom he'd converted into a home office. The answering machine was right next to his computer, and from the open doorway, he could see that the message light wasn't blinking.

When disappointment tightened his gut, he swore softly. Okay, he thought irritably, so she hadn't called. He hadn't really expected her to. It was his place to call her, and he hadn't. It wasn't from lack of wanting to.

So why hadn't he? He'd all but promised her he would. Now he tried to tell himself he'd just been caught up in the moment. Why else would he have allowed himself to forget that she was looking for a relationship and he wasn't? Once he'd put some distance between them, he'd realized that he couldn't possibly see her again. It just wouldn't be fair. Because he still loved Faith and always would.

Just thinking about her brought a pang to his heart. He couldn't remember a time when she hadn't been a part of his life. She was the first date he'd ever had, his first dance partner, the one and only woman he'd ever made love to. He'd never known loneliness until he'd lost her.

But lately, when he tried to recall the sound of her voice, the sweetness of her smile, the laughter in her eyes, he couldn't. And it scared the hell out of him. He was losing her all over again, and there wasn't a damn thing he could do about it.

Pain pressed in on him, squeezing his heart until it physically ached. Feeling lost and more miserable than he had in months, he found himself prowling through the house, looking for the life, the wife, that he would never have again. He should have been able to sense Faith's presence, to smell her scent, to almost hear her in the kitchen, cooking supper and singing along with the CD player on the counter, the way she used to. But the house was silent as a tomb, and even though her clothes were still in the closet, he could no longer pretend to himself that she would be home any minute. She was gone…forever.

He hadn't cried in a long time, but that night he lay in bed and cried like a baby. It was all gone—his wife, the hopes and dreams he'd shared with her, the children they'd planned to have one day, the life they'd shaped together. Nothing had turned out the way it was supposed to—nothing—because a drunk had run a stop sign that fateful day last summer. Thanks to the carelessness of a stranger, Logan's future, what was left of it, stretched out before him dark and empty.

Later, after the tears dried, he must have slept, but when his alarm went off at seven the following morning, he felt as if he'd been out on an all-nighter. His gut clenched just at the thought of going to work. Impulsively, he reached for the phone on the bedside table and punched in his boss's number.

"I'm not well," he told Nick in a rough voice. "I'm taking a day of sick leave." Not waiting for him to respond, he hung up.

In the newsroom, Josh Garrison was strolling past Logan's desk when the phone rang. Hesitating, he glanced around. Each reporter's desk was surrounded by four-foot-high partitions, giving them the illusion of privacy they needed to write. Six foot four in his stocking feet, Garrison glanced over the partition walls and wasn't surprised that the place was virtually deserted. It was one-thirty in the afternoon, and reporters who weren't out to lunch were out running down stories. The only reason he was there himself was because he'd accidentally left his cell phone on his desk when he'd been in earlier.

The phone rang again, daring him to answer it. He'd never been one to refuse a dare. Glancing around one more time to make sure there was no one to squeal on him, he stepped over to St. John's phone and snatched it up. "Logan St. John," he growled, and prayed that the caller wasn't someone who knew Logan well.

He needn't have worried. "Mr. St. John? This is Doug Spicer, the bartender at the Hilltop Pool Hall. You were in here a couple of weeks ago."

Searching his memory for the stories Logan had written recently, Josh lied and said, "Sure, I remember. How are you? What can I do for you?"

"You told me to call you the next time the guy came in." Hearing the pause on the other end of the phone, he lowered his voice and said, "You know—the cross-dresser who's an assistant superintendent for one of the local school districts? He came in. He just walked in five minutes ago."

Already seeing the headlines, Josh grinned slowly. "No kidding? Could you give me that address again? I seem to have misplaced it."

The bartender quickly rattled it off, then explained, "I don't want to cause any trouble, but I just think people should know what's going on in their schools."

"I agree completely," Josh said easily. "I'll be there as soon as I can. Hey, Doug," he added quickly, before the men could hang up. "How's this guy dressed?"

"A blond wig and green dress," he retorted. "Trust me, you can't miss him. He's about six foot two."

Pleased, Josh grinned. "Thanks. Keep him there, will you? I'm on my way."

Hanging up, he stepped over to his own desk and grabbed his camera from his desk drawer. Already writing the story in his head, he rushed outside to his car and headed for the Hilltop Pool Hall. He'd have to remember to thank St. John for this one, he thought gleefully. Yeah, right!

The headlines the next morning read School District Superintendent Cross-Dresser. Logan took one look at the stunning words and started to swear. The son of a bitch had stolen his story! How, dammit? Garrison hadn't been anywhere near the Hilltop Pool Hall when he'd investigated the robbery there, and Logan had made sure he hadn't told a soul about the lead he'd gotten about the cross-dressing school official. How the hell had Garrison gotten wind of it?

Here's my number. Call me the next time he comes in.

His own words came back to haunt him. The jackass must have answered his phone at work! Logan thought, feeling livid. That was the only explanation. Swearing, he didn't know why he was so surprised. He'd known the second he met the man that there was something about him he didn't like. Now he knew what it was. He was a thief!

Furious, he was tempted to go to Nick and tell him what the bastard had done, but even as he considered it, Logan rejected the idea. No, he wasn't going tattling to the boss like a second-grader complaining to the teacher. Nick couldn't fire Josh, anyway. As long as Garrison was dating old man Porter's granddaughter, they were all stuck with the jerk.

His time was coming, though, Logan promised himself. He firmly believed that what goes around, comes around—Garrison would get what was coming to him. And Logan didn't mind admitting that he couldn't think of a better person for it to happen to. There was no way to predict, of course, how or when it would happen, but he hoped he was around to see it. In the meantime, he had to take measures to make sure Garrison didn't ever again steal one of his stories. From now on, he'd give out his cell phone number instead of the office one. And Logan would change his password on his computer just in case Garrison got it in his head to try to get into his computer files.

That didn't mean, however, that he intended to act as if nothing had happened. As he left for a ten o'clock meeting with a woman who had been robbed by the same man three times in three years, he came face-to-face with Garrison.

Furious all over again, Logan stopped in his tracks and gave him a look that told him without words just how despicable he was. "If you steal another story from me, I'll go to Porter myself," he said coldly. "And don't think dating his granddaughter is going to save your sorry ass. He's an honest man. He can't stand a thief."

Far from worried, Josh only grinned smugly. "It's my word against yours. Who do you think the old man's going to believe? His star reporter or a has-been whiner who's so jealous he can't see straight?"

"Try it and find out," Logan growled. "Then we'll see who the has-been whiner is."

Giving him one more warning look, he brushed past him, barely resisting the urge to sink his clenched fist into the man's belly. He wouldn't sink that low, he assured himself—unless Garrison made the first move. He didn't, however, and Logan was forced to admit that was for the best. Garrison was more than ten years younger and obviously worked out. He probably had abs that were granite hard. One punch and Logan would break his hand.

Striding out, he dismissed him from his mind and headed for his appointment. He had more than enough work to keep busy for the rest of the day, but after his interview, he found he couldn't shake bits and pieces of his conversation with Garrison. Disgusted, he thanked God that his next appointment wasn't for another two hours. Logan was still angry and needed some time to cool down.

In the past, there was only one person he would have called—Faith. He'd trusted her judgment more than anyone's on the planet, and she'd had a real knack for putting things in perspective whenever he was troubled about something. In desperation, he headed for the cemetery.

It was a dreary day, overcast and damp, and the place was deserted. Logan hardly noticed. Standing at Faith's grave, his shoulders hunched against the rain and his hands buried in his pockets, he stared down at the tombstone that reduced her life to just her birthday and the day she'd died. She'd been so much more than that. Funny, caring, protective, beautiful. She could make him laugh when no one else could, and at that moment, he needed to hear her voice more than he needed his next breath. But silence enveloped him, and the only sound he heard was the soft murmur of the gentle rain that fell.

He'd never felt so alone. For the first time, he found no comfort in standing at her grave, talking to her. She was dead and gone, and she was never going to be there for him again. Why had it taken him so long to realize that?

His shoulders slumping in defeat, he returned to his car and instinctively reached for his phone. Without even thinking about it, he punched in the number to Abby's cell phone. It wasn't until he heard the sound of her voice that he realized she was the one he'd wanted to talk to all along.

He should have hung up immediately, before she answered. It would have been the smart thing to do. She was just a friend—he shouldn't have *needed* to hear her voice. He didn't want to, dammit! There didn't seem to be anything he could do about it, however. Sitting in his car at the cemetery parking lot, he couldn't make himself hang up.

"Hello?"

At the sound of her voice, the rainy day didn't seem so dreary. Later, that would bother him, but for now, he couldn't bring himself to worry about it. He'd missed her. "Hi, Abby."

"Logan?"

She sounded so shocked, he had to smile. "I guess you were beginning to wonder if I was ever going to call you again. I'm sorry. I had some things I had to work out."

Instantly sympathetic, she said, "Is it something you'd like to talk about?"

He hesitated, torn. How could he tell her that he'd had so much fun with her it had scared the hell out of him? He didn't want her to read anything into that, but how could he tell her without hurting her feelings? Dammit, how had this gotten so complicated? They were supposed to be just friends!

"I'll tell you about it one of these days," he finally said. "I'm sorry I'm not giving you much notice, but are you busy tonight? I thought maybe we could go out to dinner."

Her heart pounding like a drum, Abby released a silent sigh of relief. She had friends who would never go out with any man who expected them to drop everything and come running, but she didn't have a problem with that. He'd obviously come to terms with whatever had kept him from calling, and she was thrilled. Nothing else mattered.

"I'd love to go to dinner," she said softly. "What time and where?"

"Seven," he replied. "And if it's all right with you, I'd like to pick you up."

Her heart skipped a beat. He was talking about a real date! Suddenly nervous, but in a good way, she smiled. "I think that can be arranged." She gave him her address and directions, then asked, "How should I dress?"

"Nothing fancy," he assured her. "I just thought we'd go somewhere casual and get a hamburger or tacos or something. Then we can sit and talk and not be bothered by a waiter constantly interrupting us. Of course, if you'd rather go somewhere else—"

"Oh, no, that's fine. I guess I'll see you at seven, then."

Feeling lighter than air, Abby hung up, her smile stretching from ear to ear. Yes! She didn't know what had been bothering him, but he must have worked out whatever the problem was. He'd called and asked her out again, just as he'd promised. So what if he hadn't phoned as quickly as she'd thought he would? He'd finally called, and that was what was important.

Now all she had to do was figure out what she was going to wear!

The rest of the day passed in a blur. As usual, Martin was

in and out, but Abby hardly noticed him. While she worked, she mentally, systematically, went over every piece of clothing she owned. By the time five o'clock rolled around and she headed home, she still didn't have a clue what she was going to wear.

On a good day, she was home by five-twenty. She quickly discovered that today wasn't going to be one of those days. Two wrecks within three miles of each other backed the traffic up for miles. For long stretches at a time, she, like hundreds of others, just sat on the freeway, not moving. There was nothing she could do but sit there, trapped, and watch the minutes tick by.

By the time she finally made it home, it was six-fifteen and her nerves were stretched tight. She told herself that there was no reason to panic. Logan wouldn't get all bent out of shape if she was running a little late, and it wasn't as if she had to get ready for a fancy dress ball. They were just going to a burger joint. What was the big deal?

Sighing, she smiled ruefully. If only it was that simple. She didn't care what they ate—that had nothing to do with anything. What mattered was how she felt, and for reasons she couldn't explain, she felt as if she was getting ready for much more than a dinner date. Over the last two weeks, they'd become friends, and though she hadn't gotten to know him nearly as well as she wanted to, she couldn't deny that she really liked him. Given the chance, she would have liked their friendship to be much more than that.

And it scared her. Was she rushing into heartache? Yes, they'd spent a lot of time talking on the phone, but she needed even more time with him before she could say that she really knew the man. And then there was Faith. He'd repeatedly told Abby how much he loved his wife, how she was the only woman he would ever love. He was devoted to her memory and obviously missed her with every fiber of his being. How could there be room for another woman in his life when his heart was in the grave with Faith?

Unwanted doubts crept in, and as Abby stood in front of her bedroom closet, she couldn't help wondering if she was making a huge mistake. From everything that Logan had told her, Faith had been a beautiful, vibrant woman who had lived life with a kind of passion Abby could only admire.

How could she compete with someone like that? Her new hairstyle had helped her self-esteem, but no hairdo in the world was going to change the fact that she was still skinny as a rail and had a mass of freckles all over her body. Why would Logan look twice at her when he was still in love with a beautiful woman he couldn't forget? Abby didn't stand a chance.

Don't be so hard on yourself. He called you and asked you out, didn't he? He must be interested or he wouldn't have bothered.

She had to admit that the eternal optimist in her head had a point, but Abby wasn't buying it. He thought she was just looking for friendship, and that fell right in with his own plans. If he had even a suspicion that she might be interested in anything resembling romance, he probably wouldn't come anywhere near her.

So don't tell him.

Well, there's a plan, she thought wryly. Go out with the man, take a chance on falling in love with him, and if you're lucky, maybe you'll be able to make him forget his dead wife and fall in love with you. Yeah, right!

No, silly. Go out with him, guard your heart and just enjoy his company. Familiarity breeds…familiarity. He'll never give himself a chance to think of you as anything but a friend if you don't spend as much time as you can with him.

Hesitating, she had to admit that was true. She couldn't back out now. If he knew her better, maybe their relationship could turn into something romantic. If it didn't, then at least she'd tried. And they could still be friends. She'd just never tell him that she wanted more.

It wasn't an ideal plan, but it could work, she told herself. All she had to do was keep reminding herself that they were just friends. If he indicated that he might want something else, then she could give in to the feelings he stirred in her so effortlessly. Otherwise, she was better off protecting her heart.

Relieved that she'd finally come to terms with her feelings for him, she didn't have time to worry about what she was going to wear. They were just going for hamburgers, for heaven's sake! Grabbing jeans and a baby-blue scooped neck T-shirt, she hurriedly changed, then quickly redid her makeup and hair. Stepping back to study herself in the mirror, she smiled. It had been nearly a week since she'd had her hair cut, and the woman who stared back at her was still a stranger. She was getting used to her, though, and she had to admit that she liked what she saw. She hoped Logan did, too.

The doorbell rang then, startling her heart into a frantic beat. Still, she thought she had her emotions under control ... until she opened the door and Logan smiled at her. If things had been different, she would have walked into his arms. Did he have any idea how good-looking he was? she wondered. Casually dressed in jeans and a pale yellow knit shirt, he took her breath away.

Praying he couldn't hear the pounding of her heart, she said softly, "Hi. You look very nice."

"So do you," he said huskily, stepping inside as she pulled

the door wider in invitation. Glancing around her living room, he grinned. "This is nothing like what I expected. I thought you'd like froufrou and all that delicate French furniture that women seem to love and men are afraid to sit on. I like this!"

"So do I," Abby said with a laugh. "Just for the record—I'm not crazy about froufrou, either. I wanted something comfortable."

"If I didn't know better, I'd say I was in a log cabin. This is great!"

"Thank you," she said with a smile. "I just need to get my purse and I'll be ready."

Seconds later, she appeared with a small white purse, and Logan escorted her to his car. He'd been afraid she'd be uptight and nervous, but nothing could have been further from the truth. Relaxed and at ease, she seemed truly happy to see him, and he had to admit that he felt the same way. In fact, seeing her smile was all he needed to make his day perfect.

That was because they were friends and he'd missed her, he tried to tell himself. But that damning little voice in his head wasn't buying it. Friends weren't aroused by a friend's perfume. They didn't imagine carrying them off to bed or making love to them until they were boneless.

Had she noticed that he couldn't stop looking at her? he wondered. She was just so pretty. He'd thought she was attractive the first time they'd met, but now she acted more confident, and she just seemed to glow. As they reached Tom's Burger Joint and he escorted her inside, he wanted to take her hand so badly he ached with the need. And that floored him. He hadn't wanted to touch a woman since Faith died.

His thoughts buzzing, he followed Abby to the front counter to order, and later, couldn't have said what he chose. And it was all her fault. He couldn't take his eyes off her. When had she slipped past his guard? How? He was a married man—not technically, maybe, but he certainly felt like one.

"Logan? Are you all right? You look funny."

He couldn't look half as funny as he felt, he thought grimly. "It's been a strange day," he said huskily as they settled at a table overlooking the small creek that ran behind the building. "You look awfully pretty tonight."

Soft color tinged her cheeks. "Thank you."

"It's nothing but the truth."

A smile teased the corners of her mouth as she added sugar to her iced tea. "I don't know about that, but it sounds good, anyway. So what's been going on with you? I guess you've been busy."

"Josh Garrison stole one of my stories yesterday."

Startled, she dropped her teaspoon. "What? Are you sure?"

"Oh, yeah," Logan said grimly. "The second I saw the headlines, I knew he'd somehow intercepted a tip that I'd been waiting on. So I went to my source this afternoon and found out the truth. He called me at work yesterday and told me the story was going down. The problem is, he didn't speak to me. I'd taken the day off."

"Garrison pretended to be you?"

With his mouth compressed into a flat line, Logan nodded. "He answered my private line. When I confronted him about it, he couldn't have cared less. He claimed it was my word against his, and since he's dating old man Porter's granddaughter and I'm just a has-been, he has the inside track."

"That's outrageous! Did you tell your boss?" Even as she asked, Abby knew he hadn't. He wasn't the type to run tattling to the teacher. "You wouldn't do that."

"You're right. I wouldn't."

Abby sympathized with him. He was furious—she could

see the anger in his eyes—and she couldn't say she blamed him. He had to feel as helpless as she did with Martin. "He'll shoot himself in the foot before it's over with," she said, unconsciously repeating what he'd said to her when she'd told him about Martin. "All you have to do is wait."

"Damn straight," Logan retorted. "He'll get his, and when he does, it's not going to matter who his girlfriend is."

Their food was delivered to their table then, and the next few minutes were spent eating. Abby hadn't had an appetite for days, ever since she'd realized that Logan probably wasn't going to call her again, but that had all changed. Happy just to be sitting across the table from him, she took a bite of her burger and sighed in pleasure. "Mmm. I hadn't realized how hungry I was."

Watching her eat, Logan smiled. "I like a woman who enjoys her food. So how's work going? Are you still having problems with your boss?"

Swallowing, she nodded. "I don't know why I couldn't see it before, but I'm convinced he doesn't have an ethical bone in his body. The problem is proving it. He's very clever."

"He sounds like a real jackass," Logan retorted. "Is there someone higher up at your company that you could discuss this with? If you have suspicions, surely someone else you work with does, too."

Her food forgotten, Abby hesitated, wanting to tell him the truth so badly she could taste it. Why couldn't she? she wondered. He was a friend, wasn't he? Granted, she hadn't known him that long, but every instinct she possessed told her he wouldn't betray a confidence. He wasn't that kind of man.

What if she was wrong, though? she worried. It could happen. Look at her track record where men were concerned. She'd proved more than once that when it came to men, she was a lousy judge of character. Then there was the fact that Logan was a reporter. If she had misjudged him and he was just using her to get a story, everything she told him could end up on the front page of the paper tomorrow! Could she really take that risk?

She didn't have to think twice about it. Right or wrong, she trusted Logan. If he betrayed that trust, she'd probably never, ever confide in another man again, but she couldn't worry about that now.

"Actually," she said quietly, "I haven't been completely honest with you about everything. I was afraid—"

"Of me?"

"Oh, no!" she said, horrified that he would jump to that conclusion. "I wasn't afraid of you personally, but I have to admit that Logan St. John the crime reporter makes me nervous. What I have to tell you can go no further at this time. I'm sorry, Logan, but I have to ask for your word on this."

"You have it," he said without hesitation. "I know we haven't known each other that long, but I do consider you a friend, Abby. And I never betray the confidence of a friend. So if that's what you're worried about, you can rest easy. Whatever your secret is, it's safe with me."

When his gaze met hers head-on, there was no doubting his sincerity. Touched, Abby blinked back sudden tears and reached for his hand across the table. "Thank you," she said thickly. "You don't know what this means to me." Taking a deep breath, she released it slowly and finally admitted, "I don't work for a company, Logan. I work for a city councilman. Martin James."

With the admission, she saw understanding dawn in his eyes, and though nothing was said, they both knew they'd taken another step in their relationship. His fingers squeezed hers reassuringly, then seemed to forget to let go.

"You don't have to worry about this turning up in tomorrow's paper, Abby. No one at the *Gazette* will have a clue that this is going on until you give me the go-ahead to report it."

Her fingers tightened around his. "I knew I could trust you."

"What about your boss? I know you said last week that he didn't suspect that you were on to him, but your face is so expressive. Are you sure he's not suspicious of you? He's taking bribes, for God's sake! If I were in his shoes, I'd be paranoid about being caught, especially by my secretary. You have access to his records in a way no one else does. He's got to know that you're more of a threat to him than anyone."

"You don't know Martin," she replied. "He's always thought he was smarter than anyone else. He's so arrogant that it's sickening. Get this—he had me deposit a check in his personal account that was supposed to be for the sale of his Corvette, and he didn't even sell it! I know because I went by his house and looked in his garage."

"What? Dammit, Abby, have you lost your mind? You've got to go to the FBI."

"But I don't have any proof."

"You've got enough," he retorted. "You have to tell them what you know, and protect yourself. For all you know, they could already have Martin under surveillance. If they do, you can bet last week's paycheck they're watching you, too. They might think you're an accomplice."

"Oh, no!"

"Oh, yes," he insisted. "Look at it from the feds' viewpoint. It's a two-person office. How could you *not* know what's going on? You've got to report this, Abby, if for no other reason than to protect yourself."

Her cheeks devoid of color, her appetite gone, she released his hand to push her plate away. "You're right, of course. I'll go before work in the morning. It didn't even cross my mind that the FBI might already be suspicious of him. I was just concerned that they wouldn't take me seriously if I didn't have proof."

"You have sound reasons for being suspicious," he said. "Trust me, they'll take you seriously."

"Just thinking about it makes me sick to my stomach," she admitted. "I hate confrontations!"

"He won't know anything about it until it's all over and he's arrested," Logan assured her. "But if it'll make you feel better, I'll go with you."

The words were out of his mouth before he had time to think about them, but Logan wouldn't have taken the offer back if he'd had the chance. And it wasn't just because he wanted to cover the story of the downfall of Martin James from beginning to end, he realized. It was because of Abby herself. He wanted to be there for her so she wouldn't have to go through this alone. She needed someone to protect her...

Suddenly realizing where his thoughts had wandered, he stiffened. When had his feelings for her become so strong? If he didn't already care about her, just thinking about being her protector would have been enough to send him running in the other direction. It was too late for that, however. He didn't love her, he assured himself, but she was a friend, and he protected the people he cared about. That was all there was to it. He would have done the same thing for his sister-in-law, Samantha, or Colleen Angleton, the wife of his best friend, or Lisa Hamilton, a co-worker who'd started at the *Gazette* the same day he had. That was just the kind of man he was. His mother had raised him to be protective of women.

Studying Abby across the table, he had to admit that his reasoning sounded good. But if he wasn't on the verge of falling in love with her, why did he have this insane urge to snatch her up and carry her off to the ends of the earth, where no one could hurt her?

He didn't have an answer to that, and he didn't want one. He just knew he couldn't stand on the sidelines when she needed him. "So what do you say? Would you like me to go with you? I know an agent—Vic Roberts. I met him years ago when I was doing a story on a dirty agent. If you like, I can call him at home and see if we can set something up for in the morning."

Relieved, she smiled shakily. "Would you?"

"Sure." Checking the directory on his cell phone, he quickly placed the call. Within seconds, he had Vic Roberts on the line. "Hey, Vic, this is Logan St. John. I'm sorry to call you at home, but I have a friend who needs to speak to you about a problem at work. We were hoping we could come in in the morning to talk about it."

When he hung up a few minutes later, he was smiling. "I hope nine's not too early."

"Oh, no, it's perfect! You don't know how much I appreciate this, Logan. You're coming, too, aren't you? I'm going to be a basket case."

"There's no need to be," he assured her. "I'll be with you every step of the way. Why don't you meet me in the lobby of the federal building at ten minutes to nine? That'll give us plenty of time to get upstairs in time."

"Okay," she said with a sigh. "Then from there I can go straight to work. If Martin comes in before I get there, I'll just tell him I had a dental appointment I forgot about."

Chapter 8

Feeling as if a huge weight had been lifted from her shoulders, Abby was finally able to enjoy the meal. The mood lightened, and for the first time in a long time, she was able to completely dismiss Martin from her thoughts. Figuring Logan didn't want to talk about work any more than she wanted to continue the discussion about her boss, she asked him about his family, and soon they were talking about their childhoods, family traditions, outrageous moments in their past that their siblings wouldn't let die.

"I wanted to be a ballerina when I was a little girl," she confided, her eyes shining with the memory. "I even had a ballerina doll that could stand on her toes and bend her knees. She had a tutu and I wanted one, too."

Logan grinned. "Why do I have a suspicion this is one of those stories that will still embarrass you when you're a hundred and three?"

She laughed. "Well, I don't know if I'll make it to a hundred and three or not, but yeah, it's one of those moments siblings love to needle you about. Of course, my mother made sure no one ever forgot it. She caught it on tape."

"Oh, God," he groaned. "Movie cameras—don't you hate them? What did you do?"

"I pretended my slip was a tutu and danced in the backyard in nothing but it and my panties. And I never knew until it was too late that my entire family was standing at the kitchen windows, watching. I blushed so badly that my hair turned red and it's been that way ever since."

Delighted, he laughed. "Yeah, right! And how old were you when you had this recital?"

"I believe I was four."

"I bet you were cute as a button."

"All four-year-olds are cute as a button."

His eyes warmed as they locked with hers. "You're still cute as a button, Miss Saunders...especially when you blush. Watch it—your hair's getting redder even as we speak."

Her lips twitched. "I can see right now that I never should have told you that story," she said dryly. "So what's your most embarrassing moment? It's only fair that you give me the same kind of ammunition I gave you."

Sitting back in his chair, he rubbed his chin thoughtfully. "Let's see. There are so many. Carter had a real knack for setting me up when we were kids. He would sneak into my room at night and scare the beejeebees out of me. One night, he convinced me that someone had broken into the house. Our father was away on a business trip, and I didn't know he was coming home early. I heard someone on the stairs, grabbed a giant-size bottle of shampoo from the bathroom and dumped it all over Dad."

"Oh, no!"

"Oh, no is right," he chuckled. "Carter and I were both out of college and married before we got off restriction."

She laughed, loving the way his eyes danced. "Poor baby," she teased. "At least there was no home movie of you." When he just lifted a dark brow, she gasped, "Your brother filmed it? You've got to be kidding!"

"He's got a twisted mind," he retorted. "I guess this is a good time to mention that he's my favorite brother."

"Really? And should I take that as a warning that you, too, have a twisted mind at times?"

His grin broadening, he shrugged. "Maybe. Maybe not. I guess you'll just have to wait and find out."

She knew he was teasing, but she wondered if he'd realized what he'd just said. *She'd have to wait and find out.* That sounded as if he was planning on being a part of her life for a while if she was agreeable.

Her heart nearly burst with happiness at the thought. She said, "I'll be sure to be on guard."

"It won't help," he teased, "but you can try."

No truer words had ever been spoken, at least where he was concerned, but she wisely kept that to herself. "If I promise not to pull out my tutu and you agree to keep your hands off my shampoo, we can go back to my place for dessert," she suggested. "I made a pound cake yesterday, and I've got some strawberries and whipped cream. We can have strawberry shortcake."

The words weren't even out of her mouth and he was already on his feet. "Why didn't you say so sooner? Let's go!"

Laughing, he rushed her outside to his car, and before the thunder of her heart could settle into a steady beat again, they were back at her house. Unlocking her front door for her, he followed her inside, then to the kitchen.

"What can I do to help?" he asked. "How about coffee? Have you got a coffeemaker? Or do you even like coffee? I never thought to ask."

Startled, Abby couldn't hide her surprise. "I've never dated anyone who offered to help in the kitchen," she blurted out. "Dennis thought it was woman's work."

"Obviously Dennis was a bonehead," Logan retorted, not the least offended. "This isn't the Dark Ages—or the fifties! Everybody needs to know their way around a kitchen."

"I agree," she replied. "So how do you like your coffee?"

"Strong enough to strip the bark off a tree," he said bluntly, grinning. "How do you like yours?"

"Strong enough to strip the bark off a tree," she retorted.

"You're kidding! I would have taken you for one of those women who like fancy, flavored coffees that I wouldn't even call coffee. What about salsa? You do like Mexican food, don't you?"

"Yes, I love salsa. The hotter, the better."

"All right! I knew there was a reason I liked you! Have you ever tried Indian food? That'll make your hair sweat!"

She chuckled. "It's not really hot unless smoke comes out of your ears. You should taste my chili."

"Tell me when and I'll be here," he assured her. "Do you put beans in your chili?" When she just looked at him as if he'd lost his mind, he laughed. "I thought not."

"Did your wife like to cook?"

"God, no!" He smiled. "Faith had a great eye for decorating, and she was a good housekeeper, but any time she went near the stove, it was a disaster."

"My mother's like that," Abby confided. "When I was growing up, I thought spaghetti was supposed to be hard."

Stepping over to the cabinet where she kept the coffee, she

handed it to him, then set the kitchen table with cups and saucers and dessert plates. "Thank God for my grandmother on my dad's side," she said as she sliced pound cake, then drizzled the slices with strawberries in syrup before adding a dollop of whipped cream. "She was a fantastic cook, and she started teaching me almost as soon as I could walk."

The rich scent of coffee soon filled the kitchen, and Abby sniffed appreciatively. "Every time I smell coffee, I think of Gran," she told Logan as they each took a seat at the table. "She always had a pot warming on the stove."

"My grandmother did the same thing. She liked it strong enough to melt lead." Smiling fondly at the memory, he took a bite of the pound cake and strawberries and groaned. "Oh, man, that's good! Can I have seconds?"

Flattered, she laughed. "You can take some home with you."

Enjoying each other's company, they lingered over dessert, talking until Logan suddenly noticed the clock on the stove and realized how late it was. "It's after eleven! You should have thrown me out of here over an hour ago."

"Why? I was having a good time." Quickly making a dessert doggie bag to go, she sealed the Ziploc bag as he carried their dishes to the sink. "It doesn't look pretty," she said, handing it to him, "but at least you don't have to worry about spilling it all over your car."

Taking it from her, Logan should have thanked her, then gotten out of Dodge before he did something stupid—like reach for her. But it had been a long time since he'd enjoyed a woman's company so much, and he didn't want the evening to end. Staring down at her, his gaze falling to the gentle curve of her mouth, he only had to remember the one kiss they'd shared to taste her on his tongue.

"I had a great time tonight," he told her softly, thickly.

Her eyes locking with his, she smiled faintly. "Me, too."

"I meant what I said about wanting to come for dinner the next time you make chili."

"I'll be sure to let you know," she promised. "You're welcome here anytime, Logan."

Common sense told him to say good-night and go home, but he couldn't seem to concentrate on what he *should* do. Instead, all he could think about was how soft her mouth looked. Would she object if he kissed her? He had before, but they hadn't been in her house. He didn't want her to feel like he was pressuring her…

His gaze was trained on her lips, and as Abby stared up at him as if in a trance, she could have sworn she could actually feel his mouth on hers. Her lips throbbed, and deep inside, a dull ache burned with ever increasing heat. Her eyes locking with his, she swallowed a moan. Did he feel what he did to her with just a look? she wondered wildly. He had to…

"I should be going," he rasped.

Don't!

She never said a word, but somehow, he must have heard. His gaze darkened; his hands slowly reached for her. Before he could touch her, she swayed toward him. Just that easily, she was in his arms and his mouth was on hers.

Her senses swimming and her heart pounding, Abby tried to remind herself that she shouldn't lose her head here. It didn't matter that Faith was dead; Logan had loved her since he was fourteen. Abby wasn't foolish enough to think that what he felt for her was anything close to love. Call it what you will, it was nothing more than lust, chemistry, physical desire.

And that was okay, she assured herself. Because what she felt for him wasn't love, either. It couldn't be. She wouldn't let herself love him, wouldn't let him break her heart. All she had to do was control her emotions.

But merciful heavens, he didn't make it easy for her. He pulled her close and kissed her with a hunger that melted her insides, and she couldn't think. With a soft moan, she crowded closer and kissed him back.

Sweet. How had he forgotten how sweet she was? She fitted in his arms as if she was made for him, and when her own arms slipped around his neck and her tongue rubbed sensuously against his, he couldn't think of anything but how much he wanted her. Murmuring her name, he kissed her again, then again.

Later, he couldn't say when he'd realized he wasn't going to be able to let her go. With every breath he dragged in, the scent of her seduced him, teased him, made the fire in his belly burn hotter. Tearing his mouth from hers, he pressed a kiss to her ear, the side of her neck and nearly lost it completely when she shuddered delicately.

"Abby…"

That was all he could manage, just her name, but something in his tone had her pulling back slightly, her passion-darkened eyes searching his. He didn't say a word, but he didn't have to. With a single glance, he told her that what happened next would be up to her.

In spite of the fact that he wanted her so badly, he would have found a way to let her go if she'd asked him to. It would have cost him—his gut twisted at the very thought—but he wasn't a complete Neanderthal. He couldn't even imagine taking a woman to bed if she wasn't in complete agreement.

For the span of what seemed a lifetime, she didn't move, didn't speak, didn't so much as breathe. Then, just when he thought she was going to say no, she nearly destroyed him by reaching for the hem of her T-shirt. In slow motion, she pulled it over her head—and stole the air from his lungs.

"Do you know how beautiful you are?" he asked hoarsely.

Abby's heart threatened to pound out of her chest and tears welled in her eyes. She quickly tried to blink them back, but it was too late. A single tear spilled over her lashes, and before she could wipe it away, his hand was cupping her cheek, capturing it with a tenderness that completely destroyed her. With a nearly silent whimper, she buried her face against his chest.

"What's wrong?" he asked, horrified as his arms cradled her close. "Why are you crying? What did I do?"

"Nothing," she choked out. "It's j-just that no one's ever c-called me b-beautiful before."

"Then the whole damn world is full of fools."

He sounded so disgusted that she found herself suddenly fighting the need to giggle. "No, it's not. I'm not beautiful, Logan."

"The hell you're not! Where's a mirror? I'll show you."

And before she could guess his intentions, he took her hand and led her through the house until he found her bedroom. "What are you doing? Logan—"

"Just humor me," he said, and turned her to face her dresser mirror. Standing directly behind her, he met her gaze in the glass. "Look at yourself," he said huskily, "and tell me you're not beautiful. I dare you."

His hands were on her bare shoulders, his eyes heated as they skimmed over her, and she'd never been more aware of the fact that she was the only one half-dressed. "I'd feel better if you took your shirt off, too," she said quietly.

"Done," he replied, and yanked it over his head. Before the shirt hit the floor, his chest was warm against her back and his hands were once again on her shoulders. "Better?"

She couldn't find her voice. Her skin heating everywhere his touched it, she nodded.

"Now," he rasped, "I believe we were talking about how beautiful you are."

"No, *you* were," she said, only to draw in a quick, silent breath as his hands began to gently stroke her shoulders, skimming over her skin as if it were the finest silk. Watching his face, seeing the pleasure he took from just touching her, she felt her heart stumble. "Logan…"

"You have the most incredible skin," he murmured, trailing his fingers down her arms to her elbows and back up again. "How can you not call this beautiful?"

Her body started to hum. "I'm covered in freckles," she said huskily. "How can you call *that* beautiful?"

"Because I'm going to kiss every one of them," he said simply. "What's more beautiful than that?"

With that single statement, he made her ache. How could he do this to her with just words? "I'm too skinny," she said, then voiced her worst flaw. "I don't have any breasts."

"What are you talking about?" he scolded softly. "You've got a model's body. Do you know how many women would kill for that? And what do you mean, you don't have breasts? They're beautiful! They were made for my hand."

His right hand covered her left breast, making her heart pound. In the mirror, his eyes burned into hers and there was no question that he found her desirable. And for the first time in her life, she knew what it was like to feel beautiful.

Logan watched tears once again spill into her eyes, but this time they were accompanied by a shy smile that lit up her entire face. Enchanted, he turned her around, then tenderly cradled her face in his hands. "The first time I met you, I couldn't believe that someone hadn't snatched you up years ago.

You've got this old-fashioned beauty that's not flamboyant or flashy and has nothing to do with makeup or how your hair's fixed or what you're wearing. You've just got this glow that blows me away. Every time I see you, I want to touch you. Haven't you noticed?"

"No. I—"

"Then I guess I'll just have to do something about that," he growled.

As he lowered his mouth to hers, his hands moved over her, heating her skin, her blood, and slowly driving her out of her mind with need. Pressing close, she moaned when he unhooked her bra and eased it from her. Then he kissed his way down her throat to her breasts, and made her forget her own name.

Somehow, the rest of their clothes disappeared, and he swept her up to carry her to the bed, though she couldn't have said when. She felt the coolness of the sheets against her bare back, then Logan came down beside her, and every nerve ending in her body tightened in anticipation as he moved over her, into her. All her senses were attuned to the taste of him, the heat, the animal scent of him that drove her quietly out of her mind. With his wonderful, knowing hands, he made her float. With the kisses he dropped on every curve, he made her ache. And when he murmured her name in the darkness as if she were the only woman on earth, he made her feel loved.

Caught in the wonder of him and the need that throbbed with every kiss, every stroke of his hands, his hips, she didn't hear the alarm bells that clanged in warning deep inside her head. Her blood roared in her ears, and there was only Logan loving her with a fierce tenderness that made her cry.

"It's okay," she whispered when he kissed her and tasted the tears on her face. "I never expected… Don't stop. Please…"

He couldn't have stopped if he'd wanted to. Loving the way she clung to him, the way she moved with him in perfect rhythm, the soft cries that echoed every beat of his heart, he drove her to the edge and over, cradling her close as she came undone in his arms. He wanted to savor the moment, to savor *her*, but he never had a chance. His own need was too great, and before he could drag in a quick breath, he, too, was at the edge, about to shatter. He only had time to tighten his arms around her and roughly cry her name before the passion building in him like a summer storm hit like lightning. With a groan that seemed to come from the depth of his very being, he tumbled over the edge.

What had she done?

Lying next to Logan in her bed, her heartbeat slowly returning to normal, Abby swallowed a groan. She felt wonderful, closer to Logan than she'd ever felt to anyone in her life, and at the same time, horrified. How could she have let herself get caught up in the moment after the lecture she'd given herself? They were friends—*just* friends! How many times did she have to tell herself that before she got it through her head that she couldn't lose her heart to him? His wife might be dead and buried, but for all practical purposes, Logan was still married. His loyalty and heart were with Faith, and always would be.

God, she could pick 'em! What was wrong with her? Why did she keep falling for the wrong men? Logan, thank heavens, wasn't anything like the awful men she'd allowed herself to get involved with in the past, but he was just as bad for her. He was in love with another woman. What difference did it make that Faith was dead? She still had his heart.

Tears stung Abby's eyes, horrifying her. She couldn't cry

now. She couldn't let him see how close she was to falling in love with him. He didn't want that. In fact, he'd probably run for the hills if he suspected even for a second that she was getting emotionally involved.

Unable to lie there for another second without dissolving into tears, she jumped up and hurriedly began pulling on her clothes. "I'm sorry, Logan," she said in a choked voice, unable to look at him. "I didn't mean for this happen. We're friends—"

Frowning, Logan reached for his own clothes. "It's all right, Abby. There's nothing to apologize for. We both have needs. I was caught up in the moment as much as you were."

She knew he was just trying to reassure her, but his words still cut to the bone. Somehow, deep inside, she'd secretly hoped he would admit that what he felt for her was a hell of a lot more than physical, that he didn't want to be "just friends" anymore. But that obviously wasn't going to happen. And it hurt. She'd given him her heart, and he didn't even know it.

He never would, she promised herself as she pulled on her shirt and turned to face him with a composed expression. After all, she did have some pride.

"I know all you want is friendship," she said huskily. "I was afraid you'd jump to the conclusion that I was trying to change our agreement by bringing sex into the equation."

"You didn't throw me to the ground and force yourself on me," he said wryly. "If I remember correctly, I was the one who kissed you and carried you to bed."

"Well, yes, but—"

"It's all right, Abby," he said softly. "As long as you don't have any regrets, I don't, either. Do you have regrets?"

His cobalt-blue eyes locked with hers, and there was no escaping them as he waited for an answer. Trapped, she wanted to tell him yes, she had a regret, but only one. For the first time in her life, she wanted a man to be absolutely nuts about her.

She couldn't voice that, however, without revealing her own feelings, and that was something she was determined not to do. "No," she quietly, meeting his gaze head-on, "I don't have any regrets about tonight."

"Good." Satisfied, he stepped over to her and pulled her into his arms for a hug. "I've got to go, but we're still on for in the morning, aren't we? You're ready to go to the FBI?"

Her heart pounding, she realized she'd completely forgotten about her plan to go to the authorities with her suspicions of Martin. "I don't think I have any choice," she said with a grimace. "I'm not looking forward to it."

"You'll do fine," he assured her. "I could drive you, you know, instead of meeting you at the federal building. We could go early and have breakfast..."

"This isn't a date, Logan," she said with a smile. "I have to go to work afterward, remember? If I show up without my car, Martin's going to wonder what's going on. I don't want to do anything that'll raise his suspicions."

"I understand. I just know this great little hole-in-the-wall where we could get some fantastic breakfast tacos, but we can go another time."

Tightening his arms around her to draw her closer, he leaned down and pressed a quick kiss to her mouth. Abby caught her breath the instant he deepened the caress. Her blood heated, her pulse pounded, her bones began to melt. How she found the strength to step back, she never knew. She just sensed that if she didn't find a way to end this, she was going to wind up in bed with him again, and that shook her to the core. She wouldn't be able to hold back her feelings a second time.

"C'mon," she rasped, stepping away before she completely lost her head, "I'll walk you to the door."

"All right," he grumbled, a crooked grin curling his mouth. "I'll go…if you insist." When she just smiled at him, he said, "You're a hard woman, Abby Saunders."

"Good night, Logan. I'll see you in the morning."

"At ten to nine sharp," he agreed. "Don't be late," he growled. And before she could stop him, his mouth covered hers for a split second in a kiss that was already hot and searing. Then, just as she started to kiss him back, he turned to the door. "I'll see you tomorrow," he said with a grin, and left before she could say another word.

Her head spinning and her knees weak from his kiss, she locked her front door and leaned back against it in a daze. Shaken, she realized that if she'd been given the chance, she would have called him back in a heartbeat and tried to convince him to spend the night. What had he done to her? She'd meant it when she'd told him earlier that she just wanted to be friends. All her adult life, she'd jumped into relationships that were wrong for her because of low self-esteem, and she'd been determined not to do that this time. Then he'd kissed her and everything had changed.

She loved kissing him, loved making love to him. And all he'd said was that everyone had "needs." God, she hated that word! It was so impersonal. So how did he feel about her? She didn't have a clue.

And that led her right back to the worry knotting her stomach. She wasn't in love with him, she told herself as she strode into the bathroom to bathe and get ready for bed. She couldn't be! She wasn't stupid enough to fall in love with a man who had no intention of loving anyone but his dead wife.

Her heart should have agreed with her head, but honesty

forced her to admit that even to her own ears, she protested just a little too fiercely. And that scared the hell out of her. Dragging in a calming breath, she released it with a slow sigh. Okay, she admitted as she washed and rinsed her hair, so maybe she did have feelings for him, but the only ones that started with *L* were like and lust. He was an extremely likable man. As for lust, she was as susceptible as the next woman when it came to an attractive man with a great personality and a killer grin. And there was nothing wrong with that. He made her heart beat faster with just a smile. When he kissed her, she forgot her own name. She wasn't made of stone.

It was just sexual craving, she told herself for the thousandth time when she finally crawled into bed a short while later. That was all it had ever been. If he ever decided to get on with life and let himself love someone besides Faith, then Abby might let down her guard enough to love him back. For now, though, she assured herself as she slowly drifted to sleep, she just had a good old-fashioned case of lust.

After sleeping like a baby through the night, she was convinced she was firmly in control of her emotions. Then she walked into the lobby of the federal building and found Logan waiting for her. When he saw her and grinned, her heart rolled over in her breast. Stunned, she stopped in her tracks. If she hadn't, she was afraid she would have run straight into his arms. Dear God, what was wrong with her?

"Good morning," he said, his long strides quickly eliminating the distance between them. "I was afraid you might not show."

Suddenly noticing her blank expression, he reached for her, pulling her close for a quick hug before stepping back just far enough to get a good look at her face. "Are you okay? You're awfully pale. You're not thinking of backing out, are you?"

If she hadn't been on the edge of dissolving into tears,

Abby would have laughed. Backing out? Oh, yeah, that was exactly what she needed to do. A smart woman would have backed out of their agreement and run like hell from their relationship before her heart was shattered. But it was already too late for that.

"Logan..."

"What is it, honey?" Concerned, he cupped her face with his hand, his thumb gently caressing her cheek. With nothing more than that, he made her heart ache for something she was afraid to put a name to. "If you're worried that your boss is somehow going to find out about this, don't. The feds will investigate him without him even knowing it. By the time he realizes just what kind of trouble he's in, he'll be in custody. So relax. You're perfectly safe."

Her eyes searching his, she hesitated. How could she tell him that she'd never been in so much trouble in her life and it had nothing to do with Martin? If Logan suspected for even a second that she was starting to really care for him, she wouldn't have to back out of their relationship—he'd do it so fast, he'd make her head spin.

Her heart broke just at the thought.

She couldn't do it, she thought, shaken. She couldn't risk him walking out of her life. Whatever she was feeling, she'd just have to learn to live with it.

"I know," she said huskily. "I've just never done anything like this before."

"That's why I wanted to come with you," he replied. "You shouldn't have to go through it alone."

If he only knew! Dragging in a bracing breath, she forced a smile. "C'mon, let's get this over with before I chicken out."

"Good girl." Taking her hand, he led her to the elevator.

* * *

Vic Roberts was not what Abby had expected. She'd assumed he'd be dressed in a suit, serious as a mortician and strictly business. Instead, he was dressed in pressed jeans, cowboy boots and a stark white Western shirt that looked perfect on his long, lean, rugged body. All he needed was a cowboy hat, and that was hanging on the hat rack in the corner.

A crooked grin tilting one corner of his mouth, he watched as Logan and Abby settled into the two chairs across from his desk after Logan made the introductions. "What have you been up to lately, you old goat? I haven't seen that weathered hide of yours in months. I thought maybe you'd decided to take the job at the *Post* you were offered last year."

"And go to D.C.?" Logan asked, horrified. "Thanks, but no thanks. The only capital I want to cover is the one right here in Texas."

"Wise choice," Vic said dryly. Glancing at Abby, he settled back in his chair and smiled teasingly. "You can relax, Miss Saunders. I don't know what Logan told you, but I don't generally bite unless I'm provoked. I understand you're having some kind of problem at the company where you work."

It was time to put up or shut up. Her heart thundering in her ears, Abby nodded grimly. "But I don't work for a company. My boss is an Austin city councilman. Martin James."

Something steely flickered in his eyes, and just that easily, Abby knew why Logan had recommended she talk to Vic. He might look as if he'd just walked off the King Ranch, but there was a quick intelligence in his eyes that told her he was a man who wouldn't be fooled by Martin's practiced charm. In fact, she doubted there was little that got past him.

He arched a grizzled brow at her. "Your problem is with James?"

"I think he's taking bribes from law firms bidding on the new tax contract with the city," she said bluntly.

"Do you have proof of that?"

"No," she sighed, grimacing. "That's why I haven't come forward before now. I made a copy of a check he asked me to deposit for him that was supposed to be for the sale of a car he still owns, but that's all. And that was a couple of weeks ago. For all I know, he was holding on to the car until the check cleared before he signed it over to the new owner."

The agent's narrowed eyes searched hers. "But you don't think so?"

"No. He's not a rich man. Over the course of the last two weeks, he's played golf every day, had lunch at the Senators Club and every other expensive restaurant in town, and spent money I know he doesn't have.

"I've worked for him for four years," she said flatly. "He's never acted this way before. He's never socialized with anyone bidding on city contracts. Now he is. I think he's up to something. I just can't prove it. Logan said I still needed to come forward with what I know."

For a long moment, Vic didn't say anything, and when he finally did speak, he surprised Abby by saying, "I need to talk to my boss for a minute. Excuse me."

"Well," Abby said wryly, "that wasn't exactly the response I was expecting. He doesn't give very much away, does he?"

"That's why he's so good at what he does," Logan replied, grinning. "The first time I met him, I was working on a story about corruption in the Bureau, and I couldn't get a thing out of him. It wasn't until I convinced him that I was trying to expose a criminal, not bring down the Bureau, that he finally agreed to work with me."

Intrigued, Abby would have asked what kind of corruption

he was talking about, but she never got the chance. The door opened and Vic returned with an older man who wore the conservative black suit that Abby had expected of an agent.

All-business himself, Vic introduced his boss. "This is Fred Nash. He's the agent in charge of the Austin office. I asked him to sit in on this meeting."

"Does that mean you believe me?" Abby asked, relieved. "Thank God!"

"We've been watching Mr. James for some time," Fred Nash admitted. "Unfortunately, we haven't been able to collect any significant evidence against him. We really need someone on the inside—"

"Whoa! Wait just a damn minute," Logan said, already anticipating where the older man was headed. "She's not going to be your spy. Do your own dirty work."

"C'mon, Logan, at least consider the idea," Vic said. "She won't be in any danger."

"You don't know that."

"Martin James has no history of violence—"

"He has no history of accepting bribes, either," he retorted. "That doesn't mean he's not on the take."

"True, but—"

"But nothing," he growled. "Dammit, Vic, if the man's already up to his neck in bribes, he's not going to stand around with his hands in his pockets while Abby exposes him. He could hurt her."

"I can speak for myself," Abby interjected quietly. "I appreciate your concern, Logan, but since I'm the one who's worked with Martin for the last four years, I think I know him better than anyone here. He would never hurt me."

Stunned, Logan couldn't believe he'd heard her correctly. "Are you saying you're going to do this? You didn't even want to report this because you were afraid Martin would guess what you're up to! How are you going to spy on the man without giving yourself away? You're going to be a nervous wreck!"

She didn't deny it. "Just thinking about it makes me sick to my stomach, but what else can I do? I can't let him get away with this when there's something I can do to stop him."

The decision made, she turned to Vic and his boss. "What do you want me to do?"

Chapter 9

"I can't believe you agreed to spy on James," Logan said as they walked out of the federal building a short while later. "No one would have blamed you if you'd said no."

"You heard Mr. Roberts," Abby said. "They've been watching him and they still don't have any hard evidence against him. Do you realize how much money he's costing the taxpayers? Because of him and a few others, the bidding process is nothing but a sham. I can't just stand by and do nothing when he's breaking the law. I'd be as guilty as he is."

"I understand that," Logan replied. "I just don't like the idea of you being alone with him in that office while you're spying on him. What happens if he catches you going through his personal files?"

"I'll be careful."

"I know that. That doesn't make me feel any better. I've been covering crimes like this for almost fifteen years, and men such as Martin James don't take kindly to being caught. Things could get ugly really fast—which is why I don't want you anywhere near the man when he realizes the feds are on to him."

They reached her car and he frowned down at her, his blue eyes dark with worry as he wrapped his arms around her in a hug. "Just watch yourself," he said huskily. "Okay? I don't want to be called to James's office to write about him attacking you."

Touched, loving the feel of his protective arms around her, she hugged him back. "He's really not that kind of man, but I won't take any chances. Trust me, I don't want to end up in one of your stories any more than you want me to."

Uncaring that they were right downtown and in full view of anyone who cared to look, he kissed her tenderly, instantly rekindling the fires of last night. When he finally lifted his head, they were both breathless and wishing they were anywhere but on a public street.

"Can I call you at work?" he asked in a husky voice. "I need to know that you're all right."

"I'm sure Martin won't care if I get an occasional phone call," she replied. "He's not there half the time, anyway, so he won't know if I'm getting phone calls or not...or making copies of every file he's got." Giving Logan one last hug, she stepped back and grinned. "So, see? There's nothing to worry about. He hasn't spent more than two hours a day at the office in weeks."

"I'd just feel better if you weren't working there at all. Have you started looking for another job? You know this one's going to end as soon as he's arrested."

"I have a friend who owns an employment service," she told him. "I've already asked her to keep her eyes and ears open. As soon as she finds something, I'm turning in my resignation."

"Good. The sooner you're out of there, the better." Unlocking her car door for her, he skimmed a hand over her hair. "Just be careful. And call me if you have any problems. You have my cell phone number."

"I've got you on speed dial," she assured him. Giving in to impulse, she pressed a soft kiss to his mouth, then slipped into her car. When she drove off, she could see him in her rearview mirror, standing in the parking lot, worry still etching his brow.

She couldn't blame him for being worried. Her palms were sweaty, her heart was slamming and she positively dreaded going to the office. Martin probably wouldn't be in yet, but at some point today she would come face-to-face with him. Little got past him. If she wasn't very, very careful at controlling her expression, he'd take one look at her and know something was wrong.

And though she'd assured Logan and Vic Roberts that she wasn't worried about Martin doing anything crazy, she had to admit she was concerned. Even though she'd never considered him a friend, she'd thought she knew what kind of man he was. Obviously, she'd been wrong. How could she predict what he was going to do when she didn't know the real Martin James?

With her stomach knotted with nerves, she tried to take comfort in the fact that he probably wouldn't be in until after lunch, so she had time to brace herself before she had to face him. Then she turned down the tree-lined street in an older neighborhood of Austin and felt her heart stop in midbeat. The new Lexus Martin had bought last month was parked in the driveway of the yellow Craftsman-style house that served as his office.

"Damn!" she muttered, parking next to the Lexus in the

double drive. Why had he come in so early? She would have sworn he'd told her he was having breakfast with Charles Drake, the managing partner of Drake and Duke, one of the most prestigious law firms in the city. His company had made the cut and was rumored to be the dark horse in the race for the city tax contract.

So why wasn't Martin still at the breakfast meeting? she wondered as she started up the front walk with dread dragging at her every step. Had something gone wrong? Did he know why she was late and was even now waiting to confront her? Maybe she should call Logan…

The old-fashioned glass doorknob turned easily as she walked into the foyer, setting the little bell attached to the front door ringing merrily. Almost immediately, Martin appeared in the entrance hall. "Where the hell have you been?"

Startled by his angry growl, Abby froze. "I, ah, had a d-dentist's appointment. Didn't you get my m-message?"

"What message?"

"The one I l-left on the answering machine," she stuttered. "I didn't remember until this morning that I had a dental appointment. I called—"

"I didn't even think to check the damn machine," he muttered, and strode into her office, which opened right off the foyer.

"Hi, Martin," Abby's recorded voice said, when he punched the button to play the messages. "Sorry I'm not there yet. I forgot I had a dental appointment this morning. I'll be in as quick as I can."

Relieved that she'd had the foresight to leave a message before she'd met Logan at the federal building, she said, "I'm really sorry—I don't know how I forgot—but I couldn't cancel on such short notice. My dentist would have charged me for the visit anyway, so I figured I might as well go. I guess

I should have called your cell phone, but I thought you'd be in the middle of your meeting with Charles Drake, and I didn't want to interrupt you."

Suddenly noticing that the place looked as if it had been hit by a tornado, she gazed around in confusion. "What's going on? The files—"

"I need the Drake file," he told her curtly. "Charles may have canceled, but I have a lunch meeting with Lance Drake this afternoon and I need to go over the file before I go."

So he'd torn up the office looking for it? she thought, shocked. What was in that file that was so important? She was dying to ask him, but she couldn't of course. Putting her purse in the bottom drawer of her desk, she looked around helplessly. After the mess he'd made, she didn't even know where to begin to hunt for the file.

"It's got to be around here somewhere," she told him, frowning. "When was the last time you had it?"

"Last week," he retorted.

"Did you check your briefcase? Is there a chance you took it home with you?"

"No."

"Then it's here."

Resigned to spending the day setting the office straight, she started with the pile of files he'd dumped on her desk. "I'm not going to be able to find anything until I can organize everything. If we're lucky, the file's buried under something. If not, then it probably got mixed in with another file."

"How long is this going to take? I need it by eleven so I'll have time to go over it before my lunch meeting."

Then maybe you shouldn't have trashed the entire office and I could have found it. The words hovered on the tip of her tongue, and she would have liked nothing more than to blast him with them. She didn't, though. She'd always been easygoing when it came to doing whatever he asked of her at the office. Of course, that was when she'd thought he was an ethical man. Now that she was convinced he wasn't, she had little patience with him. She couldn't, however, let him know that, not without raising his suspicions.

So she kept her opinion to herself and only said, "I'll try, Martin. I can't give any promises."

That wasn't the answer he wanted. Scowling at her, he snapped, "That wasn't a request, Abby. Find it!"

He stormed into his office, slamming the door behind him. Shocked, Abby felt her heart jump in her breast. She'd never seen him so angry before, so out of control. If he was this upset just because a file was missing, how was he going to react when the FBI showed up on his doorstep? Would he know she'd turned him in? Would he come after her if he got the chance?

Fear spilled through her at the thought, but she immediately pushed it aside. No! she told herself firmly as she began to straighten her office. She wouldn't terrorize herself with what Martin *might* do. He was being watched by the FBI, and it was only a matter of time before they arrested him. Once he was in custody, he'd never have the chance to hurt her. He'd be behind bars for a long, long time.

Taking comfort from that, she went through everything on her desk and the floor, and there was still no sign of the Drake file. Glancing at the clock on the wall, she swore softly. Ten-fifty. If she didn't find the damn thing soon, Martin was going to come apart at the seams.

Resigned, she knocked on his door. "Come in," he growled.

Pushing the door open, Abby faced him stiffly. "It's not in my office, so it must be in here. If you'll let me check..."

Without a word, he stood up and stepped back from his desk. Her heart in her throat, Abby hesitated. She'd hoped he'd move into her office while she searched his, but he obviously had no intention of doing that. Standing with his arms crossed, he just stood there, stone-faced, waiting for her to proceed. Gritting her teeth, she went to work.

His office was in worst shape than hers had been—as if he'd gone through the room in a rage. There were papers everywhere, piles of files scattered on every surface. Aware of his eyes on her, watching her every move, she couldn't help but think that the mess he'd made had to be the work of a desperate man. What in the world was in the Drake file that would generate such panic in him? What was going on?

Promising herself she would find out the first chance she had, she pasted on a blank expression and went to work. But curiosity was killing her.

The digital clock on Martin's desk read 10:58 when Abby pulled out the bottom drawer on the right-hand side of his desk. He usually kept his desk locked except when he was working, and she'd wondered for years what he kept in there. She was finally about to find out.

"There's nothing in there but the phone book and some personal telephone directories," he said curtly.

She almost told him that the whole reason for searching every nook and cranny was because the file obviously wasn't where it was supposed to be. If it was going to be found, they should look everywhere. But if he didn't want the drawer searched, that was his choice. Obediently, she started to close it, only to freeze when her gaze fell on what looked like the corner of a file folder almost completely hidden under the phone books.

Frowning, she reached for it. "What's this?"

The folder she pulled out had no name on it, but before she could even begin to open it to see what was inside it, Martin crossed the room in two swift strides and snatched it out of her hand. "That's it! How the hell did it get in there?"

You hid it there, she wanted to say. Considering how he didn't want her to see what was in the folder, that was the only logical conclusion. Praying her suspicions didn't show in her face, she said with forced lightness, "Since I don't have a key to your desk, you must have put it there. Have you used the phone book lately? If the file was on your desk and you set the phone book on it to look up a number, you could have picked them both up when you were finished, without even realizing it."

She didn't believe that for a second, but he jumped at the explanation like a duck on a june bug. "That must be it. I did look up a number to the Humane Society yesterday," he said too eagerly. "I've been thinking about getting Sonya a puppy. She's always talking about doing the responsible thing and adopting a stray. I thought I'd surprise her."

Yeah, right, Abby thought. Who did he think he was conning? He didn't care anything about animals. In fact, Abby had heard him tell Sonya more than once that pets were a pain in the butt and if she was going to be with him, she could forget about having a damn dog.

He was, Abby thought, a *lying* dog. But all she said was, "I'm sure she'll be thrilled. Now that the file's found, I'll get to work."

Striding into her office, she promised herself that as soon as he went to his meeting, she was going to find a way to open his desk and copy the file—if he didn't take it with him. If he did, then she would see what else was in his desk that was so important that he kept it under lock and key.

His private line rang a few minutes later, but he immediately shut the door between his office and hers before she could ascertain who it was. Her stomach a tight bundle of nerves, Abby soundlessly rose from her desk and crossed to the closed door to see if she could hear anything that might tell her who the caller was. All she could hear was an unintelligible murmur, so, disgusted, she returned to the task of straightening out the mess Martin had made of the files. It was a tedious task.

Forty-five minutes later, Martin was still in his office and showed no sign of leaving. Impatient for him to go, Abby tapped on his closed door and stuck her head inside the door when he called for her to come in. "Did you forget your lunch meeting?"

"It's been cancelled," he retorted. "Lance's secretary called. Something's come up and he had to back out."

"Did he want to reschedule?"

Surprised, he blinked. "I didn't think to ask that. I'll call him back and see if we can meet later this afternoon instead. I've got another appointment, but I can change that."

Checking the number in his private phone book, he quickly punched it in, then waited for Lance's secretary to come on the line. "Hi, Monica," he said, turning on the charm he was famous for. "This is Martin James again. Put me through to Lance, please. I know he's busy—I just need to talk to him for a minute."

Standing in the doorway, watching him, Abby was shocked when Martin's face fell and an embarrassed flush heated his cheeks. "If that's the way he wants it, that's fine," he said stiffly, and hung up.

Abby had never seen him embarrassed before. She wanted to ask what was wrong, but she didn't need to. "Lance gave

Monica instructions not to take my calls," he told her, swearing. "Apparently, I've burned a bridge."

"Why would you say that?" she said, frowning. "Are the two of you on the outs about something? Maybe he's just busy with some kind of emergency and doesn't want to be disturbed."

Looking more than a little worried, he shook his head. "I don't think so. Two cancellations in one day is no coincidence."

Studying him, Abby said, "What do you think's going on?"

For a moment, he was so caught up in his own musings that she thought he was going to answer her. Then he glanced up, a mask dropped over his face and he shrugged. "Who the hell knows when you're dealing with lawyers? If they're not in court, they're in depositions or working a deal. Anyway, I don't have time to worry about that. I need to make some calls. Shut the door on your way out."

Left with no choice, Abby did as he asked and shut the door behind her as she returned to her own office. The second she sat down at her desk, however, she pulled a small notebook from her purse and quickly jotted down notes covering her conversation with Martin. Vic Roberts had told her to take notes on everything, even things she didn't think were important. Later in the week, she'd meet with him and hand over her notebook...unless she felt there was an immediate need for Vic to know what was going on.

Something *was* going on, she acknowledged to herself as she finished her notes and slipped the small notebook back into her purse. And there was no question that Martin was definitely worried about it. Who was he calling? she wondered. If he hadn't been on his private line, she might have worked up the nerve to listen in. As it was, all she could do was bide her time and hope he made a mistake and let something slip, and she would be able to discover what was going on.

* * *

"Hi. How's it going?"

Abby hadn't realized how tense she'd been until she answered the phone and heard Logan's husky voice on the other end of the line. Suddenly feeling like crying and not sure why, she forced a smile. "I'm okay. Really," she insisted when he said nothing. She could just see him, lifting a dark brow in doubt. "I'm just tired."

"I'm not surprised," he retorted. "Your nerves have got to be fried. Are you busy tonight? I thought maybe we'd go to a movie or—"

"Yes!"

He chuckled. "Eager, are we? You didn't let me finish. I guess it must be my winning personality. I bet I could have just crooked my finger and you still would have said yes. Go ahead. Be straight with me. I can take it."

"I'm sure you can," she laughed. "Just for the record, though, if I were you, I wouldn't crook my finger."

"You wouldn't, huh? Fair enough. I'll just whistle, instead."

"And I'll come running?" Leaning back in her chair, she grinned. How had he known how badly she needed to talk to him? "Did I happen to mention how glad I am you called?"

"I'm glad I called, too," he replied huskily. "I love talking to you. So about tonight…what time shall I pick you up?"

"How about six-thirty?"

"I'll be there," he assured her. "If you need me before that, call. Okay?"

"I will," she promised. Feeling as if he'd somehow reached through the phone line and hugged her, she smiled softly. "I'll see you later."

With her thoughts on him and the evening, she didn't realize Martin had opened the door between their offices until she looked up and saw him standing on the threshold. Startled, she felt a blush steal into her cheeks and could do nothing to stop it. "Martin!" Flustered by his hard, probing gaze, she stuttered, "I—I hope you don't mind… I've never gotten personal phone calls here before. I didn't think you would care if nothing interfered with my work…"

For a moment, she thought he'd somehow guessed that she was spying on him. His eyes were hard and cold and held her helplessly pinned before him. "You're not getting paid to visit with a new boyfriend on the clock, but I suppose I don't have a problem with you getting an *occasional* call. Just keep it short."

Relieved, she felt the tension drain out of her, and she smiled for what seemed like the first time in hours. "Thank you, Martin. I promise I won't abuse the privilege."

"Who is this guy? Someone you met through that dating service you joined?" When she nodded, he arched a brow. "And you're serious about him? Didn't you just meet him?"

"We're not jumping into anything," she assured him. "We've just been out a few times." They talked on the phone every day, and were now much more than friends, but she had no intention of discussing Logan with Martin. If he decided to be protective and check him out and learned he was a reporter, the fat would be in the fire.

Before he could ask anything else, she changed the subject. "I was supposed to remind you that there's a town meeting tomorrow night on the growing gang violence in the city. Oh, and the Parents Against Street Racing want to meet with you to see about what can be done about racing on residential streets in your district. I've checked your schedule. How does next Thursday at four sound? Smith High School has agreed to let you use their cafeteria."

He checked his private calendar to make sure he didn't

have anything scheduled, and agreed. Abby called the head of the organization to give the green light to the meeting, then collected the mail, which always came late in the day, and began going through it.

When the phone rang, she reached for it absently. "Councilman James's office," she stated, cradling the phone between her ear and shoulder.

"I need to talk to Martin," a rough voice growled.

"Who's calling, please?"

The man hesitated, then said stiffly, "Fred Jones. Is he in?"

"Just a moment, please, and I'll check," she said, and quickly put him on hold. Frowning, she checked caller ID, but all it said was Number Not Available. That shouldn't have started alarm bells ringing in her head—she answered calls on and off throughout the day that often had no identification—but there was something in the man's voice and the way he'd hesitated before giving his name that stirred her suspicions. She didn't know who he was, but she would have bet a week's pay that his name wasn't Fred Jones.

Martin's door was still shut, so she buzzed him. "You have a call on line one from Fred Jones," she told him when he answered.

"Who?"

"He said his name was Fred Jones—"

"Fred—" he began, puzzled, only to exclaim, "Oh, yes! I remember Fred now. I'll take it!"

He transferred over to line one, and it was all Abby could do not to listen in. But she'd never done such a thing in her life, and she was afraid. Knowing her, it would be just her luck that the other line would ring while she was listening, and he would realize she was eavesdropping. She didn't even want to think about what he would do.

So she ignored the blinking button for line one and pulled out her little notebook instead. Quickly jotting down Fred Jones's name, she was in the process of recording the time of the call when the door to Martin's office suddenly jerked open. Abby froze, horrified.

"I've got to go out for a while," he said, and strode past without sparing her a glance.

The front door slammed behind him, while Abby sat at her desk like a statue, listening to the thundering of her own heart. Shaken, she released her breath in a rush. That was close! If he hadn't been in a hurry, he would have noticed her jotting something in a notebook, and she didn't doubt for a minute that he would have demanded an explanation. God only knew what she would have said.

Her nerves jittery, she hugged herself, not sure if she wanted to laugh or cry. She wasn't cut out for this spy stuff. Talk about nerve-racking! She felt as if she would shatter if someone said "Boo!" Thank God Martin would be gone for a while. She needed a break from the tension.

She started to wilt in her chair, only to stiffen. What was she thinking? she thought wildly. He was gone! She could copy the Drake file!

Jumping up, she rushed into Martin's office and quickly searched through the papers on his desk. The Drake file was nowhere to be found. It had to be there! she told herself. Martin had left without his briefcase. Had he hidden the folder in his bottom drawer again? Praying he hadn't locked his desk, she jerked open the drawer, nearly pulling it completely out onto the floor. The file was right on top of the phone book.

Hurry! That single word echoing in her head to the beat of her racing heart, she rushed over to the machine and copied every sheet of paper in the file without even bothering to read it. She'd give the FBI everything later—for now, she just wanted to get it duplicated and the folder back in his desk before he returned and somehow found out what she'd been up to.

Seconds later, she shoved the file back in its hiding place and slammed the drawer shut. Stepping back, she frantically ran her eyes over Martin's desk and chair and the rest of the office. Had she moved anything? Would he be able to tell she'd been in here? His chair...where had it been when she'd walked into the office? Had Martin taken the time to push it under his desk before he rushed out or left it where it was when he'd stood up to leave? Dammit, why hadn't she paid attention?

Taking a chance, she pushed the chair under the desk, then ran one more quick glance around the room. Everything seemed to be in its place. Her heart still pounding with panic, she rushed back to her own office and grabbed the copies she'd left on the machine. Pulling her purse from the bottom drawer of her desk, she crammed them inside.

The front door opened so suddenly, Abby had no time to move before Martin hurried inside. Her hand in her purse, her fingers still curled around the copies she'd made, she froze in place. What was he doing here? she wondered, terrified that her sudden fear might be written on her face for him to see. Did he suspect what she'd been up to? Was that why he'd come back so quickly? Had he hoped to catch her going through his desk?

"Martin!" she said hoarsely. "I thought y-you'd left. Did you forget something?"

His gaze narrowed on her pale face, then dropped to her purse, which was still in her lap. Ignoring her question, he arched a brow. "What's going on?"

"What? Oh, I was just digging for some aspirin," she said,

quickly pulling a small plastic bottle out of her purse. "I've got another splitting headache all of a sudden."

For a moment, she was convinced he didn't believe a word she said. He just stared at her speculatively, terrifying her without saying a word. Then, just when she was sure he was going to call her a liar to her face, he said, "You are a little pale. Are you sure you're going to be able to go out tonight with your new boyfriend?"

"I'll be okay after the aspirin kicks in," she assured him. "It's just a sinus headache."

"Maybe you should go home early and relax for a while," he suggested, watching her carefully. "I don't want you to miss your date."

"Oh, no. I'll be fine. Really."

"I know, but today was a rough day. I came down pretty hard on you about the Drake file, and I'm the one who misplaced it. Let me make it up to you. It's almost four o'clock. If you leave now, you'll miss the worst of the traffic and have more time to get ready for your date."

Abby hesitated. She didn't want to be obligated to him in any way, but her stomach was clenched tight with nerves, and there was something about the way he looked at her that made her as jumpy as a virgin in a roomful of wolves. All she wanted to do was get away from him.

"Well, if you're sure," she said, forcing a faint smile. "I appreciate it."

Not giving him a chance to change his mind, she hurriedly shut down her computer, cleared off her desk and grabbed her purse. She was halfway home before she realized that if Martin had wanted to get her out of the office, he couldn't have picked an easier way.

Swearing softly, she almost braked to a stop right in the

middle of the road. Why hadn't she thought of that? He hadn't said anything about letting her go home early when he'd first found out she had a date. It wasn't until he returned from rushing out on some mysterious errand that he'd decided she should go home. Why? she wondered. Did he have a reason for wanting her out of the office? Was he getting rid of her? What was going on that he didn't want her to know about?

Go back and find out, the voice in her head urged. *If you called Vic, he would tell you to go back and see what's going on.*

The thought wasn't even fully developed and she was already circling the block to head back to work. A glance at a clock on the dash assured her that if she hurried, she could still get home in plenty of time to get ready for her date. After all, it wasn't as if she was going to go inside and search the place. She was just going to drive by....

But as she turned down the quaint street where the office was located, she realized too late that she'd made a huge mistake. She'd never stopped to consider that Martin might see her.

He was standing on the front walk, greeting a short, heavyset bald man in a pinstripe suit who appeared to have just arrived. They both looked up at the sound of her car coming down the street, but Abby hardly noticed she was busted. She couldn't take her eyes off the man Martin was shaking hands with.

Jimmy Blunt, she thought, stunned, recognizing him from pictures she'd seen in the media. It couldn't be. He was a cutthroat attorney who had a reputation for stabbing his own clients in the back if it would put money in his pocket. He was underhanded, unethical and political poison in an election year. What in the world was Martin doing with him?

Jimmy Blunt was friends with Edward Stewart, one of the front-runners in the bid for the tax contract. And Ed Stewart was as slick as they came. She'd heard the rumors about him, that he never got his hands dirty. He didn't have to—he had friends who would do it for him. Was that why Jimmy seemed to be so friendly with Martin? Was he delivering a bribe for Edward?

Sickened by the thought—and the fact that they'd both seen her—she almost drove straight past them. But that would have raised all sorts of suspicions with Martin, and she would have to face him eventually. She might as well do it now. Her heart skipping every other beat, she pulled over to the curb in front of the office and stepped out of the car. How was she going to explain what she was doing there when she was supposed to be home getting ready for a date? she wondered, panicking. Her house was miles from here!

His sharp eyes wary, Martin greeted her coldly. "What are you doing here? I sent you home."

He didn't introduce her to the attorney, and she didn't push the issue. Searching her brain for an excuse, she blurted out, "I forgot my dry cleaning. I picked it up at lunch the other day and left it in the hall closet. My favorite outfit's in there."

He didn't believe it—she could see the distrust in his eyes. "Let's see it," he growled. "You need to wear something sexy on that date."

Her knees not nearly as steady as she would have liked, she hurried into the office and retrieved her dry cleaning from the closet in the foyer. When she stepped outside with it, she prayed he couldn't hear the frantic pounding of her heart.

"See?" she said easily, pulling up the plastic to reveal the sparkly green-and-rose tank top and matching chiffon skirt she'd worn to a wedding recently. "Do you like it?"

His jaw set, he said curtly, "It's nice."

She hadn't planned to wear it tonight, of course—it was far too dressy for just a regular date—but Martin didn't know her plans, thank God! Even if he suspected that she'd come back for something other than her dry cleaning, he couldn't prove it. Relieved, she smiled brightly, "Well, I guess I'd better go or I'm going to be late. See you in the morning, Martin."

He only grunted, but that was all the response she needed. Slipping past Martin and Jimmy Blunt, she hurried to her car. Behind her, she could have sworn both men's eyes were drilling into her back, but she never turned to look. She didn't realize she was holding her breath until she was in her car and all four doors were locked. With fingers that trembled in reaction, she started her car and quickly pulled away from the curb. In the rearview mirror, she saw Martin and Blunt still standing in front of the office, watching her pull away.

Later, she hardly remembered the drive home. All she could think about was the meeting she'd nearly stumbled into. Just thinking about it tied her in knots. If she'd showed up five minutes later, would she have witnessed money changing hands? Why else would Blunt be there? From everything Abby had heard Martin say about the man, he couldn't stand him. So why was he meeting with him? What was going on?

Troubled, she reached her house and hurried inside. She should have been looking forward to seeing Logan again—and she was! She'd just never felt less like going out. And it was all Martin's fault! He'd almost caught her twice today, and it was only through sheer luck that she'd had a legitimate excuse for what she'd been doing.

Next time, though, she might not be so lucky, and that was what worried her more than anything. Who knew that trying to collect evidence against Martin would be so nerve-racking? She couldn't even sit still long enough to call Logan. Instead, she grabbed her portable phone and paced the length of her living room as she waited for him to answer his cell phone.

"Hey," he said the second he picked up. "How are you? I've been thinking about you all afternoon, wondering if you were all right. You are, aren't you? James didn't give you a hard time today, did he?"

"That depends on what you call a hard time," she said dryly. "He almost caught me copying files."

"Dammit, Abby! What happened? Are you all right?"

"I'm fine," she assured him. "Nothing happened. He didn't suspect a thing, but I guess I'm still a little shaken up."

"You don't have to do this, you know," he told her. "Vic can keep tabs on James's phone records and bank accounts, not to mention his coming and goings. That's what he gets paid for. You don't have to take the risk."

"I know. I just feel like I know him and his office better than anyone. And he'll destroy records if he gets even a hint that the authorities are watching him. He doesn't seem to suspect me, though he is very jumpy right now. I guess that's why I'm so nervous. I don't know what's going on inside his head."

"Which is a damn good reason why you should be nervous," Logan replied. "It's a wonder you're not a basket case."

She laughed shakily. "I'm getting there."

"You can't feel like going out. Why don't I just stop by and pick up a pizza? We can have a quiet evening at your place."

"You wouldn't mind?"

"Are you kidding? Tonight's John Wayne night on TNT. We can eat pizza and watch the Duke. I can't think of anything better than that."

Relieved, she laughed. "That sounds great to me, too. I'll see you in a little while."

Chapter 10

She loved John Wayne, but when she and Logan settled in front of her TV to watch *McClintock,* she couldn't concentrate. Seated next to Logan on the couch, their feet sharing the oversize footstool that served as a coffee table, she found her thoughts jumping all over the place. What was Martin doing? Was he still with Jimmy Blunt? Had he really believed her when she'd told him she'd come back for her dry cleaning? Surely he would have said something if he hadn't. He wasn't a man to mince words! If he suspected her of lying, she had to believe he would have called her on it.

"I love John Wayne, don't you?" Logan murmured. "He was great when he played Henry VIII."

Caught up in her restless thoughts, Abby didn't even hear him. Then his words registered. Frowning, she looked up at him in confusion. "John Wayne never played Henry VIII."

"I know," he chuckled. "I was just checking to see if you

were listening. You haven't heard two words of this movie, have you?"

She didn't deny it—how could she? She'd been fidgeting and twitching ever since they'd sat down to watch the film an hour ago. "Okay, so you caught me," she said ruefully. "I just can't seem to get my mind off Martin. Whatever deal he's working with Jimmy Blunt has me worried. I don't know what he's up to."

"Try not to think about it."

"I can't! That's what's so frustrating. My thoughts just keep going around in circles."

"Here," Logan growled, "let me see if I can distract you. Turn around. That's it," he urged as they both shifted until Abby sat sideways on the couch with her back to him. His hands settled on her shoulders. "Wow, you're tense! No wonder you can't concentrate on the movie."

"I guess I am a little uptight," she said, then groaned as he kneaded her shoulders and the base of her neck. "That's the spot," she gasped. "Right there. Mmm, that feels great."

Using his thumbs, he worked his way down her spine, rubbing and stroking until her tight muscles melted one by one. With a moan, her head dropped forward and her eyes fluttered shut. "You're good at this," she said hoarsely. "Really good."

He laughed softly and lifted his hands to her head to gently cup it between his palms. "I like touching you," he rasped. "Just relax. That's it," he murmured, slowly tilting her head from side to side to stretch her neck muscles. "Slow and easy."

"I feel like I could dissolve in a puddle at your feet."

"You ain't seen nothing yet," he murmured, and she could hear the smile in his voice. Her heart hummed in response.

Then, before she could guess his intentions, his hands slid from her neck to the curve of her shoulders. The next instant they were sliding down her arms, stroking the inside of her wrist and elbows, tracing her palms and fingers. Mesmerized, she couldn't seem to sit upright on her own anymore. With a soft moan, she leaned back against him and her head dropped weakly to his shoulder.

Her heart pounding in her ears, she turned toward him, burying her face against his throat and drawing in the spicy scent of his cologne. "I don't understand how you can do this to me with just a touch," she groaned.

He chuckled softly. "It gets better," he promised. "Just close your eyes and concentrate on the stroke of my fingers."

She couldn't have denied him if her life depended on it. He seemed to know exactly where to touch her. With infinite tenderness, he moved his hands over her with agonizing slowness, caressing her waist, her hips, the length of her legs from hip to calf. And everywhere he touched, made her ache.

The world, all thoughts of Martin, slipped from her consciousness. There was only Logan and the magic of his wonderful hands. She wanted to turn to him, to touch him as he touched her, but his fingers teased and pleased and tormented her, and she couldn't move. Helpless, seduced by his hands and her own imagination, she found herself holding her breath and wondering where he would touch her next.

When his hand settled under one breast, her breath caught in her throat and she strained toward him. "Touch me," she whispered, turning her head to kiss his throat. "I need you to touch me."

"That's what I'm doing, sweetheart. Did I tell you you feel wonderful? You've got skin like silk." And with no more warning than that, he covered her breast with his hand.

Her sigh was whisper soft and came from the depth of her being. She'd thought she knew what desire was all about, but with just a flick of his thumb, he made her yearn for a kind of intimacy she couldn't even put a name to. "Logan… please…I need…"

"What?" he rasped, turning her and sweeping her into his lap in one smooth motion. "What do you need? This?" he asked, and pressed a long, slow kiss to her mouth.

When he finally lifted his head, her blood was warm and her head swimming, but he didn't give her time to say a word. "Or maybe this," he murmured, and shifting so that they were suddenly stretched out on the couch. His eyes met hers, their legs entangled, and every so gently, he rubbed her nose with his.

It was the last thing she expected, and she couldn't hold back a laugh. Lifting a hand to his hair, she grinned into his eyes. "This is perfect."

He flashed a dimple. "I can think of something that would make it better."

"Now that you mention it, so can I," she chuckled.

When she moved closer, reaching for him, he expected her to unbutton his shirt. Instead, she traced his ear with one finger. Heat streaked straight to his loins.

He didn't say a word, but he didn't have to. He knew from the glint in her eyes that she knew exactly what she did to him. And he loved it. Did she realize how much more self-confidence she had now than when they'd met? She was amazing. She still had a shyness he found incredibly appealing, but she didn't let that stop her from teasing him.

A groan ripping from his throat, he took it as long as he could, but he was only human. And she seemed to know just how to touch him, where to touch him, to drive him slowly out of his mind. Her hands moved over his chest, stroking, smoothly undoing the buttons of his shirt one by one, making him burn. Then, just when he thought he was going to rip his shirt off if she didn't hurry, she leaned over him, letting her mouth follow the enticing trail of her fingers. At the first stroke of her tongue, his breath hissed out through clenched teeth. "Sweetheart, you're killing me."

She'd lifted her head, her eyes alight. "Really? Am I really?"

He laughed shortly, nearly in pain. "Keep that up and you'll see just how quickly you can push me over the edge."

Intrigued, she leaned down and dropped a kiss on his belly, just above the snap of his jeans.

Lightning quick, he was on her, rolling her to her back and kissing the stuffing out of her before she could do anything but laugh and kiss him back. But as her arms encircled his neck and his body settled on hers, her laughter changed to a moan.

Their clothes melted away and she never noticed. There was only Logan—the taste of him, the feel of him, the heat that jumped from his body to hers and burned her from the inside out. She moved with him, for him, and had never felt so beautiful. She wanted to ask him how he did it—how he'd changed her from a shy, insecure woman who always felt awkward when it came to her own sexuality, to a lover who gloried in the way he made her feel. But her blood was roaring in her ears and she couldn't speak.

With his hands alone, he drove her to the first peak. Breathless, she clung to him. "Logan…!"

At some point, he'd turned the lights in the living room down low, but his eyes were alight with a passion that stole her breath. "I love it when you come apart in my arms," he said thickly, and kissed his way down her body, to replace his hand with his mouth.

She never stood a chance. A sob catching in her throat, she shattered.

Struggling to hold on to his control, Logan tried to draw

out the pleasure as he moved over her, into her, but the sensations were too sweet, too unbearable. With a groan that came from the very depths of his being, he lost himself in her.

She was falling in love with him.

Cinching her robe around her waist, her eyes trained on Logan as he dragged on his clothes, Abby felt her heart ache at the thought of him leaving. *Don't go!* she almost cried, and that's when she knew she was in trouble. She wanted him to stay the night, the week, forever. And that shook her to the core. Was he over his wife's death and ready to move on with his life? She wanted to believe that he was, but he'd given her no indication of how he felt. And she couldn't ask him. Even though logic told her it would be better to know now, before she completely lost her heart to him, she couldn't deliberately set herself up for rejection. It would be too painful.

"You're awfully quiet," he said, shattering the silence that had fallen between them. "Are you all right?"

No! she almost cried. How could she be all right when her emotions were tied in knots and she didn't know if what they'd just shared had meant anything more to him than sex? And she wasn't likely to know unless he volunteered the information. Because if there was one thing she'd learned in her limited dating experience, it was that pressing a man to share his feelings was a surefire way to send him running for cover.

"I'm fine," she told him, forcing a smile. "I'm just tired."

"Who wouldn't be? You've got to be stressed to the max," he said, pulling her close for a hug. "Are you sleeping at all?"

"Some, but—"

"I'd like to kick your boss's butt!"

"It's not that—"

"Of course it is," he argued. "Are you sure you want to do

this? If you like, I can call Vic and tell him you've changed your mind. He'd understand, sweetheart. You don't need to put yourself through this. It's just too dangerous, dammit!"

What was dangerous was the way her heart turned over in her breast when he became so protective. Maybe he did feel more for her than just desire. Maybe he even—

"Well? Can I call him?"

Looking up from her wishful thoughts, she wanted to tell him that they were talking about two different things. But she couldn't. "It won't be that much longer. Martin is so cocky, he's bound to make a mistake soon."

"And if he doesn't?"

"Then I'll talk to Vic and tell him I've done all I can do," she replied simply. "Hopefully, I'll have another job lined up by then."

"I'll check and see if there's anything at the paper," he told her as she walked him to her front door. "In the meantime, you call if you need anything. Okay?"

"Okay," she promised. But as he gave her one last kiss and left, she knew she wouldn't call. What she needed was his heart, and she couldn't very well ask for that.

Logan didn't sleep much that night. His dreams were filled with visions of Abby in trouble, calling for him, making love to him as if he was the love of her life, and he tossed and turned restlessly, reaching for her too many times to remember. When he found himself staring at the ceiling at four in the morning, he came up with dozens of reasons for his insomnia. The sheets were too rough—he just couldn't get them soft the way Faith had. He'd eaten too late before going to bed. He had a headache....

He was a damn poor liar, though, especially when it came

to feeding himself a line of bull. There was only one reason he wasn't sleeping, and that was Abby.

He didn't know how she'd slipped past his guard, but she stirred feelings in him that he'd never expected to feel for a woman again, and he didn't know what to do about it. He'd loved Faith since he was fourteen years old! How could he betray her by caring for another woman?

If I die first, don't you dare spend the rest of your life mourning for me, Logan St. John! Do you think I could rest easy knowing you were alone?

Her voice came to him from out of the past, reminding him of a silly fight they'd had on their honeymoon. How could he have forgotten it? he wondered with a rueful grin. They'd nearly had a wreck when a drunk driver came across the middle line as they were heading back to their hotel after dinner, and that had started a discussion about what they would each do if they lost the other. Like a summer storm that had blown up out of nowhere, they'd suddenly been fighting. All because Logan had told her that he would never even look at another woman if he somehow lost Faith.

There was no question his wife had had a temper, he thought, chuckling. She'd raked him up one side and down another and told him exactly what she thought of him for choosing loneliness over happiness. And all over a hypothetical situation.

How could either of them have known then that it would one day come true?

The old, familiar pain squeezed his heart, but this time it was almost a comfort. For the first time in a long time, he'd heard Faith speaking to him, and he had no choice but to listen. Was he ready to risk loving someone again? If he'd learned anything from loving her, it was that there were no guarantees in life. When he and Faith had married, promising to be faithful until death did them part, their time together had turned out to be only twelve years. What if that happened again? What if he let himself love Abby, then lost her as he'd lost Faith? Could he go through that a second time without it destroying him? Did he even want to risk it?

He worried about it the rest of the night. Exhausted, he headed for work the next morning in a grim mood. He obviously had some decisions to make. He didn't have a clue where to begin.

With his thoughts on Abby, he didn't notice that Josh Garrison was coming out of the cafeteria at the same time Logan was going in until they almost collided. That irritatingly smug smile of his curling the corners of his mouth, Josh stepped back from the threshold, moving his arm with a flourish. "Please…age before beauty."

Far from fooled by his phony charm, Logan glared at him with narrowed eyes. "Save it for someone who appreciates it," he said flatly. "I don't like you, and I sure as hell don't trust you, so I'd appreciate it if you'd do us both a favor and leave me alone. In fact, I'd be perfectly happy if you never spoke to me again."

He made no effort to keep his voice down, and more than a few of their co-workers heard every word. Logan couldn't have cared less. He wasn't a hypocrite, and after Garrison stole the cross-dresser story from him, he'd be damned if he'd play nice.

A flush stinging his cheeks, Garrison snapped, "Jealousy does strange things to a man. It must be difficult being a has-been."

"It must be difficult being such a lousy reporter that you have to steal other people's leads," Logan retorted. "If I were you, I'd start looking for another job. You're going to need it when Porter discovers just what kind of lowlife you are."

Obviously far from worried, Garrison gave him that patented smug smile, the one Logan always wanted to knock off his face. "Are you kidding? I'm the love of his granddaughter's life. I'm not going anywhere but up. You, on the other hand, better start cleaning out your desk. When Papa Porter learns how you called me a thief in front of the entire cafeteria, I doubt that he'll have much use for you. And that's a shame. From what I've heard, there was a time when you were a pretty decent reporter."

Clenching his jaw, Logan dismissed him with a look, then strode out before he did something stupid and went for Garrison's throat. Five seconds, he thought as he headed upstairs. Garrison might be bigger and younger, but Logan still wanted a chance to go after him just once.

"Hey, Logan," Nick called as he passed his open office door. "Step in here a minute, will you?"

"Sure," he said, detouring into his boss's glassed-in space. He took one look at the older man and swore. "I can't believe this! Garrison called you from downstairs to whine about what I said to him in the cafeteria, didn't he? You can just save it, Nick. I meant every word. If you want to fire me over it, go ahead."

A smile tugging at his mouth, Nick arched a shaggy brow. "Are you finished?"

Far from amused, Logan snapped, "You're damn straight I am. Shall I clean out my desk?"

"No, but you can go home and pack. I want you to go to Ink's Lake to cover a story."

Surprised, Logan dropped into the chair positioned in front of Nick's desk. "Ink's Lake, huh? That's a resort area, isn't it? What's going on there?"

"There's been a murder at the home of Oscar Hunt. So far, no one's talking, not even the cops. I figured you could dig up what's going on."

Oscar Hunt was a philanthropist who had a reputation for going to church three nights a week and living a stellar life. His name and trouble weren't usually spoken in the same sentence. "Sure," Logan said. "Do we know who the victim was?"

"Hunt's wife," he retorted. "If the police have a suspect in mind, they're not talking."

"I'll dig around and see what I can find out," he promised. "How long do I have?"

"Take a couple of days, let me know what you turn up. This is going to be big, Logan. I don't have to tell you what kind of press Hunt generates wherever he goes. He's going to do his best to keep a lid on this, so just be prepared."

That settled, Nick sat back in his chair and surveyed him with sharp, searching eyes. "You know me—I'm not one to get all gushy over someone doing their job the way they were hired to do, but when someone pulls out of a slump, he needs to know it. I've been watching your work over the last couple of weeks, and it's been damn good."

Surprised, Logan grinned. "Damn, where's a tape recorder when you need one? Did you just say I was good?"

"Don't let it go to your head," his boss said dryly. "There's still room for improvement."

Far from insulted, Logan chuckled. "There always is."

"You're damn straight! So what's the story? What's going on? And don't tell me nothing," he growled. "You seem more focused, less tense."

Abby, Logan thought instantly, fighting a smile. It had to be because of her. She distracted him, amused him, took his mind off his loneliness and problems at work so much that he didn't even think about Josh Garrison unless he came face-to-face with him. As for his writing, Logan readily admitted that he hadn't given it much thought lately—which was why he had half expected Nick to call him in. He would have sworn it was obvious to everyone that his mind was anywhere but on the job.

Apparently not.

He'd have to send Abby some flowers, he decided. And his brother and sister. Who knew when they'd signed him up for the dating service that it would bring some peace and structure back to his life?

"Logan?" Leaning across his desk, Nick snapped his fingers in front of his face. "It's a woman, isn't it? You've met someone."

Logan grinned. "Maybe. Maybe not."

Far from discouraged, Nick only laughed. "You wouldn't tell me if you had, but that's okay. I'll find out eventually. And in the meantime, I've got my old, award-winning reporter back, thank God! Thank her for me, will you, whoever she is?"

Ignoring that part, Logan just looked at him with dancing eyes. "Since I'm back, how about giving me some of those front-page stories you've been throwing at everyone but me?"

Already two steps ahead of him, Nick arched a shaggy brow. "Why do you think I'm sending you to Ink's Lake, hotshot?"

The office was quiet as a tomb when Abby arrived at eight, and she sent up a silent prayer of thanks. After nearly getting caught yesterday by Martin, she hoped he didn't come in at all today. She needed a break from the stress.

Not that she hadn't had one last night, she admitted with a smile as she walked through the office, flipping on lights and computers. Logan had been wonderful. She'd spent the night dreaming of him, reliving every touch, every kiss, and when her alarm went off this morning, she'd barely resisted the urge to call him. Did he know how she felt about him? How the day didn't seem complete if she didn't at least get to talk to him? She'd thought she knew what falling in love felt like. She couldn't have been more wrong.

Was this what he'd felt for his wife? she wondered, and knew it probably wasn't even close. They'd been in love since they were fourteen years old, and had had twenty years together. How had he survived losing her? The pain must have been unbearable.

Just thinking about it brought the sting of tears to Abby's eyes. She couldn't blame him for not ever wanting to fall in love again. What were the odds of happiness like that coming along twice in a lifetime? And even if it did, would it be fair to ask him to risk his heart a second time? After all, he'd learned the price of love the hard way.

She wanted to tell him it would be that way with them. That she was falling in love with him, and wasn't going anywhere. But she could just imagine his response to that. Faith hadn't planned to die, but she was gone, nevertheless. And that scared Abby to death. How could she ask Logan to risk his heart a second time, for her?

The phone rang then, startling her. Hoping it was Logan, she snatched it up. "Councilman James's office. This is Abby. May I help you?"

"I'm sick," Martin announced hoarsely.

"You sound awful," she said honestly. "What's wrong?"

"I think it's allergies. Needless to say, I'm not coming in today."

"Of course," she said, relieved. "That's probably a good idea."

"I need you to pick up a package for me and bring it here to the house."

"All right. Where is it?"

Expecting him to say the post office, she was shocked when he gave her an address in an area near downtown that had fallen into disrepair years ago. "The building looks awful, but don't pay any attention to that. Go upstairs to Suite 323. Someone will be there with the package. I need it as soon as possible, Abby. The council votes tomorrow on the tax contract and the package contains an updated bid I want to go over."

"I'll go right now," she promised.

Fifteen minutes later, she pulled up in front of the building at the address Martin had given her and felt uneasiness stir in her stomach. She must have written down the address wrong. This couldn't be the place. At one time, the old building might have been beautiful—there were gargoyles at the corners near the roof, looking down on anyone who chanced by—but it obviously hadn't been used in decades. Half the windows were broken, the other half were caked with dirt and the front door seemed to be hanging on its hinges. No respectable person would do business here. It didn't even appear as if the building had electricity!

It looks awful but don't pay any attention to that.

Martin's words echoed in her ears, but that did nothing to dispel her doubts. What was he up to? Was someone really waiting for her inside with a package? Or had Martin somehow found out she was spying on him and come up with some way to eliminate her? What if he was planning to have her murdered? This was the kind of building where murderers dumped bodies.

Suddenly afraid, she dug in her purse for her cell phone and quickly punched in Logan's number, only to slump in disappointment when the recorded message of his answering service clicked on. "This is Logan. Leave a message. In case of an emergency, call 911."

Her gaze lifting to the third floor windows, Abby could have sworn someone was watching her. Shivering, she clutched her cell phone tighter. "Logan? This is Abby. Something weird has come up and I may need your help." Hurriedly telling him where she was, she added, "The place looks deserted, but Martin assured me someone would be waiting for me with a package containing a new bid. If you don't hear from me again, I'm probably dead in the basement."

Hanging up, she quickly called Vic Roberts only to get his voice mail, too. Where was everyone today! After leaving a quick message, she hung up.

She prayed her imagination was playing tricks on her, but when she stepped out of her car and started up the uneven walk to the building's entrance, there was no denying the place gave her goose bumps. Chilled, she almost turned around and ran for the car. Then she thought of Martin and the money he was pocketing and how clever he no doubt thought he was. If he and some of the council members really were accepting bribes to influence the city council's decision on which firm got the tax contract, the bidding process was nothing but a travesty. The lowest bidder wouldn't get the bid. Whichever firm slipped Martin the most money under the table would get the contract, and the end result was that the city—and the taxpayers—would pay millions more than was necessary. All because of greed.

And that infuriated her. She couldn't let Martin get away with that, couldn't run away and bury her head in the sand and pretend none of this was happening. She had to find out what he was up to so she could turn the information over to Vic Roberts, stopping the corruption once and for all.

Ignoring the frantic pounding of her heart, she straightened her shoulders and gingerly stepped through the building's front door. Dust-filled shadows immediately enveloped her as she moved across the foyer toward a wide staircase lit by a dirty skylight. In the silence, her own breathing seemed to echo off the bare walls.

Later, she couldn't have said how long she stood there before she started up the stairs. It could have been seconds or eons. Holding her breath, she listened for a sign that there was someone upstairs, but apart from the occasional creak of the old building, she heard nothing. Gathering her courage again, she slowly climbed the stairs.

By the time Abby reached the third floor landing and started down the hallway, she was convinced she was alone in the building. Then she heard a step behind her. Her heart in her throat, she whirled.

"What are you doing here? Where's Martin?"

Certain her knees were shaking and that she'd never felt so scared in her life, Abby faced Jimmy Blunt. He had to know it. From everything she had heard about him, he was a man who sensed fear and reveled in it. "Martin's sick," she said hoarsely, sounding sick herself. "He asked me to pick up the package for him."

For a moment, she thought the man was going to refuse. His steely gray eyes pinned her in place, and for the life of her, she couldn't move. "I don't like surprises," he growled. "And you're a surprise."

Abby didn't know where she got the nerve, but she retorted, "Trust me, I know exactly how you feel."

For a second, she thought she saw a glint of admiration in his eyes, but then he blinked and his expression turned as hard as granite. "If this is a setup, you and Martin both better find a hole to hide in. I don't take kindly to being framed."

Her heart knocked against her ribs, loudly enough to wake the dead. No, she thought, he was not a man who would stand for betrayal from someone he trusted. He had a short fuse and, no doubt, a long memory. And that scared the hell out of her.

"Martin really is sick," she said sincerely. "He can hardly talk. If you don't believe me, you can call him at home."

She rattled off the number, but Jimmy never reached for his phone. "I don't need to talk to him. You look like a smart girl. You tell him what I said. You make sure he believes every word. You got it?"

Her eyes wide, her throat as dry as toast, she couldn't do anything but nod. Pulling a fat, sealed envelope from the inner pocket of his jacket, he held it out to her. "Take it," he said coldly. "If you've got the brains I think you do, you'll forget where you got it. Now get the hell out of here."

He didn't have to tell her twice. Clutching the package with trembling fingers, she whirled and ran for the stairs as if the demons of hell were after her. Three steps from the front door, she tripped and nearly went sprawling, but caught herself with a quiet sob and kept running. She never remembered reaching her car. The next thing she knew, she had started the car with a flick of her wrist and hit the gas. Her tires were still squealing as she turned the corner and raced away.

Idiot! Idiot! Idiot! What was she thinking, ever agreeing to this madness? Logan was right—she should have stayed out of it and let the authorities handle the situation. If they couldn't collect evidence on Martin by themselves, then too damn bad! She wasn't opening herself to risk just to put Martin away for whatever crimes he was committing.

But that was exactly what she'd done, she realized, starting to shake. She'd met with Jimmy Blunt in a secret location and taken God knows what from him. Glancing away from the road long enough to scowl at the package she'd tossed onto the passenger seat, she didn't believe for a minute that it was a revised bid, as Martin had claimed. If that was the case, Jimmy Blunt would have dropped it off at the office, not set up a meeting in a deserted building far from prying eyes. No, there was something illegal in the package—she felt sure of it. Why else would Blunt have sealed it with enough tape to choke a horse?

After risking her life for it, she was tempted to tear the damn thing open and see for herself what was in it. But she couldn't, dammit, not when there was so much tape on it. Martin would know that it had been tampered with. And then there was Blunt to worry about. He would surely call Martin and make certain the package was delivered in the same condition Abby had received it in.

If this is a setup, you and Martin both better find a hole to hide in. I don't take kindly to being framed.

The lawyer's sinister words echoing in her ears, she drove straight to Martin's house, pushing the speed limit the entire way. Braking to a quick stop in his driveway, she threw the transmission into Park, cut the engine and grabbed the package. Had Blunt had her followed? she wondered. She told herself it didn't matter—she was delivering the package just as he'd instructed—but merely thinking about it made her skin crawl. Was he watching her even now? Would he follow her home?

Her stomach turned over, and suddenly she felt as sick as Martin. Rushing up the front walk, she knocked sharply. "Martin?" she called when there was no answer. "Open up! It's me—Abby!"

She was sure she could feel eyes drilling into her back, and it seemed to take him forever to answer the door. When he finally did, she only had to take one look at him to know that he was sick as a dog. There wasn't a drop of color in his face and dark circles surrounded his eyes. "You look awful."

"I told you I was sick," he said hoarsely, pulling the door open wider. "Did you get it?"

She didn't have to ask what "it" was. He could hardly stand, but he was already reaching for the thick envelope in her hand. "Mr. Blunt wasn't exactly thrilled to see me," she said flatly, following him as he turned and staggered into the living room, where he dropped into the nearest chair and tore open the package. "He was expecting you."

In the process of examining the contents, Martin looked up sharply. "I tried calling him, but I couldn't reach him. What did he say?"

"That you and I better both find a hole to hide in if this is a setup."

"What? Why would he think he's being set up?"

"I have no idea," she retorted. "He's your friend, not mine. I'm just the messenger. If that's all you need, I've got to get back to the office."

"Wait! I was wondering if—" He started to cough, a hacking, wrenching cough that grabbed him by the throat and cut off his air. Pressing a hand to his chest, he rose abruptly to his feet, trying to get his breath, and inadvertently dropped the package, which fell to the floor at his feet.

Several one hundred dollar bills spilled halfway out of the package, but he never noticed. Abby did, however, and her heart stopped dead in her chest. Her eyes flew to his face, but he was still coughing and obviously didn't realize what she'd seen. Her gaze trained anywhere but on the package, she said quickly, "Can I get you some water? Or some juice? Where's the kitchen?"

Still coughing, he choked out, "In there," and pointed down the hall.

Hurrying to the kitchen, she opened several cabinet doors before she found where he kept the glasses, then quickly filled one with ice water. "How about some soup or something? Do you have any medicine for that cough?" she asked when she returned to his side and handed it over.

"The doctor gave me a prescription," he said faintly, "but I can't take it again for four hours. I'm fine. Really."

Abby had done her duty. All she wanted to do was get out of there before he realized that she'd seen the contents of the package. If she was lucky, he'd never know for sure. Forcing a bright smile, her gaze still focused anywhere but on the money on the floor, she said, "Well, then, I guess I'll get back to work. If you need anything, just let me know."

She rushed out before he could say anything, and never looked back. She should call Vic, she thought frantically. He had to know about the money! But she didn't dare risk phoning while she was still in full view of Martin's house. If he happened to step over to the window and saw that she was still parked in his driveway, talking on her cell phone, he would know immediately that she was up to something.

Hurriedly starting her car, she backed out of his driveway and headed to the office. The second she was out of sight of his house, however, she put in another call to Vic Roberts.

He answered on the first ring. "Abby? Where are you? Are you all right?"

Laughing shakily, she said, "That depends on how you look at it. No one's killed me yet, so I guess I'm okay."

"I'm sorry I couldn't take your call earlier—I was on a

stakeout and had my cell turned off. What happened? Did you pick up the package? Did you get the name of the person James was supposed to meet with? What did he look like?"

"I didn't need to ask his name," she retorted. "It was Jimmy Blunt."

"What?"

"He was expecting Martin. Trust me, he wasn't happy to see *me*."

The FBI agent swore. "He's another one we've been watching, but he's damn slick. What happened?"

She told him everything, including the threats the man had made against her and Martin, and the money that had fallen out of the package when her boss dropped it. "I can't take this, Vic. I've never been so scared in my life. Martin's playing with some rough people, and he doesn't seem to have a clue what kind of danger he's in. I do, and I don't want any part of it."

"I don't blame you," he said, "but I just need you to hang in there one more day, Abby. The city council votes tomorrow on the tax contract, and all we need to wrap up our case against James is his vote to award the contract to Blunt."

"But Martin's sick. You should have seen him. He may not even make the meeting tomorrow."

"Oh, he'll be there," he assured her. "Even if he's on his deathbed. He took a bribe from Jimmy Blunt. If he doesn't show up for that vote, he's a bigger fool that I think he is."

"This is just so nerve-racking."

"I know. But if you quit now, he's going to be suspicious, and that could blow everything. C'mon, Abby, it's just one more day. I promise."

If he'd told her that when she was in that warehouse with Jimmy Blunt, she would have retorted that she didn't care if it was one more hour—she was out of there. But it was just one more day, and he was right. If she quit now, Martin would be suspicious.

"All right," she sighed. "I'll keep quiet—for now. But if Martin is still a free man tomorrow night, I'm done. I'll come up with some excuse that won't make him suspicious, but I'm quitting, effective immediately."

Chapter 11

The second Abby finished her conversation with Vic, she hung up and quickly punched in Logan's cell phone number. She couldn't wait to tell him everything that had happened today. He would, no doubt, chew her out for doing Martin's dirty work for him and putting herself in danger, but if she hadn't picked up that package for Martin, Vic Roberts wouldn't have the verification he needed to arrest Martin. With Martin's vote at the city council meeting tomorrow, the FBI would have all the proof they needed to complete their case against him. It was almost over.

She sighed in relief at the thought. Tomorrow would be a big day for both her and Logan. She would no longer have to worry about Martin discovering that she was spying on him, and Logan would break the story about the rise and fall of Martin James. City Hall would never be the same.

"The cell phone number you are trying to call is temporarily out of service. Please try your call again later."

Already anticipating reading Logan's exposé, Abby swore softly at the recorded message and hung up. Maybe he was at the office. Quickly punching in his work number, she waited impatiently for him to answer. If he was out of pocket—

"Hello?"

"Logan? Thank God! You're not going to believe what's happened. Martin called in sick this morning, then had me pick up a package for him. You're never going to believe who gave me the package. Jimmy Blunt! And he threatened me! He's an awful man. Anyway, the package was full of hundred dollar bills. I'll tell you all about it later. Right now, I just want you to know everything's coming down tomorrow. The city council votes on the tax contract, and Vic's going to arrest Martin right afterward. I knew you'd want to know."

"Thanks," he said gruffly. "I'll be there."

His reaction wasn't quite what Abby had expected. Frowning, she said, "You sound funny. Are you all right?"

He coughed, then choked. "Sore throat."

"Oh, I'm sorry. It must be allergies. Martin has the same thing. Can I bring you some soup tonight—"

"No! Ah...thanks. I'm just going to go home and go to bed."

Disappointed, she sighed. "That's probably for the best. Tomorrow's going to be pretty hectic. I don't usually go to the council meetings, but I will definitely be there for the tax vote. So I guess I'll see you there."

He mumbled something Abby didn't quite catch, then hung up. Blinking in surprise, she found herself holding her phone, listening to the steady buzz of the dial tone. That was odd, she thought, confused. He hadn't even asked if she was all right after her encounter with Jimmy Blunt. She'd expected him to be furious with Martin for putting her in such a dangerous position, but he hadn't expressed a single opinion about the situation. Apparently, he couldn't have cared less. And that hurt. Was he mad at her? What was going on?

Across town at the *Gazette,* Josh Garrison smiled in satisfaction as he hung up the phone on Logan's desk. He didn't have a clue who he'd just talked to, but he'd have to give her a big wet kiss if he ever got the chance to meet her. She'd just given him the story of the year, and she didn't even know it.

When Nick had told him about the murder at Oscar Hunt's palatial estate on Ink's Lake, Logan had grudgingly agreed that it would take several days to conduct the investigation, and he had no choice but to get a hotel room for the next few nights. But the drive to the lake hadn't taken as long as he'd thought it would, and once he arrived, he'd hit the ground running. He'd worked until well after dark, investigating the story, and gotten far more done than he'd expected. Hunt was in seclusion, which was to be expected—after all, his wife had been murdered!—but he was also a man who respected the power of the press. When Logan had called, requesting an interview to discuss the murder that had taken place at Hunt's lakeside estate, the old man himself had taken the phone and agreed to meet with him three days after the funeral, which was tomorrow. Logan had already talked to most of the employees, the police and the EMTs who'd arrived at the scene first, and he'd been left with nothing to do for the next three days. That's when he'd decided to go home and come back in three days for the interview with Hunt.

Glancing at the clock on the dash of his car, he swore softly. Where had the time gone? It was already eleven o'clock, too late to call Abby. He'd tried calling her earlier, but the lake was in the hills and his cell phone hadn't worked worth a damn. He hadn't even been able to reach Nick to let him know his change of plans, and it was too late to phone him, too. Logan would just have to wait until morning.

Racing toward Austin, he had the highway and his thoughts to himself. Had Abby missed him today? he wondered. He sure as hell had missed her. He should have asked her to take the day off and come with him. He'd had to work, of course, but she would have enjoyed the lake, and they could have spent the night. But he'd had to leave so quickly, and even if he'd thought to ask her, he doubted James would have let her have the day off with no notice. He didn't seem the type.

There was nothing Logan liked about the man, and he readily admitted that he was worried about Abby being in the same office with him. Had she had a rough day? She would have called, he assured himself. Even if she couldn't reach him on his cell phone, she would have called him at work and home. There would be a message.

When he finally reached his place, however, there was no call from her on his answering machine. He should have been relieved. Apparently, everything was all right. She was safe. He didn't need to worry about her.

But when he crawled into bed and stretched out with a tired groan, he felt her presence as clearly as if she were right there with him. He only had to close his eyes and he could see her, hear her, as she spoke of Martin and her outrage over what he was doing. Had she been able to hide her dislike and suspicion of the man? he wondered. She had such an expressive face. He'd come to know her so well—he only had to look at her to read her every thought. She'd worked for Martin James for four years. Surely the councilman could do the same.

Swearing at the thought, Logan knew there was no way in

hell he was going to sleep now. Rising from his bed, he strode into his home office and booted up his computer. He might as well work on his screenplay.

Sitting in the dark at her bedroom window, Abby stared out at the cloudless night sky and hugged her updrawn knees. The clock on her nightstand read two-thirty, but she'd long since given up any idea of sleeping. It was only a matter of hours before she had to report to the office. Just thinking about it made her sick to her stomach.

Martin would be there, she decided, hugging herself. As Vic said, he'd have to be on his deathbed to miss the council vote on the tax contract, and even then, Abby knew he would find a way to get there. He had to. He'd taken God knows how much money from Jimmy Blunt, and if he wasn't there to vote for his buddy, Edward Stewart, and sway the other council members to do the same, Abby didn't even want to think about what Blunt would do. According to the rumors she'd been hearing about him for years, he wasn't the kind of man you'd want to betray.

Not, she reminded herself, that Blunt was going to have the chance to do much in retribution. As soon as the city council vote was complete, Vic Roberts would no doubt arrest him and Edward Stewart, as well as everyone else who'd slipped Martin money under the table in an effort to try to buy his vote and influence. Blunt and Stewart would post bond, of course, and hire a shyster lawyer who would do everything he could to discredit her and, no doubt, try to make her the villain in all this. But she could handle that. What she couldn't take was the waiting. It was driving her crazy.

She just wanted to get on with her life, she thought, leaning back against the windowsill with a sigh. She had to find another job, of course, and then there was Logan. Just thinking about him made her smile. He hadn't called her tonight, but she wasn't really surprised. Tomorrow was the big day. He had to have the background story of Martin's downfall ready to go so that the exposé could be published following his arrest. Considering the trouble that he'd had at work with Josh Garrison, a lot was riding on this story. She didn't doubt that it would be fantastic.

Tomorrow they would celebrate, she decided. She wouldn't have to worry about Martin anymore, and Logan would win the approval of his boss and publisher with a story that people would, no doubt, be talking about for months. Maybe they'd go out dancing. They hadn't done that before, and there was nothing she wanted more right now than to be back in his arms. Her heart turned over just at the thought. He would be a good dancer, she thought, closing her eyes with a smile as she let her imagination run wild. She could feel the strength of his arms around her, smell the clean, spicy scent of his cologne....

She fell asleep thinking of him and slept right through her alarm the next morning. When a car horn blasted somewhere down the street, she came awake with a start and winced as every bone in her body creaked in protest. With a groan, she straightened, and only then noticed the time.

"Oh, my God!"

She had ten minutes to get dressed and get to work!

Later, she didn't remember changing from her nightgown into green slacks and a white shirt, let alone driving to work. Had she brushed her teeth? she wondered as she raced toward town. All she could think about was Martin and what would happen later at the council meeting.

"Please, God, don't let him come to work today," she

prayed aloud, clutching the steering wheel until her knuckles were white. "He's got to still be sick. It would be so much better for me if he stayed at home this morning and rested, then went directly from there to the council meeting later this afternoon. Then I wouldn't have to see him at all."

Murmuring the same prayer over and over again, she slowed down to turn onto the street where the office was located, only to have her heart stop dead in her chest at the sight of Martin's car parked in his usual spot in the drive. Without looking at herself in the rearview mirror, she knew every drop of blood in her face had drained away.

"No!" she cried softly. She didn't want him there, didn't want anything to do with him, but what else could she do? Martin might be suspicious if she—who never got ill!—called in sick the day of the city council meeting.

Resigned, she found herself fighting tears. Horrified, she hastily blinked them away; she couldn't cry now. Before the sun set today, Martin would be in custody. It was almost over. All she had to do was hang tough for a few more hours!

But it was so hard. Her palms were damp, her throat dry, and when she parked and started up the front walk to the office, her legs were anything but steady. How she walked inside with a bright, friendly smile on her face she never knew.

"You're here early," she said with forced cheerfulness as he looked up from some paperwork he was going over at his desk. "You must be feeling better. You certainly look better. How's the cough?"

"Better," he said roughly. "I thought about staying home, but I really need to go over all the bids one more time, and most of the paperwork was here. It seemed dumb not to stay once I came to collect it all."

"But you'd be more comfortable there," she pointed out.

"And it's still hours until the city council meeting. Are you sure you don't want to go home? It's not like we're going to do a lot of work today. Things are generally pretty quiet on council meeting days. If something pops up that I can't handle, I can always give you a call."

"No, that's okay," he replied. "I'm already here. And there is a couch here in my office. If I get tired, I can stretch out on it. I'll be fine."

He might be, but she wasn't so sure about herself. Resigned, Abby tried desperately to act as if this was any other workday and prayed it would be over soon. "Okay. I'm going to make some coffee. Would you like some?"

He shrugged. "I guess. Thanks."

Glad to escape from him, she hurried into the small office kitchen and retrieved a can of coffee from one of the upper cabinets. Down the hall, she heard Martin retrieve something from the file cabinet in his office, and she wished again he'd go home. Did he realize he was making her a nervous wreck? Was that why he was sticking around when he should have been home in bed? Was he trying to make her crack?

Her fingers shaking at the thought, she started to scoop coffee into the coffeemaker just as the phone rang, startling her. Coffee grounds went everywhere. "Damn!"

"You all right?" Martin called sharply.

"Oh, I just spilled the coffee," she said, disgusted. "I'll clean it up in a minute. I've got to get the phone."

"Don't worry about it," he told her gruffly. "I'll get it. You take care of the coffee."

That was fine with her, she decided. She'd like nothing more than to spend the rest of the morning hiding out in the kitchen. Unfortunately, it didn't take long to clean up the mess and finish filling the coffeemaker with water and coffee. Left with nothing else to do, she turned back toward her office, only to stop short at the sight of Martin standing in the doorway.

"Oh!" she said, startled. "I didn't realize you were there. The coffee will be ready in a few minutes." When he just stood there, his blue eyes narrow and searching as they met hers, she felt her heart skip a beat and couldn't say why. "Is something wrong?"

"You tell me," he said coolly. "I just got a call from a reporter with the *Gazette.* He wanted to know if it was true that that I was taking bribes from some of the firms bidding for the city's tax collection contract. Where do you think he got an idea like that?"

Every drop of blood in Abby's body turned to ice. "Wh-what?"

"You heard me," he said coldly. "I asked him where he got his information, but he refused to identify his source. It's you, isn't it, Abby? You put two and two together and came up with five, didn't you?"

Horrified, Abby couldn't believe Logan had gone back on his word. He'd sworn he wouldn't say anything! How could he betray her this way? She'd promised him the story. Was he afraid she wouldn't give him the exclusive, after all? All this time, had he just been stringing her along, using her, to get the scoop? Was that why he hadn't called her last night? Now that everything was coming down to the wire, had he decided he didn't need her anymore?

"Well?" Martin said sharply, making her jump. "Don't just stand there. Say something! Who else did you talk to?"

"No one! I swear!"

"Liar!" he screamed. "Do you think I'm an idiot?" Suddenly grabbing her, he shook her like a rag doll. "Tell me, damn you! Who else did you tell about this?"

"The FBI!" she cried. "I talked to an FBI agent. I saw the money Jimmy Blunt paid you. You're going to be arrested after the city council meeting."

"The hell I am!" And with no more warning than that, he slapped her.

In the past, Abby would have sworn that Martin would never do anything to physically harm her. Now she realized she'd only been kidding herself. Terrified, she wanted to run, but he was standing in the doorway, blocking her path, cutting off escape.

The thunder of her heartbeat loud in her ears, she tried to reason with him. "Martin, please, if you'll just let me explain—"

"Explain what?" he mocked. "That you decided to be my judge and jury? That you wanted some fame of your own? You know what? You're going to get exactly what you wanted. You're going to be the most famous corpse this city's ever seen. C'mon, let's go."

Before she could do anything but gasp, he grabbed her by the arm, twisted it behind her back and dragged her out of the kitchen. "Don't! Wait!"

"I don't have time to wait," he growled, forcing her out the front door and over to where his car was parked in the driveway. "Get in!"

Not giving her time to comply, he shoved her into the driver's seat, then across the console to the passenger side. When her head hit the window and her knee scrapped on the console, Abby hardly noticed. She had to stop him, had to make him see reason, or they were both going to regret it.

"Martin, please don't do this!" she cried. "There's no way

you're going to get away with it. The FBI is watching you right now! You can't get away."

"You're lying! See?" he taunted as he backed out of the driveway with screeching tires. "The street's empty. There's no one here but you and me."

Sick with fear, Abby looked down the street and felt her heart sink. He was right. There wasn't a soul in sight to witness her abduction. Where was Vic Roberts and his men? They were supposed to be on the scene, watching Martin's every move. Especially today, for heaven's sake! They had to know anything could happen. How could they have been so careless to leave him without surveillance even for an hour?

"They'll find you," she told him, and desperately tried to believe it. "If you hurt me, it'll only make things worse for you in the end."

Far from seeming troubled by that, he laughed shortly. "You just don't get it, do you, Abby? How are they going to find me? There's no tail. No one will know where to even begin looking."

Oh, God, he was right! she thought, swallowing a sob. If Vic Roberts was waiting for him to show up at the city council meeting this afternoon, he wouldn't even realize Martin had kidnapped her until five hours from now! How far could he drive in five hours? Too far! They could be in Mexico by then! Or halfway to Big Bend. If Martin didn't want to be found, he could disappear in either one of those areas and never be heard from again. And he would take her with him.

Sick at the thought, Abby knew she had to stop him, had to keep trying to discuss this with him until she finally made him see reason. "Martin, let's talk about this," she pleaded. "How long have I known you? Four years? You have to know I would never wish you any harm—"

"Yeah, right," he retorted. "I bet you say that to all your kidnappers."

"I'm serious—"

"Save it for someone who cares. You're just protecting your own neck." Turning at the next corner, he headed for the freeway, but it was still several blocks away when he glanced in his rearview mirror and stiffened. "Dammit to hell!"

When he stomped on the accelerator, sending the car surging forward, Abby quickly glanced behind them and immediately spotted the same thing he had—a navy-blue Ford sedan that was racing after them and making every move they were. "This is crazy, Martin. Why are you doing this? You know you can't possibly get away, and in the long run, it's only going to make things worse."

"Shut up!"

"No, I won't shut up!" she cried as he swerved around a minivan that suddenly pulled in front of him. "You're going to get us killed. Watch it!"

His notes on the high-class murder at Ink's Lake neatly spread out on his desk and his fingers flying over the keyboard of his computer, Logan quickly banged out the story. He couldn't help but notice the similarities between Martin James's downfall and that of the millionaire who'd decided to kill his wife, whom he planned to divorce, so that he wouldn't have to share the extensive profits from the upcoming sale of their business. Greed, Logan thought with a shake of his head as he read over the story carefully, making sure he'd left nothing out. The whole damn world seemed to be populated with greedy bastards who didn't care who they had to use or hurt in their quest to have it all. As far as he knew, Martin hadn't stooped to murder yet, but Logan wouldn't put anything past him. Power-driven, money-hungry men like Martin didn't usually have many scruples.

Anyone who got in their way would pay a price.

Was Abby all right? He'd meant to call her, but he hadn't had a spare moment to do so all morning. There'd been an unscheduled staff meeting five minutes after he'd walked in the building, lasting nearly half an hour. Then he'd had the Ink's Lake story to write before the city council meeting after lunch. Writing for a deadline wasn't usually difficult for him—he'd never had any problem blocking out distractions—but it seemed as if every time he got into the story there was an interruption. The phone had been ringing off the wall, and none of the callers had been Abby.

Five minutes, he told himself. He'd just take five minutes to phone her and make sure she was all right. Hopefully, she wasn't having to deal with Martin this morning. That was the last thing she needed today. He knew her now, knew how she worried about things, and there wasn't a doubt in his mind that her stomach was tied in knots at the thought of what was going to happen after the city council meeting. And she didn't deserve that. Logan didn't have to see her at work to know that she was a hardworking, loyal, reliable secretary. And Martin had taken advantage of her. For no other reason than that, Logan wanted to kick his butt.

Quickly punching in Abby's work number, he found a smile playing around the corners of his mouth. God, he'd missed her! Given the chance, he would have liked nothing more than to take the rest of the day off and spend it with her. That, of course, wasn't going to be possible, but they could plan for later. Maybe they could get together tonight.

But after three rings, the answering machine kicked on. "You have reached Councilman Martin James's office," Abby's recorded voice said in his ear. "Please leave your name and number at the beep and your call will be returned. Thank you."

Surprised, he frowned. "Abby, this is Logan. Please call me as soon as possible." He would have said more, but he couldn't take a chance that Martin might hear it. Where was she? Logan wondered as he hung up. He knew she must have dreaded going in this morning, but she would never have called in sick. She wouldn't have wanted to take a chance of raising Martin's suspicions.

There had to be a logical reason why she didn't answer, he assured himself. It was only a two-person office. If Martin hadn't come in yet and she was in the bathroom, the machine would have picked up the call. Or she could have made a run to the bank or office supply store. Or maybe she just couldn't get to the phone. She'd call him back in a minute.

But ten minutes passed, then fifteen, and his phone never rang. Starting to worry, he was about to call her cell phone when he suddenly heard the police scanner that was always on across the room.

"A 2003 black Lexus, license plate number J-A-M-E-S-1, is headed north on Interstate 35 at a high rate of speed. The vehicle is believed to contain Councilman Martin James and a female hostage. All units be advised that the councilman is considered possibly armed and dangerous. I repeat—this is an all-points bulletin. A 2003 black Lexus…"

Later, Logan never remembered rising to his feet and moving across the room to listen to the APB again. Suddenly, he found himself standing with several of his co-workers, listening to a further description of Martin James, his shiny black Lexus and the redheaded woman who had been taken against her will. Frozen in place as if he'd turned to stone, he heard a roaring in his ears and suddenly realized it was fear. The bastard had Abby.

No! he told himself furiously. There had to be a mistake. Martin James might be guilty of taking bribes and conspiring to manipulate the bidding process to award the city tax collecting contract to one of his crooked buddies, but he hadn't completely lost his mind. He wouldn't kidnap Abby. He wasn't that stupid. And he certainly wouldn't take her on a high-speed chase through the city like some kind of O.J. wannabe. Martin valued his elected position too much.

But the woman with him was a redhead. And Abby wasn't answering the phone at the office. It had to be her!

"Can you believe this? What do you think made him snap?"

"Who knows? He's an arrogant son of a bitch—I know that. Maybe his girlfriend dumped him."

"Maybe. Whatever happened, he can kiss his council seat goodbye."

Fear clutching his heart, Logan hardly heard the other reporters standing around the radio, commenting on the situation. Then he looked up and found himself staring right at Josh Garrison. Never in his life had Logan seen guilt so clearly written on a man's face.

"You son of a bitch! You had something to do with this, didn't you?"

"Go to hell, St. John. You don't know what you're talking about."

When Garrison turned away, dismissing him with a snear, something in Logan snapped. Muttering a curse, he grabbed him, whirling him back around to face him. "You're a lying dog! So I don't know what I'm talking about, huh? Well, how about this? I know you've intercepted my phone calls in the past and pretended to be me so you could steal a story idea from me. If you did it once, you'll do it again. That's it, isn't it?" he said furiously when Josh's expression changed. "You took one of my calls! Damn you, who was it from?"

For a moment, he didn't think the jackass was going to answer. Garrison hesitated, refusing to look him in the eye. Then Logan took a threatening step toward him. "All right," he said sullenly. "I was walking by your desk yesterday when you got a call, and I picked it up. So sue me."

"I'll do more than sue you, you rat," he growled. "What happened? Who was it?"

"I don't know. Some woman. The second I said hello, she was chattering on about picking up a package of hundred dollar bills from Jimmy Blunt. She said everything was going down today. Someone named Vic is going to arrest Martin after the city council meeting today."

Logan's blood turned cold. "That was Abby. And now she's been kidnapped by Martin James. You had something to do with that. Don't deny it," he said silkily. "Everyone here knows what a slimeball you are. You haven't a scruple to your name. You got an incredible tip when you answered my phone. If you expect all of us to believe you just sat on that information, you're a bigger fool than I thought you were."

Josh's eyes narrowed angrily. "I don't have to take this from you, St. John. You're not my boss."

"No, I'm not. I'm just the man who loves Abby Saunders. You remember her, don't you, Garrison?" he taunted. "She's the woman who's in danger because of you. What the hell did you do? You've got sixty seconds to tell me or I swear I'm going to take you apart limb by limb. Then I'm calling Vic Roberts, the FBI agent working this case. If you won't talk to me, maybe he can convince you that it would be in your best interests to spill your damn guts. Talk, damn you! What did you do?"

The crowd surrounding them had doubled in size, but Logan never took his eyes off Josh Garrison. *Give me an excuse to knock your teeth down your throat,* he thought, *then go crying to Porter. I dare you.* If Garrison wanted trouble, Logan would be more than happy to give it to him. Not only would he go straight to the old man and tell him what kind of jerk his granddaughter was dating, but Logan would also press Vic Roberts to charge him with obstruction of justice. And it was no more than Garrison deserved. He was the biggest loser Logan had ever met in his life.

His determination must have shown in his face, for after swearing in disgust, Garrison said, "I don't know what the big fuss is about. I was just doing my job and following up a lead."

Logan felt his stomach turn over sickeningly. "It wasn't your lead to follow up," he said coldly, "but we'll deal with that later. Just get to the point. How did you follow up the lead?"

"How do you think? I called Martin James this morning and asked him if it was true that he was taking bribes. I figured I'd catch him off guard—"

That was as far as he got. With a furious snarl, Logan went for his throat. "You bastard! You stupid, crazy bastard! You don't even realize what you've done!"

It took three men to pull him off the other reporter, but Logan couldn't have cared less. Ignoring the co-workers who held him back, he jabbed a finger at Garrison as if it was a dagger. "If something happens to that woman, I'm going to make you wish you'd never been born!"

Chapter 12

Logan had never considered himself a violent man. But as he ran for his car, rigid with fear as he thought of Abby in the hands of a man who had no scruples, he felt as if he could have killed Martin James with his bare hands. Bastard! Did he really think he could drive off with her and make her pay for *his* mistakes? Like hell! If he harmed a single hair on her head, Garrison wasn't the only one who would be wishing he'd never been born.

God, Logan loved her! Why had it taken him so long to realize it? She was the reason he got up in the morning, the reason he looked forward to getting off work. Just hearing her voice on the other end of the telephone made him smile. When a day went by without the two of them talking, he was bored, lonely, miserable. Idiot! he told himself. He'd been in love for weeks and he hadn't even known it.

Turning on the police scanner in his car, he headed for Interstate 35, his gut knotting as he listened to the emotionless drone of the dispatcher as she described the chase. Weaving in and out of traffic, Martin James was driving like a crazy man, at times exceeding one hundred miles an hour. One mistake, a sudden flat tire, misjudging the distance between his car and another driver's—anything could happen and he and Abby might both end up dead.

No! Logan cried silently. He'd lost one woman he loved—he couldn't lose another. With Faith, there'd been no time to save her, no time to even say goodbye. From what the paramedics had told him afterward, she was gone in the time it took to blink. But Logan could save Abby. He had to! He wasn't letting her go.

His expression grim, he raced down the entrance ramp to the interstate at sixty miles an hour. Ten seconds later, he was going seventy. Breathing a fervent prayer, he pressed the accelerator all the way to the floor.

He couldn't interfere, he told himself. He had to let Vic Roberts and the police handle this. They would made sure that James didn't get away with this insanity and that Abby was safe.

A sick knot of worry clenching his gut, Logan raced north toward Round Rock, his eyes searching ahead for some sign of the police and Martin James's Lexus. For as far as he could see, there was nothing but normal morning traffic. Where the hell were they? he wondered furiously. Had James somehow managed to evade the police and exit the freeway without anyone being aware of it? Was he even now circling back around the city and heading south, toward Mexico? He could reach the border in a matter of hours and just disappear, taking Abby with him....

Stiffening at the thought, Logan cursed himself for a fool. The police weren't going to let that happen. Hell, Abby wouldn't let that happen! When he'd first met her, she might have been shy and unsure of herself when it came to dating, but she was gutsy. How many other women did he know who would meet with Jimmy Blunt to pick up a bribe? Or spy on their boss for the FBI? She was one of a kind, and all he could think of was how much he loved her.

Racing down the interstate, he came up over a rise, and there in the distance saw the flashing lights of what looked like dozens of police cars. A half mile in front of the lead cruiser he spied the Lexus weaving in and out of the slower traffic like Mario Andretti at Indianapolis.

"Fool!" Logan muttered, increasing his own speed until he was passing the cars in front of him as if they were standing still. What the hell did Martin James think he was doing? He couldn't get away. He could race all the way to Dallas, and every law enforcement officer in the state of Texas would be there to grab him when he finally ran out of gas. Couldn't he see that?

"Martin, this is insane," Abby gasped as he swerved to go around a white sedan that a white-haired woman was driving at a snail's place. "You can't get away! Can't you see that? There are cops all around us. Where do you think you're going to go?"

"Shut up!" he screamed at her. "None of this would have happened if you'd just kept your mouth shut!"

Abby couldn't believe he was serious. "This is a joke, right? You take money under the table, let every sleazy lawyer in town wine and dine you, then bribe you to give them the tax contract, and *I'm* to blame?"

"You should have minded your own business!"

"You're an elected official," she snapped. "When you

take a bribe to give a city contract to some good old boy you're in cahoots with, you're spending *my* money and everyone else's who pays taxes! You're damn right this is my business!"

"Bitch!"

He swung his arm to backhand her and nearly lost control of the Lexus. "Watch it!" she cried.

Muttering curses, he slapped both hands back on the wheel and managed to keep the car in its lane, but he refused to cut his speed. With her heart in her throat, Abby hugged herself and struggled to control the outrage boiling in her. Telling him off wasn't going to do anything but infuriate him and put her in even more danger. She had to reason with him, try to convince him to at least slow down. If she could get him to pull over, she might be able to talk him into releasing her. It was a long shot, but she had nothing better to do while he was racing down the interstate like a maniac.

"I'm sorry," she said quietly, trying to sound as if she meant it. "I'm really not throwing stones. We both did what we thought was right, and we can't change that. When I spoke to the FBI, they were already watching you."

"Why?"

"They didn't say. I presume it was for bribery—you weren't exactly discreet. Of course, that all changed today when you added kidnapping to the mix."

"The bribery charges will never stick," he said confidently. "It doesn't matter who gave me money if I don't vote at the city council meeting, and I'm not, of course."

He was grasping at straws, but Abby had to wonder if he was right. "That's a possibility," she agreed. "So why don't you call your lawyer and let him discuss the matter with the FBI? In fact, if you'll take the next exit, we can go back to

Austin and drive directly to his office. For all you know, he might be able to get this all straightened out."

He shot her a sharp look. "Do you really believe that?"

She shrugged. "Why not? It's at least worth a shot. You have to do something, Martin," she said quietly. "We can't just keep driving up Interstate 35."

Returning his eyes to the road, he frowned. Seconds ticked by, then minutes. Just when Abby thought he was going to completely ignore her suggestion, he said grudgingly, "You might be right. I probably could talk my way out of the bribery charges, but what about kidnapping? That's serious stuff. The feds aren't going to look the other way on that one."

No, they weren't, thank God, she thought, but that was hardly something she could say to him. If he wanted to believe there might be a way for him to avoid kidnapping charges, then she'd tell him whatever he wanted to hear.

"You were upset," she said carefully. "You needed to get away, to talk about the situation, and you insisted I come with you. Is that kidnapping? That, too, is a question for your lawyer."

For a moment, she thought he was going to buy it. Frowning, he drummed his fingers on the steering wheel, weighing the argument in his mind. Then, just when he'd started to lighten his foot on the accelerator and their speed began to drop, his expression hardened. "No," he said flatly. "It'll never work."

"Why?" she asked, bewildered by his sudden mood change. "Dammit, Martin, you have to give yourself a chance!"

"I'm not the problem. You are."

Confused, she frowned. "What are you talking about?"

"I don't trust you," he said simply. "You already went behind my back to the FBI. You obviously want me in jail."

"I do not!"

For the first time since he'd kidnapped her, he laughed with true amusement. "God, you're a lousy liar. Save it, okay? We both know that you'd say just about anything right now to convince me to pull over and let you go. You might as well know that that's not going to happen."

Fear curled around her heart. "Martin, please, you're not thinking clearly. The kidnapping charge is going to stick if you don't let me go. You don't want that."

"You're absolutely right," he retorted.

"Then you have to set me free."

"That's one option," he agreed. "The other is I could kill you."

He said it so casually that she was sure he was joking. "C'mon, get serious. You're not going to kill me. Then you'd be facing murder charges…and the death sentence."

"Not if I kill myself, too."

There'd been a time when Abby would have laughed at the mere suggestion that Martin James would ever kill himself—he loved himself too much. But there was nothing to laugh about when they were racing down the interstate at a hundred miles an hour and Martin sounded anything but sane.

Hugging herself closer, she shivered. "Don't talk that way," she said huskily.

"It's the perfect solution," he continued. "It's obvious I'm not going to get out of this mess without spending a hell of a lot of time in jail. I'd rather die first."

"Well, I wouldn't! I'm in love for the first time in my life. I don't want to die!"

"Too bad," he said simply, and steered the Lexus straight toward the cement divider that separated the northbound lanes of the interstate from the southbound ones.

"No!" Abby screamed, and jumped toward him to grab the steering wheel.

Throwing his right arm out again, he hit her on the side of the head, but the pain hardly registered. Sobbing, she fought him for control of the wheel, but he was stronger than she was. Even though she jerked on it with all her strength, within a matter of seconds they were racing right toward the concrete wall. Horrified, she could do nothing but give the wheel one last desperate jerk just seconds before they slammed into the barrier.

Abby wasn't aware until later that her last-second heroics probably saved her life. Instead of hitting the cement head-on, as Martin had intended, the left front fender and headlight on the driver's side took the brunt of the damage. The driver's airbag inflated, the car bounced off the wall and went skidding across three lanes of traffic, and all she could do was scream and wait for another impact.

She never noticed the stream of police cars behind the Lexus, never saw them slow down and spread out, blocking other traffic from getting too close. Suddenly, the Lexus shuddered to a stop sideways, across two lanes. With every bone in her body still vibrating from the force of the crash, Abby just sat there, too stunned to move.

In the time it took to blink, they were surrounded by a dozen or more police officers, their guns drawn and all pointed at Martin. They needn't have worried. Blood was streaming down the left side of the councilman's face from a cut over his brow, and he seemed totally unaware of where he was. He groaned, closing his eyes, and clutched at his left arm, which was hanging at an odd angle.

Relieved, Abby slumped in her seat. It was over. Dear God, it was over and she had lived to tell about it. Sending up a silent prayer of thanks, she didn't know whether to laugh or cry.

Beside her, Martin stirred and only just then noticed that

the police were quickly closing in on him. Groaning, he fumbled to release his seat belt. "Gotta get out of here—"

Abby couldn't believe he was serious. "Don't be an idiot! It's over, Martin. In case you haven't noticed, we're surrounded. You're not going anywhere."

Like a fool, he didn't listen. He tried to kick the door open, and in an instant, the police were on him, jerking him out of the car and onto the pavement. Someone grabbed his injured arm to flip him onto his stomach, and he screamed in pain. Wincing, Abby couldn't help but feel sorry for him…until she remembered how much terror he'd put her through. He'd tried to kill her, for God's sake!

"He's unarmed," she told the police through the open driver's door. "Or at least I think he is. I never saw a gun."

"We'll check," one of the officers said grimly, and began patting him down. Seconds later, he pulled a small, pearl-handled revolver from Martin's pocket.

Stunned, Abby blanched. "Oh, my God!" she whispered. "I had no idea. He could have killed me."

"That appears to have been his intention," Vic Roberts said grimly as he stepped through the crowd that had gathered around the accident scene, and opened the passenger door for her. Leaning down, he examined her with a frown. "That was quite a ride you took. I guess I don't have to tell you you're lucky to be alive. Are you all right?"

Her smile shaky, she nodded. "It was pretty hairy there for a while. He didn't lose control—he was trying to kill us."

"He came damn close. Are you sure you're all right? An ambulance is on the way."

"Oh, but that's for Martin."

"We'll let the EMTs check you out, too," he said easily

"How do you feel? No broken bones? Bleeding? Headache?" He nodded at the cracked passenger-door window. "That had to hurt."

Until then, Abby hadn't even realized her head was throbbing. With trembling fingers, she lifted her hand to the side of her skull and winced when she felt a knot the size of egg. "So much for having a hard head," she told him with a grimace.

"What happened, Abby? I was all set to arrest the bastard after the city council vote, and the next thing I know, I get a call from my men that you're being forced into his car and he's making a run for it. What set him off?"

The whine of a siren interrupted them before Abby could say a word. Blocked by the maze of police cars and traffic that had stacked up behind Martin's Lexus, which still sat sideways in the middle of the interstate, and an access road that was equally busy with rubberneckers who slowed to a crawl, the ambulance had no choice but to drive along the grass meridian that separated the highway from the feeder road.

It pulled to a stop on the shoulder next to the Lexus.

EMTs spilled out, and within a matter of seconds, Abby found the knot on her head being examined and cleaned, then various other cuts and bruises treated. A few short minutes later, the ambulance raced away carrying Martin, and she was relieved to be left behind.

After waiting patiently to one side during the exam, giving her some privacy, Vic Roberts stepped forward again. "You were about to tell me what happened."

"Logan called him and asked him if it was true he was taking bribes."

Vic jerked back as if she'd struck him. "Are you sure? That

doesn't sound like Logan at all. He wouldn't deliberately put you in danger."

"I didn't think so, either," she said flatly. "But I was there at the office when he called."

Stuck in traffic nearly a mile from the accident scene, Logan heard the mournful wail of an ambulance siren and felt his heart turn over in his chest. "No!" he cried hoarsely. She was hurt and he couldn't get to her. The highway had turned into a parking lot and no one had moved in over ten minutes.

In his rearview mirror, he watched the approaching ambulance swerve onto the grass median and speed past toward the scene. A feeling of déjà vu hit Logan right in the gut. He was losing her, he thought starkly. Just as he'd lost Faith. And there was nothing he could do but sit and watch the ambulance go by. He'd never felt so helpless in his life.

So don't just sit here. Go after it! She's right down the road. Go to her! She needs you, dammit!

His heart in his throat, Logan grabbed his keys and pushed open his door. Then he was running as if the hounds of hell were after him. And with every step he took, her name pounded in his head. Abby… Abby… Dear God, if he lost her now, he didn't know what he would do.

He wasn't a man who worked out at the gym. He played an occasional game of basketball with friends on a Saturday afternoon, but that was just for fun. He couldn't remember the last time he'd run anywhere, but nothing was keeping him from Abby when she needed him, especially a traffic jam. Darting through the cars, his eyes trained on the crash site in the distance, he ran like a man possessed. In his head, all he could see were pictures of Abby hurt, possibly maimed, calling for him, and it tore him apart.

Long moments later, he burst onto the scene just as the ambulance pulled away. "No!" he roared, but he was too late. With sirens screaming, the ambulance picked up speed and raced off.

Staggering to a stop, Logan felt as if he'd just been kicked in the heart. He had to get to her! But how, dammit? His car was trapped in the traffic jam. God only knew how long it would be before Martin James's Lexus was hauled away and the traffic cleared. Logan couldn't wait that long. There had to be another way.

Vic! he thought suddenly. The agent had to be there somewhere. His men had been watching James for weeks. The second the councilman took off with Abby in tow, they would have notified Vic. So where the hell was he? His car, no doubt, was among the police cars and highway patrol cruisers that had chased James down. If Vic was still busy booking James for kidnapping, bribery and whatever else he could think of, he could at least let him borrow his car to go after Abby.

But when Logan searched the crowd for the FBI agent, he found him almost instantly…with Abby. Stunned, Logan froze, relief sweeping through him like a summer storm. If he'd had any doubts that he loved her, they died forever at that moment. He knew what it was like to lose the woman he loved. Never in a million years could have he imagined what it felt like to find her safe.

He was a man who made a living working with words, but he could think of only one word to describe the emotion that squeezed his heart at that moment: *joy.* It wasn't a word he'd ever applied to himself before, but there was no other way to express the mixture of love and happiness and laughter that flooded every fiber of his being, then rose like a helium balloon in his heart. He felt as if his feet weren't touching the ground.

He wanted to run to her, sweep her up in his arms and never let her go, but even as he hurried toward her, he could see that she was none too steady on her feet as she rose from the wrecked Lexus and turned to face him. Her eyes locked with his, and for a split second, he thought he saw the same joy he felt reflected in her face. Then she stiffened.

That was the last reaction he'd expected from her. Coming to a stop three feet away, he hesitated. "Abby? Sweetheart, what is it? Are you all right? I've been worried sick."

Beside her, Vic Roberts said gruffly, "I think you two need to talk." Excusing himself, the agent walked away, leaving behind a silence that seemed as deep as a chasm.

Needing to touch her, to hold her, Logan wanted to reach for her, but she looked as fragile as spun glass. "Something's obviously wrong," he said huskily. "And we'll get to that, but first I need to know if you're all right. I was afraid the ambulance was for you."

"I hit my head on the window," she said quietly. "One of the paramedics checked me out—he was pretty sure I didn't have a concussion. I've got a headache, but that's to be expected, considering the bang I took. If it gets worse, he recommended I go to the hospital."

"Thank God it's not critical," he sighed in relief. "I was so worried."

"Then why did you call Martin and ask him if he was taking bribes for the city tax contract?" she retorted. "You had to know that would put me in danger."

Logan couldn't have been more surprised if she'd slugged him. "Is that what James told you? That *I* called him?"

He sounded so outraged that Abby found herself suddenly wondering if she'd somehow misunderstood. "He talked to a reporter. I thought..."

"That it was me," he finished when she hesitated. "Do you really think I'd do that to you?"

Anger glinted in his eyes—and a hurt look that struck her to the bone. Too late, she realized that she hadn't even considered the possibility that he might not be the reporter Martin had spoken to. He'd never given her a name—she'd just assumed it was Logan.

Sick to her stomach, she looked at him in horror. "It was Josh Garrison, wasn't it? Somehow he found out."

He nodded grimly. "You told him, sweetheart."

"I did not!" she began indignantly. Then the truth hit her. "The phone call," she said, horrified. "I called you at work to tell you about my meeting with Jimmy Blunt. I thought you sounded odd, but it wasn't even you, was it? Oh, God, Logan, I'm sorry! He said he had a sore throat! I didn't know—"

Eliminating the space between them with two quick steps, she reached for him with tears in her eyes. "Can you forgive me? I never meant to hurt you."

"Of course I forgive you," he said huskily, gently cradling her close. "Don't feel bad. Garrison is damn good at pulling the wool over people's eyes."

"Oh, my God!" she cried abruptly. "You've got to get back to the paper. If you're not there to stop him, he's going to steal the story!"

"I've got time to take you home first," he assured her. "Then I'll go to work."

That sounded easy enough, until he turned back toward his car and found himself facing a sea of traffic. A wrecker had arrived and was in the process of pulling Martin's Lexus from the middle of the highway, but it would still be several long moments before the roads cleared.

"Stay here," Logan told her. "I've got to go get my car before the traffic starts moving. Will you be all right?"

"I'll watch over her," Vic Roberts promised, stepping forward. He'd been hanging around just out of earshot. "I need to get Abby's statement, anyway. C'mon, Abby, you look like you need to sit down. We can talk in my car."

"She needs to be home in bed," Logan told him. "Can't this wait? You've got Martin—he's obviously not going anywhere. He's in the damn hospital."

"I have to talk to her while everything's fresh in her mind," Vic retorted. "I'll keep it as brief as possible."

Logan wasn't pleased, but he knew Vic was right. No one knew more about James than Abby. It would be her testimony that would convict him. Vic needed to know everything that had happened today.

Next to Faith dying, listening to Abby tell the story of her kidnapping was one of the most difficult things Logan had ever been through. Sitting next to her in Vic's car, her hand in his, he felt his gut clench with rage as she told about James's reaction to the phone call from Josh Garrison.

"He was furious," she said huskily, her hand tightly clutching Logan's. "He shook me, then slapped me and accused me of going to the FBI because of some kind of twisted desire for fame. He told me I was going to be the most famous corpse in the city."

"The son of a bitch!" Logan swore. "You had to be terrified."

"It was awful." Brushing at the tears that spilled over her lashes, she swallowed thickly. "I tried to convince him to turn himself in, but there was no reasoning with him. Once he saw he wasn't going to be able to escape, he decided to kill both of us. If I hadn't grabbed the steering wheel at the last moment, he probably would have succeeded."

Jotting down notes, Vic said, "I have to give you credit. You're one gutsy lady. Martin James obviously didn't have a clue what he was taking on when he hired you."

"I couldn't just stand by and not do anything when I realized he was taking bribes," she said simply. "And I couldn't let him kill me without putting up a fight."

"All I can say," Logan said grimly, "is that he's lucky he's in the hospital. You are going to put this jackass away, aren't you, Vic? Even though he didn't get the chance to vote at the council meeting?"

"We have plenty of evidence that he accepted goods and services from several different law firms in exchange for manipulating the city council's vote on the tax contract," he retorted. "The fact that he didn't actually vote to award the contract to one of the firms that gave him bribes does hurt our case, but we have several people prepared to testify that Martin came to them, offering to vote to award the contract to their firm if they made it worth his while."

Surprised, Abby blinked. "You're kidding. Who?"

He smiled slightly. "Jimmy Blunt, for one."

"But he threatened me!"

"You won't get any argument out of me that he's a dirtbag," Vic said, "but the man's damn clever when it comes to protecting his own hide. He taped every conversation he had with Martin, and there's no question that Martin made it clear his vote was for sale."

"Son of a bitch," Logan repeated.

"My sentiments exactly," Vic replied, "but thanks to his testimony, we will get a conviction of bribery. When a kidnapping conviction is added to that, Martin James will be viewing life through prison bars for many years to come."

"It couldn't happen to a more deserving person," Logan

retorted. "Now that we've got that settled, can Abby go home? She's really wiped out, and the traffic's finally clearing up."

He nodded. "I may have more questions later, but that's all for now. Sit tight and I'll take you back to your car."

Twenty minutes later, Logan pulled up before Abby's house and escorted her inside. "Are you sure you don't need to go to the hospital?" he asked, studying her with a frown as she shut her front door and leaned back against it with a tired sigh. "You're awfully pale."

"I feel like I've been beaten up," she said, grimacing. "But my head isn't hurting like it was earlier. I'm sure I'm fine."

"I don't want to leave you," he said huskily, reaching for her. "Let me hold you for a minute."

He would have sworn he had his emotions under control—she was safe, back in his arms, and Martin James would never hurt her again. But then she buried her face against his neck and he felt the wetness of her tears. "Oh, baby," he groaned, tightening his arms around her. "I thought I'd lost you."

"Me, too," she sniffed, clinging to him. "I was so scared."

He wanted to tell her he'd felt the same way, that he hadn't even known he loved her until he realized he could lose her, but the words wouldn't come. Not yet. He didn't want to confess how much he loved her, then rush out the door. She deserved so much more than that.

"You're safe," he said huskily, kissing her. "I've got you and I'm not letting you go."

With his arms around her, holding her close to his heart, Abby felt as if nothing and no one could ever hurt her again. Given the choice, she would have stayed right where she was for the rest of the day. But Logan had work to do, and after everything Josh Garrison had done to the two of them, they couldn't let him get away with anything else.

"You have to," she said, giving him a quick kiss, then pulling back before he could stop her. Her brown eyes somber as they met his, she took his hands when he reached for her again. "You have to go to work, Logan. You can't let Josh Garrison steal this story from you."

"Trust me," he said grimly, "I don't plan to let him get away with it, but I've got a fight on my hands. If Porter sticks with him because he's dating his granddaughter, then I can probably kiss my job goodbye."

"If that happens, you don't want to work for that kind of man, anyway," she retorted.

He grinned crookedly. "In case you hadn't noticed, sweetheart, the *Gazette*'s the only game in town. There's nowhere else to go."

"There's always somewhere else to go," she replied with twinkling eyes. "You're good, Logan. And Porter knows it. He'd be a fool to let you get away. Go talk to him and tell him what's going on."

"I will if you promise to spend the rest of the day in bed. You need to rest."

"You've got yourself a deal," she murmured, and sealed the promise with a kiss. A few seconds later, she laughingly pushed Logan out the door. "Go to work!"

She didn't have to tell him twice. In spite of the fact that Garrison had Porter's ear, Logan had no intention of stepping out of the way for the jerk. He headed for the *Gazette,* braced for the fight of his life.

The second he walked into the building, the receptionist stopped him. "Mr. Porter would like to see you immediately," she said coolly. "You can go on up."

Logan swore silently. Well, hell! Garrison had already gotten to the old man. He might as well go clean out his desk. It was all over.

Furious with Garrison, he stepped onto the elevator and jabbed the button for the top floor. Seconds later, he stormed into Thomas Porter's office. "I heard you wanted to see me," he said coolly. "I suppose you want to fire me. If that's the case, just do it and get it over with. Garrison warned me I would be the loser if I was stupid enough to get in his way. It looks like he was right."

"I don't know about that," the older man drawled, his lips twitching. "It looks to me like you're here and he's not."

Taken aback, Logan stared at him warily. He and Porter had always been blunt with each other and he saw no reason to change that now. "What the hell is that supposed to mean? Where, exactly, is Garrison?"

"Out looking for another job, I would presume," he retorted. "I thought about turning him in for interfering with an FBI investigation, but decided against it. I can't completely antagonize my granddaughter," he added with a grin. "I don't want her to disown me."

The old man seemed quite pleased with himself. All his hostility draining away, Logan didn't quite know what to make of the sudden turn of events. "Obviously, something happened here today that I don't know about. D'you care to fill me in or do I have to guess?"

Puffing on his favorite cigar, Porter offered one to Logan, then waited for him to light it before he said, "There's nothing like a good cigar to help a man relax. You should have told me Garrison was stealing your leads, Logan. You know I don't put up with that kind of crap. This is a family-owned business, and I consider everyone who works here family. I expect everyone to work together, not stab each other in the back just to get a byline on the front page."

"I handled it," he replied, and blew out a smoke ring. "How the hell did you find out about it? I know Garrison didn't tell you."

"No, you're right there. The slimy road lizard knew better."

"So who squealed?"

"Nora."

"Nora? Your secretary? How the hell did she know?"

Leaning back in his chair, the old man grinned around his cigar. "She overheard the ruckus this morning around the police scanner." Sobering, he asked, "How is the woman Martin James kidnapped?"

"Alive by the skin of her teeth," he retorted. "And much better now that James is in police custody."

"Josh put her in danger," he said tersely. "From what I understand, she came damn close to being killed. When were you going to get around to telling me about that?"

"When I turned in the story. I was afraid that Garrison would beat me to the punch, though. I don't have to tell you that he's pretty damn slick. I knew he would do whatever he had to cover his butt, and to be perfectly honest, I was afraid you'd fall for whatever he said. When the receptionist told me you wanted to see me, I figured it was to give me my walking papers."

"Your job was never in jeopardy," Porter assured him. "I know the last year had to be incredibly difficult for you. Losing a spouse isn't something anyone recovers from quickly. I know you didn't believe me when I told you at the funeral to take as much time as you needed, but I meant it."

"But you brought in Garrison—"

"True, but he was never in competition for your position here. *He* just thought he was. I never liked the man. The only reason I took him in was because my granddaughter asked me to. If I'd known he was stealing stories, though, he'd have been out of here the first week."

Blowing out a cloud of smoke, he grinned. "My granddaughter wised up and finally saw what kind of man he is, so we don't have to worry about him any longer. He's history. So when am I going to get to read the exposé on Martin James? There's another idiot. I'm telling you, the world's full of them."

Logan had to agree. "Hopefully, greed and stupidity aren't contagious. As to the story, now that I know I don't have to clean out my desk, I'll finish it. I'll follow the story all the way through James's trial and sentencing, of course, but the first installment will be ready for press by late this afternoon. I'll send you a copy as soon as I'm done."

"Then you'd better get to work," Porter said. Rising to his feet, he held out his hand. "It's good to have you back, Logan."

"It's good to be back, sir," he said gruffly, shaking it. "Thank you for being so understanding. I won't forget this."

Feeling like a ten ton weight had been lifted from his shoulders, Logan hurried to the hospital to get the particulars on Martin James's injuries and to see if he could talk him into giving an interview. James, however, had already contacted a lawyer, who'd posted bail for him, and Logan arrived at the hospital just as he was being released. His arm was in a cast, he had a small bandage on his temple and he had no interest in granting an interview. Looking right past Logan and the television news crews that had gathered outside the hospital entrance, he and his attorney hurried outside and rushed over to the shiny black Escalade illegally parked at the curb. Seconds later, they drove off without saying a word.

Amused, Logan turned and walked into the hospital. He didn't needed James's cooperation to write his story. He had sources in the hospital, as well as the police department. And then there was Vic Roberts, of course. As soon as Logan learned more about James's medical condition, he'd call Vic to find out the charges filled against James, as well as what he might have revealed when he'd been questioned. Vic wouldn't, of course, be able to reveal anything that might damage the case they had against the councilman, but that was understandable. Thanks to Abby, Logan still had a hell of a story.

Hours later, he was done. Both Nick and Porter had read the piece and given it rave reviews. It would not only be the lead story tomorrow morning, but Nick expected it to be the major story for some time to come. James wasn't the only city councilman suspected of taking bribes. Logan would start investigating the others tomorrow.

For now, however, he had personal business to take care of. Leaving the *Gazette* office, he headed for Abby's place, but turned left when he should have turned right. Before he knew it, he was driving through the gates of the cemetery where Faith was buried. That was when he realized that before he talked to Abby, he needed to spend some time with Faith.

Had there ever been a day when he hadn't loved her? he wondered as he parked the car and walked the short distance to her grave. If there was, he couldn't remember it. From the moment his eyes had first met hers, he'd been in love. Twenty-one years later, he still loved her and always would.

He'd sworn he could never love anyone as much as he loved her, but he'd never planned on meeting a woman like Abby. She was nothing like Faith at first glance, but she touched his heart in a way no other woman ever had...except

Faith. Now that he'd found Abby, he couldn't imagine going through the rest of his life without her.

Which meant he had to say goodbye to Faith.

Standing at her grave, staring at the tombstone that said so little about her life, he felt a bittersweet pain squeeze his heart. Never had he needed to hold her more.

"I don't need to tell you how much I love you," he said huskily. "You've always known. But I've met someone else, honey, though I guess you know that. Her name's Abby. You'd like her, Faith. She's a wonderful woman. And I'm going to marry her. I just thought you needed to know."

A redbird suddenly landed in an oak tree twenty feet away and began to sing as it looked right at him. Logan grinned ruefully. The cardinal had always been Faith's favorite bird. "Leave it to you to find a way to signal your approval. You always did say you didn't want me to go through life alone if something happened to you. I guess you knew."

Peace settling over him, warming his heart, he said huskily, "God has really blessed me, sweetheart. He gave me two great women to love in a single lifetime. Just because I've found Abby doesn't mean I'll ever forget you and the life we shared together. I just have to move on."

The redbird continued to sing, and with a sigh of contentment, he turned to leave...only to find himself face-to-face with Samantha, Faith's sister. "Sam! What are you doing here?"

"I was feeling down," she said stiffly, "so I thought I'd come and talk to Faith. Did I hear you correctly? Have you fallen in love with someone else?"

There was no denying the hurt and anger in her eyes, and too late, Logan realized that Abby had been right when she'd said she thought Faith's sister was interested in him. He felt like a heel, but he couldn't help that. He'd never thought of

Samantha as anything but a sister. He would have never fallen in love with her even if Abby had never come along.

He couldn't, however, tell her that without hurting her more, and that was the last thing he wanted to do. "Her name is Abby," he said huskily. "And yes, I'm in love with her."

He was afraid she was going to say *What about me?* but she didn't, thank God. "I don't have to ask if she loves you, too," she said stiffly. "Only a fool wouldn't, and I can't see you falling in love with a fool. I hope you'll be happy, Logan. I know it's what Faith would want."

"I'll always love you, Sam. We're family. That's not going to change just because I'm going to marry someone else if she'll have me."

She didn't have to tell him that the kind of love she wanted from him had nothing to do with family—he could see it in the tears that misted her eyes. But he had to give her credit. She blinked them back, straightened her shoulders and forced a smile. "I know that. Who would cheat at poker with you besides me?"

He grinned. "My point exactly."

Stepping close, she gave him a fierce hug. "Be happy," she whispered, then moved back. A moment later, she was gone.

Watching her drive away, Logan realized that another part of the past had just let him go. It was time to move on with his life.

The day stretched out interminably for Abby. She tried to rest, to forget the horror of the morning, to just veg and give her body a chance to recover from ramming into a concrete wall at a hundred miles an hour, but she was too restless to sit still. And her agitation had nothing to do with Martin or everything he'd put her through. No, it was Logan she couldn't stop thinking about, and with every passing hour, she became more and more upset.

Did he still love Faith? Since he'd never told her that he loved her, she had to believe that he loved his wife. And that tore her apart. She couldn't stand this! She loved him with all her heart, but she couldn't continue in a relationship with a man who couldn't let go of the past. It hurt too much.

She had to end it. She had to walk away now, before she lost all pride and ended up staying with him even though she knew he would never love her. But how? she wondered. How could she break things off with him when just thinking about it made her heart hurt? After the loving they'd shared, the laughter, the confidences on the phone, he wasn't going to just let her walk away without some kind of excuse. So what was she supposed to say? *I can't see you anymore because you don't love me?*

Hurt, frustrated, fighting tears, she swore softly and said, "Think, for heaven's sake! And be quick about it! He's bound to come by when he finishes writing his story, and you'd better be ready for him."

But even as the words echoed off her living room walls, her doorbell rang. Her heart stopped in midbeat. He was here! Panic seized her by the throat. How could she face him, knowing she couldn't see him anymore? What could she possibly say to him?

The thunder of her heartbeat loud in her ears, she almost ignored the doorbell and pretended she didn't hear it. But he knew she was there—her car was in the drive! If she didn't answer the door, he would, no doubt, think something had happened to her because of the blow she'd taken to her head that morning, and he'd kick the damn door in. Like it or not, she had to face him. Dragging in a bracing breath, she crossed to the front door and pulled it open.

"There you are!" he said with a broad grin. "I didn't wake you, did I? When you didn't answer, I thought you might be taking a nap. C'mere." And with no more warning than that, he pulled her into his arms and kissed the stuffing out of her.

Stunned, Abby melted—she couldn't help herself. And when he finally let her up for air, he had a smile as big as Texas stretched across his handsome face. She'd never seen him so happy.

She told herself she couldn't let herself care why he was happy, but she loved seeing him like this—like he was on top of the world. Her own mouth curling into a grin, she said, "All right, what's happened? And don't say nothing. It's written all over you. I've never seen you this happy."

"I don't think I've ever been this happy before," he answered with a chuckle, and pulled her into his arms for a bear hug. "You're never going to believe what happened at work today."

"Your boss loved the story?"

"Yes—"

"Josh Garrison got what was coming to him?"

"Okay," he explained, "so maybe you did guess, but it gets better. Old man Porter called me into his office and told me he'd fired Garrison for stealing my stories—his secretary heard me confront him this morning. He's glad I've got my old fire back and wanted to make sure I knew my position there was secure."

"Oh, Logan, that's wonderful! You must be thrilled."

"Oh, it gets better," he assured her. "I'm doing a series of articles on the corruption in city hall—it's going to be incredible. But no more incredible than you," he added huskily. "Did I mention how much I love you?"

Caught up in his excitement about work, she found it was a second before his question registered. Stunned, she looked up at him blankly. "What?"

"I stopped by the cemetery before coming over here—I needed to tell Faith about you and how much I love you. I know that sounds crazy, but she was not only my wife, but my best friend, and I've been sharing my deepest secrets with her since I was a teenager. Just because she's dead doesn't mean I don't talk to her anymore."

Joy filling her heart, Abby couldn't stop smiling. "No, of course not. Trust doesn't stop just because someone dies."

"You're damn straight," he agreed. "She was the first girl I ever kissed and the only one I ever loved…until I met you. Did I say I love you?"

Abby couldn't stop herself—she had to kiss him. Rising up on tiptoe, wrapping her arms around his neck to pull his mouth down to hers, she kissed him sweetly, hungrily, hotly. "Say it again," she murmured against his mouth, tilting her head to change the angle of the kiss. "I love hearing it because I love you, too. I've been thinking about you all day, aching for you."

He groaned at her words, the rough sound of need making her ache even more. Suddenly, his arms were fierce around her, holding her as if he'd never let her go. "I was terrified when I heard that James had kidnapped you," he said huskily. "After losing Faith, I couldn't face losing another woman I loved."

"You're not going to lose me," Abby assured him. "I love you. I'm not going anywhere."

"It's so easy to take someone you love for granted," he said, framing her face in his hands. "You go to work every day, you come home and have dinner together, you go to bed. The next day, you go through the same routine all over again. You get caught up in the rat race of living, and you forget to say those three little words that make it all worthwhile. Then one of you dies, and you find yourself trying to remember the last time you held her and kissed her. Did she die knowing she was loved?"

"Oh, no, Logan! Don't do that to yourself. Of course she knew. The two of you had been together so long—you didn't need to say the words every day for her to know that she was loved. She knew every time you touched her, smiled at her, kissed her. She had to. I do."

"Doubts creep in in the middle of the night," he said with a grimace. "For months after she died, I would wake up telling her I loved her just because I couldn't remember the last time I'd told her how crazy I was about her. I won't do that with you," he promised. "I'm going to tell you every day for the rest of our lives."

Her heart in her eyes, Abby smiled and kissed him until they were both humming with need. "It took a long time for me to find you," she murmured. "I never thought I'd get the chance to say I love you, let alone hear you say it back."

"Because of Faith?"

"You loved her so much," she said simply. "I was afraid you would never let yourself love anyone else."

"I felt like I was betraying her," he said honestly. "But she never wanted me to be alone. Then when I realized I was starting to have feelings for you, I was so afraid of losing you the way I'd lost her. But everything changed today when you were kidnapped. I love you, and like it or not, there are no guarantees in life. If we only have three years, ten years, a half a century together, it still won't be enough. So I'll take what I can get. How about you? Are you all right with that?"

Feeling as if her heart was going to float right out of her chest, she grinned. "I don't know what kind of old lady I'll be. Will you still love me when my hair is white and I have to put my teeth in a glass at night?"

A wide grin spread across his face. "I can't wait. But what about me? I could lose my hair and my teeth and snore loud enough to wake the dead. Will you still love me then?"

"Just try stopping me."

"Then I'd say it's settled. You're going to marry me." It was a statement, not a question, but just to be sure, he held out his hand. "Deal?"

As far as marriage proposals went, it was unlike anything Abby had ever expected, but it couldn't have been more perfect. Her grin as wide as his, she shook his hand. "Deal!"

Their eyes met, they both laughed and sealed the deal with a kiss.

* * * * *

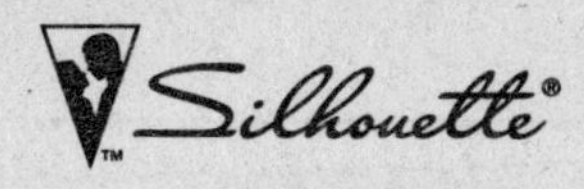

INTIMATE MOMENTS®

COMING NEXT MONTH

#1339 DANGEROUS DISGUISE—Marie Ferrarella
Cavanaugh Justice
Mixing business with pleasure wasn't in detective Jared Cavanaugh's vocabulary—until he saw Maren Minnesota walk into the restaurant where he'd been assigned to work undercover to catch the mob. But when their smoldering attraction for each other threatened his disguise, would he have to risk everything to protect the woman he loved?

#1340 UNDERCOVER MISTRESS—Kathleen Creighton
Starrs of the West
After a hit-and-run accident forced Celia Cross from Hollywood's spotlight, her only refuge was the beach. Then homeland security agent Roy Starr washed ashore, bleeding from an assassin's bullet. Little did she know her mystery man had gotten too close to an international arms dealer. With the killer determined to finish the job and Roy's feelings for his rescuer growing stronger, would this be their beginning—or their end?

#1341 CLOSE TO THE EDGE—Kylie Brant
Private investigator Lucky Boucher knew his attraction to fellow investigator Jacinda Wheeler was a mistake. He was a bayou boy; she was high society. But when a case they were working on turned deadly, keeping his mind off her and on their investigation proved to be an impossible task, because for the first time since he'd met her, their worlds were about to collide.

#1342 CODE NAME: FIANCÉE—Susan Vaughan
Antiterrorist security agent Vanessa Wade felt as false as the rock on her finger. Assigned to impersonate the glamorous fiancée of international businessman Nick Markos, she found herself struggling to remain detached from her "husband-to-be." He was the brother of a traitor—and the man whose kisses made her spin out of control. Could she dare to hope their fake engagement would become a real one?

#1343 RUNNING ON EMPTY—Michelle Celmer
Detective Mitch Thompson was willing to risk his life to uncover the mystery surrounding Jane Doe, the beautiful amnesiac he'd rescued from an unknown assailant. But the more time they spent together trying to unravel the secrets hidden in her memory, the more evident it became that they were falling in love…and that Jane's attacker was determined to stop at nothing to destroy their happiness—not even murder.

#1344 NECESSARY SECRETS—Barbara Phinney
Sylvie Mitchell was living a lie. Pregnant and alone, she'd retreated to her ranch to have the baby in hiding. Then her unborn child's uncle, Jon Cahill, appeared, demanding answers, and she had to lie to the one man she truly loved. She'd lived with the guilt of his brother's death and the government cover-up that had forced her into hiding. When the truth surfaced, would she lose the only man who could keep her—and her baby—safe?

SIMCNM1204